Les Beaux Châteaux

Les Beaux Châteaux

a novel

Dorothy Mackevich Marks

DMM
PRESS

Published by DMM Press, Chicago, IL
Dorothymackevichmarks.com

Edited and designed by Girl Friday Productions
www.girlfridayproductions.com

Cover design: Paul Barrett
Project management: Katherine Richards
Editorial: Tiffany Taing
Image credits: cover © Shutterstock/HJBC

ISBN (paperback): 979-8-9854566-0-8
ISBN (e-book): 979-8-9854566-1-5

To my family, especially my husband, Peter,
for their loving patience and unconditional support.
Also, to my many teachers, who inspire me to
make each day a learning day.

Chapter One

JP zips his vintage roadster into his parking spot behind Les Beaux Châteaux, his salvage and antiques store. Getting out, he admires the new contrasting convertible top, even though the color's not "period," as purists call it. Owning, garaging, and driving a car in New York City is a recent guilty indulgence. Driving this '67 Porsche, he savors each city block with a sort of American independence.

His pocket vibrates with a call. *Damn!* That's Victor calling again. He checks the log. Sure enough, his dad has left another message. Impatiently, he reads the voice-mail transcription: "Along with a classic bakery, items in this week's container shipment include chairs from India Mahdavi's irreverent collection. I bought them because they remind me of you."

Irreverent? Too late to call France, JP justifies. After pulling the car top back up, he brushes his hands on his tailored jeans, imagining Victor at an auction buying cushy pink lounge chairs. Checking for dust, he pats his pants clean. His inseam hits midheel on his soft leather boots. Clothing alterations are one more extravagance he's allowed himself.

He crosses the parking lot to look inside the moving van containing an ancient stone fountain wrapped so tightly with baling twine that the furniture blankets protecting it squeeze out between the rope with a strangled look. JP nods a faint greeting to the foreman, Hank. His guys are ready for work, with gloves and weight belts on. Hank opens the loading gate. JP sidesteps the muddy puddles that polka dot this parking area to peer inside Les Beaux Châteaux to see where the fountain will fit. Does Hank know how to assemble it? JP nods again at Hank, feigning confidence. The last fountain from France was a disaster—it fell from the truck, breaking to bits. He stops to look back at the truck. The unloading is progressing smoothly. Hank's solid and in control.

***

Iris looks at her watch and tosses her second empty coffee cup into the trash. Clouds darken the skylight of the showroom. She hasn't supervised Hank, one of JP's worst hires. She overheard him and Rodolpho laughing and saying they didn't know a thing about old fountains. She's heard the purr of a vintage car crossing the parking area.

Picking up the stack of pink message sheets that JP likes to thumb, she wonders if Office Depot will continue to stock these antiquated pads.

"Hey," she greets him as he enters the showroom. Dolly, her Weimaraner dog, heels, and Iris notes her round belly. JP gives her too many treats.

Salespeople, furniture movers, and office clerks are in their places. JP glances at Iris, the superb manager, a straight-postured, silver-haired woman who has been selling pedigreed antiques since her middle school days. She's a quiet observer who knows how to flatter customers while remaining personally unremarkable. Dolly greets him. He pulls a treat from his pocket and slips it to her. Iris watches silently.

JP picks up candy wrappers and a cigarette butt, which she takes from him. "What's up?" Iris is finding these predictable conversations irksome. Shining her saccharine smile, she says, "Victor's called twice. What's got his goat?"

Although she's turned away from him to toss the trash, she knows that he's shrugging. Facing him again, she waves the stack of message sheets.

"And Johnny, that squirrelly customs broker, called about antiques in customs purgatory. Do you know anything about that? I'll call him later to straighten him—"

"I'll call him. Victor's harassment has me in a sour mood. Better I make these calls than insult customers, eh?" He points to two blondes walking the aisles as he takes the pink sheets from her and shakes them above his head, then slips Dolly a second treat.

"You don't know harassment. My mother was a relentless beast. Count your blessings, my man. Victor's a peach."

Walking blindly away from JP to calm herself, Iris stumbles into the lighting supply room, the area of Les Beaux Châteaux that she notoriously avoids.

When she was young, her mother, watching for get-rich-quick opportunities, often bought cheap box lots (unidentified items) at rural auctions. Hives appeared on Iris's adolescent abdomen while she was accompanying her mom to these Podunk places. Every time her mom raised her bidding paddle, Iris's stomach clenched. Worry, combined with rancid smells from the auction-circuit food trucks, made for predictable car sickness on the long rides. When they finally arrived home, filth and dust would trigger Iris's sneezy-wheezy anxiety as she unloaded the Cadillac's cavernous trunk.

Her parents' combustible dialogue ignited once when Iris and her mom returned home, her dad's anger wafting out of the kitchen. "These useless auction swing-throughs and chores will give her asthma."

Her mom wouldn't have it. "I'm teaching her survival skills!"

Iris then washed up in the garage slop sink as her dad left, calling over his shoulder, "Let's hope that she does survive!"

As social skills were never a part of her mom's curriculum, that weekend, a long-anticipated Girl Scout trip was nixed in favor of assembling an ugly chandelier. Iris was charged with making something to sell from the box's bits and bobs.

These days, Iris stays strictly away from wires and pliers, instead embracing beautifully complete chandeliers and artifacts.

Listening, she tunes her ear to hear JP settling back at his desk, probably putting his feet up next to the gargoyle head that holds his business cards. Iris calls Dolly, half ignoring what she imagines is his shameful posture. His hostile tone on the phone can be heard by every customer in the store. She returns to him, jaw tight. He pantomimes a query while continuing his phone conversation. She gives him an arch glare. He turns a few degrees away from her, settling into an ergonomically designed chair whose bright chrome lines don't fit with the store's ambiance. No matter—Iris selected it for him.

***

"Hey, Johnny! What's up?" he chimes in in his salesman's voice. He and Victor share this unique tone. "Iris tells me that Victor's sent us some trouble."

People wandering in the store can hear the irritated clips in his conversation.

"Yeah . . . buying French artifacts. Unnnhunh. Yep. Sure. I wouldn't be surprised if he sent us entire rooms. Bakeries, you say? That's the problem? We've been buying artifacts for nearly fifteen years and bringing them in without a hitch. What's up now? Uh-huh, national heritage. The French? Nahhh. They'll sell anything."

Finally off the phone, he turns to Iris. "Do you remember that guy from White Plains who's been calling about old fountains? Do we have notes on that guy?"

Iris nods in the direction of his desk. "Check the top of your pile."

He sees a pair of well-heeled customers walking aimlessly. Iris intercepts them. He's hired her exactly for her American values—her know-how and customer service. When she sends him a stern look, he usually cleans up his rude attitude.

Sometimes he thinks that Iris is the heart of Les Beaux Châteaux. He remembers when he hired her. Les Beaux Châteaux was limping along. He employed minimum-wage movers and had a lackluster sales style. Though the product mix was relatively the same as it is now, there was no sense of place. New Yorkers didn't know what kind of store Les Beaux Châteaux was back then, and no one came in to investigate.

Iris had wandered in on the pretense of buying a mirror. She ambled around the store, waiting for JP to approach. He was clueless back then. Finally, she went to him and directed their conversation; she queried about his mission and vision in the community. He'd never considered these ideas. Public relations and profile . . . what? Neither he nor the store could afford PR *anything*. And staging . . . how? Even without the cost of PR or advertising or community outreach, he was bleeding cash and had been for more than a year.

Soon, their conversation got cozy; he learned about her family antiques business in Savannah, Georgia. He tried not to let on that he had no idea where Savannah was. Facile Iris put him at ease, explaining, "Savannah's a backwater, but it used to be a historical hub in the South."

She left Les Beaux Châteaux that day without a purchase or a promise. He couldn't afford an experienced sales manager like Iris, but he knew that he couldn't afford *not* to hire her. Two weeks later, she and Dolly, the new store mascot, closed the deal when he hired her. He resigned to paying himself minimally and slept on a cot in the back for years, until their profits grew enough so that he could afford an apartment off-site.

There had been a few unsalesmanlike episodes before Iris created the Les Beaux Châteaux script. JP once told a belligerent customer to shop at Sears, where cheap crap is one size fits all. Maybe JP was, as Victor said, irreverent? Iris proclaimed that there was no place in sales for bad manners. She came from the school of *get it done*. American marketplace etiquette was her specialty. Iris started a campaign that French antiques should be lauded and marketed to the richest financiers in the Wall Street orbit, and she set out to be noticed by decision-makers in that culture. Soon, Les Beaux Châteaux and JP were hosting exclusive cocktail parties for various high-profile causes, such as the marriage-equality movement and Artists Without Homes, and eventually, he hosted a quarterly "professionals" happy hour for interior designers, by invitation only. Les Beaux Châteaux became a haven for arts and human rights–affiliated events. He donated prized French artifacts du jour—kitchen sinks if kitchens were in vogue, or chandeliers if living rooms were featured on design magazine covers. It was her sales strategy to never rush a buyer, yet they mostly returned to complete their purchase. Decor, lifestyle magazines, and blogs began to follow JP and Les Beaux Châteaux, and social media virally reached some of the hottest influencers.

Learning Iris's culture and processes were well worth his own stripped-bare sacrifices. She created the destination, Les Beaux Châteaux. They helped the Meatpacking District (as well as the Highline) emerge as Manhattan's hippest neighborhood. JP was hesitant and slow to surrender the cultural sway of Les Beaux Châteaux to Iris. Eventually, the store went from the school of *anything goes* to organized. She won his trust. Iris masterfully designed mini stage sets throughout the store—arranging a period vanity with a sexy nightgown, a silver cocktail shaker, and vintage highball glasses. She learned the truck drivers' names, streamlining deliveries to customers' homes and the transport of artifacts from the port of Newark to their store in Lower Manhattan.

When money-laundering laws whipped panic into international banking, Iris calmed their bankers with personal familiarity. Antoinette, Victor's banker in Chartres, shared pictures of her grandchildren with Iris, and in return, Iris sent pictures of Dolly. She saw cost-cutting measures and ways to make profits, whereas JP didn't have the imagination to change unworkable habits. Despite these deficiencies, JP intuitively activates customers' want-to-possess algorithm. Iris's American efficiency combined with JP's French accent, poetically long hair, and honeyed voice made them a profit powerhouse.

"Thank you, Johnny. I'll get back to you on this. Do your best, man. We've been selling this same stuff for years. I can't imagine why now, all of a sudden, they're worried about their heritage. Politicians are always changing the rules. Yeah. Right. Bye."

Signing off, he joins the customers whom Iris greeted. One is in her early fifties, and the follower is midthirties. Sizing them up, he names the leader Big Diamond. Fabric swatches are escaping from her tote, along with paint chips, architectural plans, and a measuring tape. A dazzling diamond ring is so large that it catches and drags these tools out of her bag.

JP clears his throat and sends out his cultured sales voice: "Hello, ladies, may I show you something special today?"

Remembering the wide north wall, a perfect location for the stone fountain being unloaded, he walks them toward a wrought-iron console sitting snugly in the shadowy corner. Big Diamond answers, "We're just looking. I'm not sure exactly what we want." Pretty But Quiet (JP's name for her accomplice) nods in agreement.

"Don't let me get in your way! I don't know what you want either, but I'm sure that you'll find it here at Les Beaux Châteaux. I have hundreds of these." He turns and picks up a porcelain hand mold for gloves. Many similar life-size models are jumbled in a galvanized trough. Behind it stands a Wisconsin summer camp totem pole made from birch bark.

"Are you perhaps outfitting a boys' summer camp? If so, I have just the thing."

Both Big Diamond and Pretty But Quiet smile.

"Mostly we sell French artifacts. Well, I guess you know that, right?"

They nod.

"Do you know the work of Edgar Brandt, fer forgé artisan?" He reaches for a well-thumbed book sitting on the shelf of the iron console. He flips the book to a page showing Edgar Brandt's most famous iron staircase in a beautiful art-deco room.

Big Diamond's eyes light up. "Yes! Something special like that. Well, not a staircase, but a magnificent piece like that is just what we need for the foyer."

Pretty But Quiet nods again.

Looking around, JP feigns ignorance of the inventory. "Let's see."

Gesturing for them to follow, he walks across a bridge from one showroom to another. Dozens of vintage sinks line one row, and spiked wooden stands to dry wine bottles fill another, while large school chalkboards with wooden frames, a few wooden school desks, and stacks and stacks of stained-glass elements line the aisleways. To the right is another trough, brimming with printers' type blocks, and to the left, yet another, full of hundreds of glass doorknobs. Baskets dangle among light fixtures, and street signs from cities around the world hang low so as to be unavoidable. Several gravestones with old moss clinging to the edges lean against the wall next to church pews and giant crucifixes.

Like a mama duck teaching ducklings about the world, he traverses the entire sixty-thousand-square-foot showroom with the blondes in tow. He leads them to the basement and back to the north wall. Full circle.

"OK. You can stop me anytime when you see the perfect thing for your foyer."

Pretty But Quiet asks, "Where did you get all this stuff?"

JP laughs. "I've been on the hunt all my life. My dad did this as a hobby in France, of course. We've been buying this stuff together since I was in short pants. My dad, Victor, is the real mastermind of this outfit. He's selected and purchased every item in this place. He is driven on a quest for rarity, curiosity, antiquity, but more than anything, beauty. He knows beauty. So, you like fer forgé? Did you notice this piece?"

Big Diamond's brow furrows. She fishes eyeglasses out of her bag, along with another fabric sample clinging to her ring. Looking carefully, they approach the console. JP runs his hand over the iron roses and rests it on a splendidly wrought leaf.

"You know that ironmongers have their own special recipes for the metal they fashion. Some like the iron to be dark, or red, or shiny, or green. Like ceramicists or, say, bakers with their proprietary recipes, these guys keep their secrets locked away. This piece, in particular, is dazzling. It does everything that you want in wrought iron. Wait—do you know the difference between wrought iron and, say, pressed iron?"

Seduced by sales magic, the blondes are wide-eyed yet silent. JP's knowledge has them riveted like children at story time.

"All these shapes, these roses, branches, thorns, leaves, they are hand-wrought. No press or form or template makes these. Oh no! These are heated to white-hot, then beaten on an anvil into these realistic shapes. And this branch, see how it goes from chocolate brown to black? That's entirely intentional. This artisan has such control over his materials. This is made by a master. It's not signed Edgar Brandt, but I'm guessing that it comes from his forge."

The blondes lock eyes in approval. JP steps away. It is a very big piece. Few homes or apartments can accommodate this size. It's been in the showroom for several years. Too long.

Iris has excellent timing. She and Dolly approach to tell JP that there's a call for him.

"Excuse me, ladies. I have to attend to this. If you have any questions or want to know about any of our antiques, we're here to help."

Big Diamond asks, "How much is the console?"

JP reaches toward it, flipping over the tag that he wrote. He knows just what it says. "Thirty thousand. But let's see if it's exactly what you want. We can accommodate you. I love this piece, and I want it to go to the perfect place."

JP, Iris, and Dolly walk back to the desks.

"I'll figure out the best lighting for the fountain on that wall," Iris says. "I'll call the guy in White Plains and have it displayed when he comes in."

JP congratulates himself for giving Iris so much room to thrive. She's a great strategist.

The blondes begin measuring.

***

Victor hangs up again. *Damn, JP! Why doesn't he pick up?* He moves a pile of auction flyers and bank notices from atop his calendar. He reviews the auctions for the next week, then pulls out his well-worn Michelin road map and opens the mapping software on his computer.

Victor used to live in the 11th in Paris, but that location made getting out of town so aggravating, not to mention time-consuming. His monster vehicle lumbered down the ancient city streets, just barely squeezing through, and the cobblestones messed with the suspension.

In truth, the quiet of Luisant, outside of Chartres, gives him peace. That old apartment in Paris kept dreams of his dead wife, Frida, vividly alive, and that did nothing for his libido. Sleep and sex with the girl of the month are easier here. Well, Caterina isn't exactly the flavor of the month—she's been around for more than a year or so now, it seems. Victor stops and considers that. This is the first sincere and, yes, trusting relationship he's had with a woman since Frida died. Before he moved to Luisant, there were several women from his and Frida's circles who made a play for him. In each of these encounters (so strange being potentially romantic with someone he'd known as a friendly acquaintance for many years), the mechanics functioned, but he felt nothing, just ambivalence.

He had met Caterina at a local lecture on rare books. The head priest at Chartres Cathedral happened to be a rare-book hobbyist. His expertise about the cathedral's own collection was the subject of that evening's lecture. Victor found himself among an audience of Russian speakers—or Russian book collectors? He thought, *This group is too fashionably styled to be authentic book mongers.* Victor later learned that they had intended to leverage some rare-book collections for possibly nefarious purposes. Dark doings that he purposely ignored.

Father Allard gave a glib and interesting lecture. Victor liked him. He often sold books to the cathedral collectors. But that particular evening, Victor overheard Catty chatting up the leader of the Russian group, not for his antiquarian knowledge but rather to congratulate him on his purchase of a huge villa near Paris. Victor was curious because they were speaking stilted English rather than Russian or French. Victor listened as Catty offered her services as an interior designer to the big Russian.

"You've made a wise purchase, Meester Osofsky. Your villa's a rare beauty. I have many ideas about how to decorate it to refleeect your style. Here's my card, when you're ready to bring new life to the interior."

Victor watched her walk outside alone. He followed after her. "Excuse me, miss, do you have time for a glass of wine? I'd love to learn more about antique books."

Catty smirked. "I don't know books, but a glass of wine sounds fine."

Right from the start, their conversation was easy and casual. At the bar, they chatted about her decor business and her artistic sensibility, which she learned from her mother, whose admiration for French culture inspired Catty to move to France. She just couldn't live any longer in the Putin kleptocracy of Russia with its anti-Semitic dangers.

Although Victor no longer lived in Paris, he and Catty began spending several evenings a week together. She was knowledgeable about architectural styles and popular culture, as described in fashion magazines. Though her ways were often out of step with Victor's own conservative lifestyle, her authentic innocence and kindness toward him were reassuring and without demands. He had grown to appreciate her regular presence and loving smile.

Victor thumbs the dog-eared auction flyers sitting on his desk. He already knows the vital information: time, place, and auction company. Damn if the best auctions aren't the farthest away! He'll have to leave in the dark of night to preview properly and bid on yet another closed bakery's carcass.

No doubt he and JP are making a killing selling former bakeries' crown moldings, paneling, shelving, and hand-painted fanciful clocks, the focal point of these artistic masterpieces of symmetry and carpentry.

French boulangeries used to be iconic and ubiquitous on the main street of every village in France. The buildings that housed them were often crafted to suit the needs of several generations, not only in the fortitude of the materials used—marble and mahogany, granite and walnut—but also in their classic, elegant proportion and simplicity.

Today's bakers either can't make a living selling bread or they won't. A skilled, some say magic, touch is necessary to make the perfect baguette, balanced between a crunchy crust and soft center, with a crumb and aroma to evoke yearning. It takes more than simply following the directions written down by one's ancestors. The process is laboriously taxing; one must master big machines, heavy bags of flour, and blazing hot ovens. The baker puts in extreme hours, and the work is blindingly repetitive—first milling the flour, proofing the yeast, then making the dough, and finally, racing the relentlessly hot ovens so that your product doesn't burn. If that charm's not enough to maintain a steady workforce, there's also the joy of rarely increasing prices from year to year.

France's traditions used to demand that a baker's family train their children to take over the trade, but those customs have faded. The monotony keeps young people away. Village life doesn't command the bucolic attraction it once did for young people. New families won't take it on. The boulangerie, this icon of French culture, is vanishing fast, and Victor fully understands his role in the change.

His stomach grumbles. There's no baguette in his pantry—no bread at all—not a *ficelle*, a *flute*, or a *batard*, for that matter. The baguette has the highest proportion of crust to crumb, and that means crunch! The local bakery in Luisant closed two years ago. Fresh bread is available at several bakeries in Chartres, or at that horrid plastic vending machine on the autoroute, but surely no one actually thinks that it dispenses real bread!

He dials JP again. The call goes directly to voice mail. He smells Caterina's jarring perfume and then hears her platform shoes clunking on the tiles in the entry foyer. No doubt she's stopped at that horrid bread vending machine.

"Bonjour! Cuu va?"

Her French pronunciation drives him crazy. The flat approach of her Russian tongue mauling French lyricism is brutal. She butchers French food and the language! He laughs to himself. Her young tongue is good at several things that matter to them both. They share English, and they laugh together, sometimes at the expense of what he calls boorish Russian insensitivity to French etiquette—speaking loudly in crowded places or cutting in line, everywhere from bakeries to the cinemas. She's learned to see through his French eyes.

He enjoys her presence; her company is a comfort. She fled post-Soviet Russia's extreme anti-Semitism and is sincerely grateful for the freedoms that French life affords her. She's easygoing, and they enjoy a hearty meal together and a neighborhood stroll. After Frida's death and his break with JP, Victor had resigned himself to curmudgeonly aloneness, but he's learned that life's surprises are inexhaustible, the appearance of Catty in his world being one of the best.

He tucks his newspaper, maps, and auction flyers under his arm and heads toward the door.

Caterina's dramatic face sinks into a frown. "No, dalink. Not leaving already? Wait! Before you go. Next week at the Louis Vuitton opening, I need you!"

"They've ruined that park! Louis Vuitton in the Bois de Boulogne?"

"Victor, it's not a store. Bernard Arnault opened the most beautiful museum in the park. I got a peek last week. The official opening is next Wednesday, and all the big Russians have bought tables. The opening is for charity. I need you to come with me, or that wretch Olivia, with her organic, homespun, trashy whatever, will win Oleg Osofsky's redecorating contract."

"That tax-dodging crook built a vanity monument in a park owned by the City of Paris, and you want me to celebrate that? I don't get those kinds of tax breaks. Imagine! Yes, I know all about that crap, using an American architect. I heard that it cost a hundred million euros."

"Oh, but Victor," Caterina coos. "I need your help. I have great eedeas to transform Oleg's villa into a playground for a modern man."

"Oh, joy. Imagine that contribution to humanity." He bites his tongue, wondering where his nasty attitude has sprung from. He takes a cleansing breath and thinks to himself that he's found no relationship between decorating and real beauty. He calms himself and says tenderly, "Catty, sweetheart, you don't need me, but if you want me to join you . . ."

She pouts and blinks her false eyelashes. "Oh, dalink. He thinks that you've got good taste. He's right!" She giggles and primps. "He'll think of me as his decorator if you and I are a known ting."

Victor's stomach grumbles louder, and he grabs his coat from the rack, kisses her forehead, and walks out. "I'll be back very late. You mustn't wait up."

He throws his papers into the truck's cab and quickly backs out onto the street. The few kilometers to Chartres aren't so far after all. And Jennie's Café off the main square has *bon rapport qualité-pris*, good value for the money.

He consciously tries to quiet his anger that the richest man in France is getting tax breaks to put monstrosities in the city's park. To lower his blood pressure and ire, he breathes in again—through his nose and out through his mouth—deep, soothing breaths. But then, in his peripheral vision, he sees that hideous Marine Le Pen, the power-hungry right-wing Populist, plastered on a billboard. Signs so huge should never be allowed here in Luisant village, he thinks.

He slams his hand on the steering wheel and whispers to himself, "Merde! The damn French are like sheep, following idiots to slaughter. That Fascist bitch'll push us deeper into a hole that we'll never get out of."

He drives off to Jennie's Café, more agitated than before.

Chapter Two

JP thinks regularly about what makes him unhealthy. What is it that creates this hollow emptiness in his gut? If only meditation came to him more easily—or maybe a yoga teacher? People rave about the yoga classes at the Ninety-Second Street Y. Forget that. He's not going all the way uptown—too much aggravation!

Victor's ongoing complaints about France—the idiots who run the country and the lost way of life—burn JP's stomach and corrode his magical memories of all things French. He can't ask Victor to stop ruining his reminiscences. Victor is so full of bile and anger that it can't help but spill out across the phone lines, across the Atlantic to JP.

JP remembers his mother, Frida. She loved Paris and explored even its far-reaching arrondissements. She claimed to be on the hunt for the perfect Parisian baguette, but really, she loved exploring new neighborhoods—Muslim, Jewish, and many South Asian areas as well.

Victor often admonished her adventurous ways: "Someday, I'll find you in the back of a kebab grill." JP and his mother secretly noted Victor's old-school racist tendencies, and though she silently tolerated Victor's curmudgeonly ways, JP never missed an opportunity to poke at Victor. "What happened to equality, fraternity? You've lost your very Frenchness."

One night, JP listened to them arguing: "Victor, I don't think that you believe that kebab restauranteurs are any less French than, say, architects. Why do you spout foolish racist things like that?"

Victor growled, "Why are you in cahoots with JP against me?"

JP could picture the rise of her brow and a smirk as she replied, "I adore his irreverence, his fearless ease."

JP imagined that Victor, in his usual manner, shook his head and walked off. JP slept soundly, knowing that his mother endorsed his approach to life.

Victor's attempts to rein in Frida were partially humorous and partially born out of sincere concern for her safety. But she wouldn't be controlled, always wanting to be an example to her son on her excursions, to make every day a learning day. Most times, she returned home with JP's after-school snack—called goûter—from a distant boulangerie. More often than not, she'd bring goûter for JP's entire soccer team, meeting them in the park on practice days.

A few of JP's friends from his soccer league lived in the same neighborhood—two guys from Spain, Manuel and Hector. Both of their families were involved with medicine at the nearby hospital. And both guys intended to return to Madrid after high school. JP practiced with them on Wednesdays and never missed a Saturday game, but their friendship stayed on the pitch. They didn't socialize beyond practice and games.

In school, JP drifted between cliques. The *populaires* didn't look twice at him; *les intellos* showed no hospitality to him at lunch. Even though the comradery of his neighborhood soccer club gave him a limited sense of belonging, school jocks were not his crowd. He found the odd artist kids most interesting. There was a great photography program at Lycée Henri IV. The teacher, Monsieur Vichorn, was a former news photographer with tales of never taking no for an answer. JP admired his stories of harrowing difficulties to *get the shot*, including ride-alongs with police and garbage collectors. JP framed his mother or streetscapes and public art in careful photo compositions instead. Hanging out in the darkroom in the art studio, he heard plenty of good school gossip, which he liked to bring home to share with his mom.

Frida studied in the States and spoke perfect English. On the days that she wasn't out exploring Paris, she worked as an English-speaking docent in the Louvre. Her delicate stature and stylish fashion attracted foreign visitors to her museum lectures. Bringing Napoleon's raids of distant lands to life made her one of the most popular docents on the Louvre roster. She was always winning the sympathies of foreign nationals for Emperor Napoleon's mission to create the world's most important national repository in France. An avid student of history, she constantly revised her lectures, keeping them fresh and lively. Her magnetism was irresistible.

After Frida's death, Victor's bitterness was unharnessed. Somehow, all the softness in him, all of what little parental tolerance he had, hardened and shrank into a poisonous rock. Victor lost more than Frida when she died. His personality changed, or maybe it was that she expected tolerance and open-mindedness in him. The limitations that she placed on his bitterness vanished when she died.

Their big old apartment, with soft, worn rugs and books everywhere, echoed with Frida's absence. Watching her slow and painful death drained Victor. Was that why he seemed to lose his sensitivity? Or was it Frida all along who encouraged his empathy? JP was eighteen, too young then to be patient with Victor's bitter mourning. Was there a chance that they could have found sanctuary in each other's sadness? In each other's presence? Without Frida, their anchor, neither of them could go on together. Paris became unlivable for JP.

He passed his baccalaureate with high marks and qualified for entrance to the Sorbonne. But without Frida's steadying influence, their family's dream of him becoming an architect seemed frivolous and bourgeois to JP. Frida showed JP that Paris's morning mist could frost trash with beauty. Without his mother, everything about Paris and France sickened him. Victor simply did not know how to insert himself into JP's thoughts and plans. Frida had been the bridge that joined the two of them—the three of them.

JP was brokenhearted after she died. That, combined with adolescent angst, sent him on a dangerous trajectory of isolation and self-indulgence. Frida often said that it was JP's velvet-timbred voice, exactly like Victor's, that drew all the girls to him. It didn't hurt that his physique became chiseled and handsome in his last years in high school. His narrow hips and wide shoulders were a close copy of Victor's. After graduation, JP let his hair grow wild and curly. He had a medieval, poetic style that caught women's attention, and JP leveraged his wild-child aura. He fucked dozens of women. A few of those experiences gave him the vitality of Superman in the moment, but most of the encounters lacked lasting connection or satisfaction.

JP drifted from a library job restacking dusty books to a bicycle delivery job at a hardware store and a barista at a coffee shop for two undisciplined years after his mother's death. Finally, he found a position that he enjoyed, as a busboy at the fancy French Open lunch tent on the Roland Garros sports grounds. Both he and Victor loved watching professional tennis. And eavesdropping on celebrities had a particular cachet. On a devastatingly hot day, a forty-something woman dressed in a hip-hugging pencil skirt caught his eye. The air in the tent was steamy, and the diners had a louche temperament in the sweltering humidity. Without a word exchanged between them, the vogue woman managed to find an empty broom closet and wordlessly directed JP with an arch of her eyebrow to meet her there. They fucked for five heated minutes, splitting the seam on her hiked-up skirt and smearing makeup all over his white waiter's uniform. Two brooms and a mop fell loudly out of the closet as she pushed the door open and slipped out of his embrace. JP never saw her again. Didn't even know her name. He wasn't fulfilled, but this crazy behavior continued.

After his time as a busboy at Roland Garros, JP managed to get an internship with his father's architectural firm. He didn't spend one day in their glass-skinned high-rise headquarters. Rather, he helped a partner to design a seasonally erected pavilion at Roland Garros for VIPs to be photographed in. The PR manager for this new space, a French American media whiz, whose chic and savvy reputation preceded her, was Belle Korski. She knew media influencers, agents, and celebrities—in Paris and New York. Belle was an original tastemaker herself. Fashion houses, movie stars, sports figures, and restauranteurs all hung on her predictions. JP's second season at Roland Garros, as an intern rather than a busboy, gave him an ease among the staff and around the grounds. He was an obvious choice when Belle needed a minion to be her gofer. She selected him to work closely with her in the weeks leading up to the French Open.

She and JP supervised the pavilion's every detail—from drapery and lighting to stage height and dressing room accouterments. In the process, JP became her boy toy for a few months. He was with her at high-level meetings in Paris's most exclusive C-suites and in the beach cafés of the Riviera as she worked with celebrities all over the country. It was an exciting and harrowing time for JP.

At one contract negotiation for Chanel product placement, they sat on the storied terrace at the Eden Roc in Antibes. Belle's presentation was forceful: "I can assure you that Chanel logos will be on every actress on the red carpet next month at Cannes. But I never, ever, discount my fee." While sitting in a semicircle with three business-suited silverbacks of finance, she leaned over and licked the inside of JP's ear. Silently, he sat stone-still, staring off, looking at nothing at all. The business types pulled their pens and papers from their attachés and looked down until Belle finally reviewed and signed the contracts. She was fond of sex on the conference table after the subject parties departed. After some months, she ghosted JP without explanation. The Roland Garros project was complete, but JP was hollow.

He and Victor lived in the Paris apartment alone together. JP didn't know how to find happiness in himself and without Frida had no one to help him feel whole. After the tumble with Belle, JP avoided emotional intimacy. He allowed women to *catch* him while remaining remote and distant.

None of the women who seduced him—not the Italian countess or the various suburban housewives—none of them helped him find the gravity or groundedness that he sought. Angela, the MacArthur Award–winning artist, was very forward. Their meet-cute collision happened at the Metro turnstile. He leaned his shoulder into the exit turnstile as she, not realizing that it was indeed the exit, leaned into the same spinning apparatus. Together, embraced by steel rods, they untangled themselves and then laughed heartily at the mistake.

"Bonjour." He looked directly into her eyes. "Would you like to have a coffee with me at the—"

She interrupted him, asking, "Perhaps you'd like to come to my studio instead, errr, to see my paintings. I'm an artist."

At first, he agreed to meet her, anticipating that he'd cancel at the last minute. But that morning, Victor left the house without a word, like the previous four days that week. Without the comradery in the darkroom and with school and soccer finished, his days alone were long. When Angela called to confirm their date, he agreed to meet at her Marais studio. Out of breath after walking up five flights of stairs, he knew why he was there, and yet he was surprised by her aggressive manner. No chitchat or queries about his happiness or life. Rather, a quick fuck and even quicker dismissal. He walked home through the park, feeling invisible.

Victor's own grief stifled any nuanced instinct he might have had to support JP. They suffered their mourning in isolation from each other. Victor's singular message, *go to school*, kept JP in bed most days until

Victor left the apartment. JP grew to hate all things French. The traditions, like greeting people in the streets, even strangers. The smells. How could anyone dislike the smells of French bakeries? And yet, JP found the buttery, sugary odors wafting out of bakery doors cloying. He resented the older men in janitor jumpsuits who proudly swept the streets collecting dirty tourist trash. These random French elements combined to become his memory of his mother. He and Victor clashed about things large (JP's professional future) and small (the length of his hair). This transitional time was sharp and painful, but it wasn't just Victor and JP who were changing.

All of France was emerging from a chrysalis, the whole culture being reborn. The clashes weren't so obvious in Paris, Bordeaux, Lyons, or Marseilles, but in the villages and towns where young people had always continued family traditions, suddenly, they were abandoning their homes, some that had been held by a family for multiple generations—possibly as long as three hundred years. Along with these desertions went artisanal trades and traditional crafts. The homes and buildings in villages across the country were being cannibalized by salvage (some would say savage) resellers from all over the world. The once-functional household elements, from doors to floorboards, roof tiles to mantels were sold off to hipsters in the urban USA and UK as expensive architectural artifacts.

Crackled, glazed kitchen backsplash tiles; ancient stone floors, burnished smooth; horse troughs now long dry; fireplaces; roof tiles; and door knockers—even front doors—were torn from their ancestral hinges and foundations and sold piecemeal across high-end zip codes in the United States.

Victor and JP seized their opportunity. This was their chance to change *their* everything too. JP intended to leave France, whereas Victor chose to leave the trappings of his traditional architectural firm. In truth, the firm would have let him go in spite of his years of service. He was no longer flexible; client meetings that necessitated careful listening and observation were met with Victor's humbug impatience and intolerance.

JP and Victor were surgical in their separation. JP morphed into a business partner and abandoned his role as a willing son and honoring child.

"There's no value in duty these days, Dad!"

Together, they solicited loan applications from banks, investors, and business strategists. Their new paradigm of cold-toned business conversations never diverged from their commercial agenda. They never shared a family meal, holiday, or walk in the park. Their fairy-tale family existence disappeared into the atmosphere like the wafting aroma from a bakery oven.

***

Calculating like newly minted MBA graduates, they researched and crunched prospectuses and pored over loan offers from both sides of the Atlantic. It seemed that in France, the banks were giving money away, but as they drilled into the fine print, it was clear that the banks weren't interested in financing their salvage process. Additionally, the EU had so many hurdles to prevent money laundering that they simply couldn't initiate their business plans in France.

Finally, JP moved to New York City. Victor, deeming JP too young to create and grow a business on his own, expected that together, they would find the best building and neighborhood in which to establish themselves. They could not even agree on that plan. JP would have none of Victor in New York. JP leaned into big risk and bought a huge and hugely expensive building in the potentially hip, meatless Meatpacking District. They had calculated that JP could leverage some of the money that Frida left him, and JP didn't hold back a centime.

The old family apartment in Paris had surprisingly little equity. JP realized that Victor must have remortgaged the apartment for living

expenses over the years. He wondered why Victor hadn't, as the traditional head of the family, guarded that nest egg more carefully. But that
was yesterday's news, and now it was revealed that Victor did not abide
by tradition either. Victor and JP were joined by financial agreements,
and they treated each other with a wide *professional* distance. JP held
Victor at arm's length and never spoke with him about his worries or
loneliness or lack of knowledge about American culture. Their conversations were kept strictly to logistics: when the next shipment would
arrive, which items were particularly unique or historical or junk, and
which banking and shipping arrangements were worrying them.

Victor left his old architectural firm with a congratulatory office
party with the smirking senior partners that he resented and a thirty-
five-years-of-service gold watch. The next day he sold the watch to buy
an American-style pickup truck that was too big for Paris's ancient
streets. From there, he set up house outside of Chartres in Luisant,
the center of France. Luisant isn't too far from Paris, and it's classically French, with its medieval cathedral and conservative yet fashionable streets. Now he follows country auctioneers to the dead and
dying towns in every corner of France. A hobby he began doing eleven
years ago. Victor's practiced eye evaluates the condition of buildings
to know if the contents, the cannibalized elements that he will buy,
are in fact authentic and beautiful. He can tell by the condition of the
terra-cotta of a building, or the character of the bricks, if the inside
has been well maintained and used. Buildings that were renovated in
the fifties or seventies were so often denuded of their character that
they were cheapened in the process. Gone were the subtle dips in the
marble counters where hands slid payment to proprietors who in turn
slid back tarts and breads. Cheap Formica was often found in buildings
that were *updated*. Victor pitied these old families that traded down
for inferior materials and craftsmanship to make their homes appear
more modern.

In spite of their personal animosity and naivete about the salvage business, Victor and JP readied their business as the world welcomed them. Victor's network of architects and suppliers informed him about the French villages that were forced to purge their treasures. This, while JP slowly rode the real estate wave in New York, leveraging and trading up to new and more valuable building ownership. JP still wonders how some of those bankers decided to finance his risk. But that precarious leverage is in the past, at least for JP. For years, he teetered on the edge of profitability and success: If Les Beaux Châteaux failed, if he couldn't make enough money to cover his risky mortgagees, would he return to France? Alone? How did he get to the safe side of that worry? Was it his tenacity? Iris's logistical know-how? Luck and timing? He owns several buildings, and the mortgaged ones have strong equity stakes. He's solid now. He even owns a seaside mansion in the Hamptons. He's never spent a night there, but he owns it. And his timing for immigrating and being granted alien status was not at the fraught state that it is currently. Money to lawyers, and the easy political winds pre-9/11, made his transition to becoming a legal alien easy. A green card, cash money in the bank (the immigration monitor's most important measure), and a growing business made JP a successful immigrant—the very best kind of American.

All the while, Les Beaux Châteaux was slowly gaining traction. He sold garden urns, farmhouse sinks, bakery clocks, and slowly, bigger-size items with bigger price tags—bars, fountains, even entire rooms. Their bread-and-butter sales were small- to medium-size urns, chandeliers, and stained glass. JP had buyers—multiple buyers—for almost everything that Victor picked and sent stateside. They had big expenses with international shipping and trucking and customs and breakage, but their markups justified all of the involved coordination. Victor bought and sent to JP authentic artifacts for a fraction of what other antique store buyers paid at auction to stock their stores.

In the beginning, it was complicated to price, say, an old farm-house sink. It was old and cracked and had a big hole where there wasn't supposed to be one, but it was copper, it was French, it was old, and most of all, it was unique. Billionaires, he learned, want things that are better and different from their neighbors' possessions. Iris's clever marketing created a buzz where every hedge-fund mama had to have something unusual for her new kitchen. JP gave up looking for comps and similarly priced retail sales. He dreamed big, adding 45 percent from his original pricing ideas, and wham-bam, thank you, SOLD! Sometimes he would raise the price on an important artifact, like a sculpture or a desk that had an important provenance. If a big piece had been on the showroom floor for too long, JP would raise the price and move it to a new location in the store. It was this unconventional logic that helped him grow Les Beaux Châteaux into a financially successful enterprise.

Iris knew a few high-end kitchen designers, the sort who took out full-page ads in *Architectural Digest,* and those whose names were rarely known in popular circles but were passed between very rich homeowners. JP wasn't sure how she knew them or how she got them to come in to buy some of Les Beaux Châteaux's best pieces. He suspected that she gave a select few cash kickbacks. But he never questioned her methods. Once a few well-placed sinks and stained-glass pieces were installed in Upper East Side town houses, the word spread quickly—Les Beaux Châteaux was *the* place to shop for that *special thing.*

His first years in New York, JP didn't date at all. Romance was expensive and would have altered his financial goals. He kept to his stringent budget, reinvesting in Les Beaux Châteaux and advertising in expensive publications. When he wasn't working, he was scouting to purchase new buildings. Financial independence from Victor was his impossible goal, and he was driven. He hoped that only Iris knew he slept on the rollaway for those few years.

***

Finally, after he paid the bank in full for the building that housed Les Beaux Châteaux, he relaxed. The store was one of the anchors of the now-fashionable Meatpacking District. Rents were high and escalating. If LBC failed, he could rent out the building, giant as it is. No matter what Victor pulled on him, he had *fuck you* money in the bank.

And then, when his financial foundation appeared to be stable, his eyes opened again, and beautiful women seemed to be everywhere. But he didn't want to make the same mistakes he had made in Europe. He wanted someone real. Not too thin and not too trendy and not too fake. That ruled out nearly every LBC customer, interior designer, and banker. For a while, he ironically wondered if there were any sincere women in all of New York.

Reaching out beyond his comfort zone seemed like enlightened self-fulfillment. He wasn't predatory. He was curious and wanted to meet different people from different lifestyles. He began volunteering at refugee shelters—Bengali drop-in centers, Guatemalan mother-child safe spaces, even Rohingya legal aid centers. Finding the time to do this two mornings a week was difficult, and those volunteer hours were filled with reading to small children, filing paperwork for overstressed immigration lawyers, or reading aloud housing contracts to people with limited language skills and next to no money.

He had fallen in love with the vibrant and exceptional New York, but its brutality and inhumanity were shocking. Maybe it was the same in France, but his recollections of Paris were those of tolerance and a far more capable, benevolent society. He decided to limit his volunteer time and stayed on only with the Rohingya—they were the group most in need. Glad to share his American largesse, yet modestly disappointed that he didn't make any close friends at these organizations, he withdrew slowly. Was that because of his own defensive shell, or were the cultural differences so wide that he couldn't bridge the gaps?

Only Iris knew where he was on those Wednesday mornings. She didn't pretend to understand his motivation to be involved with refugee communities, but she always filled in at LBC when he was busy. Though she did not reciprocate in kind, JP felt at ease in sharing the quieter aspects of his life with Iris.

Chapter Three

Holidays in the States can be lonely. Most of the time, JP is too busy, purposely busy, to feel alone. But holidays—Thanksgiving, Fourth of July, even New Year's—are a drag. So much of the city's commercial life is simply closed on Thanksgiving. A dreary day for anyone not celebrating.

This Thanksgiving, he goes to the most French bistro that he knows, Bistro Bordeaux, in the West Village. The bartender there speaks passable French, and a glass of wine will be a welcome diversion. He turns the corner, and it looks dark. Ugh! Another restaurant closed for the holiday. But when he approaches and finds it open, his relief loosens his tense shoulders.

But merde! Muriel, his bartender, isn't here. Instead, an amazingly tall and dark woman crawls under the bar and asks him, while lifting a bottle of wine, "Monsieur, perhaps, would you like une verre du vin rouge?" She has a lilting, unfamiliar accent. Her wide white teeth shine brightly against her almond-shaped cheeks. Her black hair is clipped so closely to her head that he can see her scalp, emphasizing the diamond shape of her large skull. Above the beer and sour wine smells of the bar, the smooth melon scent of her skin wafts under his nose.

"Bonsoir." She stands tall and straight. Wide black jeans and a loosely draped turtleneck disguise her slim shape.

He is dumbstruck, and she perhaps mistakes his awe for disappointment. "Muriel will be back next week. She's gone out of town for the holiday." JP breathes deeply, taking in her smell again. He looks down at his hands. He had been moving that damn fountain yesterday with Hank, and his fingernails are still dirty. The bar's dim lights may keep his secret. He hangs his jacket on the hook behind his stool. Maybe he'll be comfortable this Thanksgiving after all.

"Good evening, mademoiselle. Je suis Jean Paul. It's a pleasure to find a friendly face on this Thanksgiving night. We immigrants can find comfort together. This is the one night of the year when most everything stops. I am glad that you are not in a far-flung suburban house, eating turkey and potatoes ce soir."

She doesn't reveal much. "How do you know that I am an immigrant?"

He smiles quietly. "I promise not to ask for your green card or work documents."

"You don't know me, yet my name is an immigrant name: Rama. Still, your assumption is questionable. I might be American with a foreign name?" She nods slowly and deeply.

"Where are you from?" he says, nodding slightly in her direction.

Rama transforms in a second, with a thick and authentic Brooklyn accent. "You don't know me. After my shift here, I'm drivin' out to White Plains to get my fill o' turkey, gravy, and smashed potatoes."

She is so believable that he is stunned silent. He swallows twice in the unsettled pause. She looks him in the eye and stands still as a statue. Seconds pass, and then she cracks up, laughing so hard that she's doubled over. She picks up the pen and order pad. That is all the casual time that she can spare.

Other patrons come in and order food to be served at the bar. Rama is busy. He's finished his drink and he doesn't want more, but how else to get her attention?

"S'il vous plaît? Un autre verre du vin rouge?"

She looks more carefully at him. "Seriously, dude, are you French? You sure sound it, but you look like Mom, home, and apple pie to me."

He'd worked assiduously to shed his Frenchness, and apparently, he's a success. "Oui! Mon Dieu! Je suis Français! Are you French?"

Rama's eyes get glassy and unfocused as she answers, "I'm becoming African American."

Other people begin to fill the bar. Turning to give her his full attention, he asks, "How about you tell me the story of how you're from France? And then you can tell me the story about how you're from Africa, and then you can tell me the story of your home in Brooklyn. I'd like to listen to all your stories some evening soon, over dinner. Would you be my guest? May I call you?"

She smiles, ignoring the other patrons' calls for more beer. "There's règles, rules, here. We're not supposed to date the patrons." She hesitates to see if he'll just roll over or try harder. *Oh yeah,* he thinks, *I'll play her game.*

He reaches for his wallet and pulls out his business card. His name and "Les Beaux Châteaux" are printed in an exquisite French art deco font on thick white card stock that screams high quality. He used to be especially proud of this presentation. That pride has diminished, and he's not sure why. He places the card on the bar next to a ridiculously large tip. "Call me when you're ready to tell your stories."

He walks home with a spring in his step, enjoying the glow from the streetlights.

***

The rainy sleet blows in torrents across French Autoroute D744. Victor is wired. It took so long to settle his accounts at the Niort village auction.

At the settlement desk, Victor had asked the cashier to itemize his bids again. Through the sale, he kept good notes; still, this discipline at settlement came after multiple overpayment errors. He kept quiet, calming his excitement inside. This business-y paperwork was only the beginning of his efforts to care for the bakery that he just purchased. He didn't want to look the sad bakery owner, La Madame, in the eye. He'd paid so little for the elegantly symmetrical walls and shelves of her family bedrock. He politely accepted the coffee she offered, sipped, and wrote his check.

The other bidders collected their property and filed out. Victor pulled his truck into the back alleyway, where the loading gate opened for him. Parallel to the main commercial street, this workers' access area was also silent—empty of all vibrancy.

His furniture blankets, folded in ascending size from largest to smallest, created a blanket pyramid in the flatbed of his truck. He had multiple tool bags: different-size hammers, mallets, and screwdrivers; a bag of power tools and extra battery packs; four different-colored tapes; and ziplock bags for hardware like unique clips and bolts and other tiny findings.

In the early years, he would hire young men looking for work—local muscle—to disassemble his trophies. In the first two or so hours of the work, the process would be predictable and satisfying. Large boards came apart easily and were stored in geometrically logical bundles in the truck. But as the hours passed, the work became more specific and tedious. A mature carpenter or salvage man's real worth was evident as the disassembly got to the nitty-gritty. Small marquetry boards needed coding with colored tape, numbering, and a reconfiguration system. It took Victor years to develop a reliable system for such numbering and color coding. Ancient plumbing fixtures necessitated firm yet gentle handling. Small joining tacks had to be carefully released from their yearslong duty rather than recklessly yanked and snapped. Backsplash tiles or board pieces might be in even lengths of two feet, whereas the last piece removed might be four and a half feet long, making the last odd pieces difficult to bundle and place in the truck bed. In the end, Victor found that this long, careful, surgical work was for him alone. No matter how strong the young locals' backs were, their work was often so sloppy that he'd spend hours reassembling the pieces that they'd jumbled like a giant jigsaw puzzle. Those young bucks were no match for his patience. It took skillful hands to disassemble ancient plumbing fixtures. His system for removing book-matched wood paneling, or even his own way of lowering and packing up crystal chandeliers, added to these artifacts' value.

His stomach growls with acid, but the ride to Luisant should only be two hours at this time of the night. He'll get some antacids at home. His Ford pickup is a workhorse. So dependable and American. Amazingly, everything fit in the truck bed. He had battened down the mahogany walls, shelves, and drawers, and even the heavy marble slabs slid into the felted slots he arranged for them. He'd watched the bakery owner herself wrap the clock from the center wall in a furniture blanket. She handed it to him but he couldn't catch her eye. He set the clock on the seat in the cab. Bungee cords tied down the giant canvas over the payload, and he put a makeshift plastic cover on top to protect against the rain. That final, ill-fitting wrap irked Victor. He had rushed the bungee hooks arrangement holding it. His stomach was roaring. But he was on the road. Finally!

His mind wanders to the arrangement he'll make for these items in the shipping container. Will it go into a container with the stone fountain he bought last week or a separate one? The fountain won't be shipped to the Port of Le Havre till next month. He can get this bakery into the next container to JP on Monday.

He is driving on autopilot, ignoring his stomach, and rearranging the geometry of the pieces of the bakery in his head when flashing lights catch his attention. "Merde!"

He pulls over and steps out into the cold, windy rain. The policeman is unfamiliar. *Damn!*

Matter-of-factly, the cop says, "Your plastic tarp is flipping in the wind. It'll surely blow off and cause an accident. C'est un danger."

Trying to ignore the pain in his gut, Victor is polite. "Merci, officer. I hadn't noticed. You're a tremendous help." He jumps up on the running board and pulls the plastic taut with the bungee hook.

"Merci, encore." Victor begins to walk back to the front of the cab.

"What's in the back?" the cop calls after him.

Victor is well rehearsed. "Ahhh! Just some old wood."

The cop seems interested. *Damn,* Victor thinks. Couldn't he be interested on a dry, sunny day?

"Where are you coming from?" the cop asks.

Victor mumbles, "Niort village."

The cop shakes his head with knowing intelligence. "At the auction, right? Pickin' at the bones of those old widows? I heard a terrible thing about that village. Maybe you heard it too?"

Victor shakes his head to show that he doesn't know anything special about Niort, and he wishes that this cop would just get a move on.

"Yeah, I heard that they're talking about allowing nuclear waste to be buried there. Imagine, they're so desperate that they'll sell their legacy, their terroir; they'll poison their land. I can't understand that trade-off. The government would never allow such a thing, but those old folks must be ruined."

The rain is letting up now, but the wind continues unabated, and the plastic on Victor's truck bed loosens again. The cop begins taking the plastic off and bundling it in his arms. Victor stands watching, dumbstruck, as the cop hands Victor the wet plastic bundle. "Get home safely, man."

Victor drives straight home without interruption.

He walks through his front door, and the smell of Caterina's perfume smacks him in the face. Ugh! So caustic. He heads straight to the kitchen cabinet where he keeps the antacids. It is dark and late. She's left her car blocking his entrance to the porte cochere again. "Catty! Catty!" he calls.

He sees her keys on the coffee table. He still has a long night ahead, drying and protecting that damn bakery. Outside, he has a locker full of soft cloths and brushes, polishing paste, sandpaper, and shellac, each product carefully placed with its like brothers. Preservation is usually little more than proper cleaning and drying. Some of the bakeries are more than a hundred years old. The wood has already been dried, cured, and aged to perfection.

Finally, when the work is done, he comes back inside, throws his keys on the kitchen counter, and quickly chews a few more antacids, then takes a big swallow of water. His shoulders burn from lifting the marble slabs. Luckily, he didn't drop them, brittle and fragile as they are. This work is not for him, not the muscle part. Not anymore.

Throwing his damp and dirty clothes onto the tiled bathroom floor and stepping into the shower, he shakes off some tension from this long day's work. Why in God's name isn't JP here, hauling this crazy stuff? But Victor wouldn't trade places to live in New York. Even the thought of retail gives him the creeps. His stomach gurgles.

He towels off and slips on his flannel robe, then clomps into the bedroom, purposely waking Caterina. One quick fuck, and he'll get some rest.

Victor pulls back the blankets, and she scowls. "Aw, Victor, it's cold."

"I've got something warm for you, Catty."

She turns over with a sour face but puts her hand on his ribs. He looks down, and she has neon-green nail lacquer on her fingers; she looks diseased. He tries to unsee those hands, closing his eyes.

He grumbles again. "It was a long trip. Just do me quick so that I can relax, huh, honey?"

She pulls herself up on her hands and knees, reaches her head down, and licks his cock. *Ahhh, yes.* He stands up on command. He reaches out to smooth her hair and then delicately strokes her nipple, and there, again, he watches her green-nailed hand reach to stroke him. He looks away, but he can feel himself shrinking from her touch. She licks and sucks, nibbling a bit, but this is a fait accompli.

Catty murmurs, "Oh, hhhoney, eet happens to eeeveryone once in a while. You're just tired."

Victor turns his back to her, bundles the pillow under his head, and tries to sleep.

***

JP isn't surprised when Rama calls the next day. Sure, she can meet uptown. Art? Yes, she says, "Everyone likes art."

JP meets her in front of the Neue Galerie, one of his favorite New York museums. Small and utterly exquisite. A true gem. He stands across the street to watch her for a minute. She's wearing a nondescript trench coat with a small, tasteful backpack, no jewelry, and little makeup. She doesn't have her nose in her phone, and she seems to possess a curiosity as she watches the world pass. JP crosses the street and greets her with familiarity, reaching around her shoulder and giving her a kiss on the mouth. She doesn't resist.

"I don't want to tell you too much about this place. Well, except that I love it. It's not that old, as a museum, that is. The building is vintage. And the museum was founded by Ronald Lauder. Do you know Estée Lauder, like the makeup?"

"Maybe. Sure, I guess so."

"Well, anyway, he's super-rich. He bought this building. Beautiful, right? And this very famous painting. It's not quite as well known as the *Mona Lisa*, but close. Well, I think all the exhibits here are beautiful, and there's a visiting show of Max Beckmann. He's German, but in spite of that, he's another of my favorite artists here too." *That joke didn't land too well,* JP thinks. *Well, I guess you have to be French.*

He flashes his membership card, and one of the formally dressed guards gives him a knuckle bump. He and Rama climb to the main exhibit area. The iron banister that guides them around the curved stairway is cool to the touch. The sun's rays glow on Rama's cheeks through the skylight above. They walk through the art deco–styled rooms and stop in front of the Adele painting by Gustav Klimt.

Rama walks directly to the famous painting, sometimes called *The Woman in Gold.*

"Right! This one. But I know this image. It's on trash cans and coffee cups. It's everywhere."

"You're right. Of course, you're right!" JP answers. "But it was here, in Klimt's vision, first."

They walk through the gallery and into the Beckmann exhibit.

"Please stop me if you already know this. Sometimes it helps to appreciate the art if you know a bit of the backstory."

Rama turns to him with a sly expression. "I wonder about art that needs explanation."

JP admires her self-confidence. Then he considers whether she's just snarky. She definitely deserves the benefit of the doubt. He turns on his velvet voice. "Beckmann painted in Germany between the wars. See here?" He points. "Men bandaged, and women grotesquely seductive. I love his technique, his painful colors, and tragic vision, but we French, we sort of love to see the suffering of Germans between the wars."

Rama is quiet. He wonders if she knows what he's talking about. She looks carefully at each image but doesn't comment. JP's not pushy. It's nice to be in her company, and her smooth melon smell is intoxicating.

After they've seen all the exhibits, they head to the basement to Café Sabarsky, the art nouveau–themed café with dark wood paneling and French/Viennese food, music, and ambiance. JP orders strawberries, chocolate cake, and two flutes of Veuve Clicquot champagne. Rama remains quiet.

"So, what did you think?" he asks her.

She smiles and pulls her hands out from under his. She's thoughtful for a few seconds more. "It's very Western. I mean European. I appreciate the skill and, as you call it, technique, but I'm not drawn to Western motifs. I like less-schooled art. Call me pagan, but I like African art."

JP listens carefully. "African art? Like more primitive?"

"I guess that's what you call it."

JP smiles at the waiter as he places the food and drink on the table. "You still haven't told me where you're from. I'm gonna say Africa. Right? Good guess? Big target."

They drink their champagne, and the conversation smooths out a bit. Rama tells him how she came to NYC from Dakar, Senegal, by way of Canada. She's getting divorced from her husband, and her residency and work papers are finally in order now.

"I don't have time to really know art. I've paid off my husband, my lawyer, and I send my mama money every month. I've worked as many as four jobs at one time. I have made this happen. I'd like to know art, I guess. I'd like to know that Ronald Lauder. Imagine his billions."

JP is slightly crestfallen. He wanted Rama to be educated, charming, and unaffected. Instead, he finds her slightly coarse in spite of her natural beauty. Kind of like every artifact that Victor has sent him—not as refined as he'd like, but beautiful in its functionality and craftsmanship. He senses a snobbishness in himself that he doesn't like but can't fully control. He can hear Victor in his head, admonishing his affectations.

"Don't you want to know about me?" he asks her.

"Oh, I've asked around about you," she says offhandedly. "Everyone knows about you."

This is surprising to JP. He feels heat rise on his neck. "Really? Who have you spoken with?"

"Oh, I know the car parkers in the Meatpacking. My husband owns Marty's Car Parkers."

JP is not only surprised, but he feels a sort of violation. Prickly stinging races across his abdomen. He's well aware that his cheeks and ears are blotched red. He doesn't even know the people who are reporting on him.

"And what do these car parkers say about me? Wait, your husband owns the car parking company? I know that creep. He's always trying to scam me!"

Rama smiles. "Right, you do know my husband. Well, ex-husband."

"You were married to that joker? He's a shakedown criminal, that guy. I can't imagine you with him."

"It was for the paperwork. I almost married someone wonderful, but he was a musician, traveling, and we would never have passed the immigration tests to verify that we were really married. I was in a rush. Hell, I would have married any frog that promised to convince the immigration people that I deserved to get a green card. And yeah, Marty, he shook me down for lots of money."

An air of disappointment descends upon JP. He feels his attraction to Rama waning. The wind has shifted, and an obscure gale has blown her magnetism away; the whole thing feels off. She runs with a different crowd. Would they find they have anything in common? She doesn't even like Klimt! He resolves in his mind to finish politely and call it a one and done.

They're both finishing up their champagne, and he figures the night will wind down from here. Instead, Rama signals to the waiter for two more glasses. She has a glint in her eye. "So, do you want to know what the car parkers say about you or not?"

JP shakes his head no.

She giggles. "That's smart. I'll tell you what I think I might know about you instead—how's that?"

"I don't like your sources. Your opinion can only be colored by bad intel."

"Fair enough," she says.

They drink in silence. He pays the bill, and they walk out of the café. On the street, JP hails a cab. He opens the door and hands the cabbie twenty dollars. He stands back and reaches to take her hand.

"That's it? We're done because my ex-husband is a gangster car parker? Where do you live, man? Let's go downtown and have another drink. C'mon, baby." She reaches to stroke his cheek. He withdraws.

"Have it your way. Ciao!" she says as she slams the cab door.

In the Uber headed back downtown to his apartment, JP feels hollow and lonely again, separated from the France he no longer loves and without any family anywhere. He thought that success with Les Beaux Châteaux would lessen his insecurity, but no matter how big his bank account grows, he's remained untethered.

He walks through the glass-cube lobby of his building. A charcoal-gray modern elevator opens into his apartment. He places his jacket on a vintage French coat hanger from a men's choral club in Provence. Twenty of them are loosely grouped in his coat closet. These hangers are the only soft-edged vintage objects in the house. In contrast to everything at LBC, JP's house is a study in minimal, monotone modernism. White, gray, black, silver, and gold populate the tableau from kitchen to balcony, and the bedroom too. Abstract ink paintings in black and silver hang on the few solid walls. The apples and oranges on the kitchen counter stand like screaming beacons of color.

He throws his keys onto the dining table. This absurdly expensive hipster address is empty and cold. It's probably too late to call Victor—9:00 p.m.—but what the hell?

Victor picks up on the first ring.

"Good evening. Sorry to call so late."

"Nahhh. Can't sleep anyway," his father replies.

JP chooses his words carefully, trying not to sound blaming and accusatory in his tone, but everything he says seems to come out that way. "That customs officer says that there's trouble with the last container. What do you know about that?"

JP hears Victor spit and harrumph. "That goddammed bitch Marine Le Pen's on a rampage about national treasures and cultural identity, and suddenly I'm not allowed to sell these bakeries? It's an entire room. It's beautiful. You'll be able to sell it for a fortune. It's complete." JP hears him spit again.

"I'll do fine with the sinks, roof tiles, and front doors. Business is good, and the markups on the small stuff without the hassle are rock-solid."

JP hears Victor growl in a guttural tone that alarms him for what is to come. Victor's voice is clear, and the words are slowly enunciated. "Get out there and find the better buyers, you lazy slob. I'm hauling this stuff myself."

"I told you to hire some muscle. Don't blame me if you can't keep any hires."

"Well, aren't you the sass? I'm quicker and better by myself. I'm first at every auction. I'm able to buy the best. If you can't sell what I send you, I'll find a—"

JP stops him again. "D'accord, Papa. I get it."

Victor breathes audibly, deeply, and clears his throat. "I read in the *Wall Street Journal* how those tech billionaires are seeking authenticity in their lives. I'm sending you the real goddamned stuff. Get a fucking different customs officer and move that stuff because I sent two more entire bakeries to you in a container just yesterday!"

"Right. And what of Ms. Le Pen's concern for national heritage?"

Victor hangs up.

***

Victor stands in front of the full-length mirror in Caterina's tiny pied-à-terre on Rue Victor Hugo in Paris. Catty's hair is teased to the height of a three-tiered wedding cake. Her platform shoes clomp, an ungodly sound. She fidgets with an apricot kerchief in his suit pocket and broadens the collar of the black-on-black shirt he's wearing.

He looks at the two of them in the mirror. Happily, he notes that her fingernails have a tame red tone on them today, and the perfume of a few weeks ago is gone. He feels attractive with the vital and young Catty on his arm.

Catty is eye-catching, though hardly elegant. She wears a red bustier that pushes up her already substantial breasts. Rhinestone buttons close the front, and the contrasting black lingerie bones run down her abdomen, highlighting her narrow waist. Purple satin pajama pants with a high waist and wide black belt encrusted with rhinestones scream *look at me!* Her black platform sandals with gumball-size "pearls" on the boxy heels clomp in a loud, unrhythmic cadence. Finally, the green-and-purple feather necklace is the icing on her cake.

"We won't stay long? Right?" he asks.

She smiles and rubs his chest. "Just long enough for me to fix the deal with Oleg Osofsky."

As Victor and Caterina get out of the taxi at the Louis Vuitton Foundation Museum in the Bois de Boulogne, he hears chanting and sees a crowd holding signs. They are being held back by caution tape and a small crew of police. There is Marine Le Pen herself, leading the chants: "Choose France! Together France! In the name of the people!"

Victor pulls Caterina close as they stride to the entranceway. Inside the huge party tents are waterfalls, grottos, ice sculptures, floral arrangements, and nearly naked women standing in ponds dotted with lily pads. Seating for what looks like a forty-piece orchestra surrounds the catwalk, and giant high-res billboards with pictures of children with cleft palates hang among the decor. Oh, d'accord, he remembers, this is for a children's charity. Merde!

Ahhh, and here comes Catty's Russian Mafia, eager to embrace her. Should he make a run for the bar now? But Caterina holds his hand firmly. Olga, Anya, Marina, Dominika, Natalia, Sofia, and a few more converge on them. Air-kisses fly. Catty's friends never smear their makeup. The various perfumes are so strong that Victor's eyes burn. The Mafia's saccharine smiles glow with unnaturally whitened teeth. All are thin and tucked and dressed in au courant costumes that remind him of youthful visits to the circus. Catty is the leader of her gang; they all follow her like obedient sheep . . . A shiver briefly shakes him.

Caterina holds his hand tightly again. They begin their parade around the tent and into the museum. Hundreds of fashion people nibble the food and drink. Caterina hands him a tall champagne flute with flowers floating in it. He hands it back.

"I've gotta find a different drink." He slips away from her grasp and into the ocean of carefully coiffed revelers. He walks aimlessly in the crowd, looking for a bar, but all he sees are waiters with trays of flower-floating champagnes. His stomach gurgles and growls.

He reaches into his pocket and pulls out two antacids. He just needs some water to wash these down. He's drowning in a sea of flamboyant costumes, jewels, textiles, and synthetic hair color.

Finally, he finds a bar. He stands waiting as the waiter, who talks with his colleague, ignores him. A tall, nearly bald Slavic man with a robust physique plants himself next to Victor. The close tailoring of his blue sharkskin suit gives his taut build sleekness. He watches Victor chew one antacid and then the second.

Victor feels the man's eyes burrowing into him. "I have un de plus in my pocket. Want it?"

"No, thank you very much, though."

The man doesn't avert his gaze from Victor.

Victor turns a few degrees away and thinks, *Ugh, another Russian. I can't get away from them. What could this one want from me?*

The Russian reaches his hand out. "I am Oleg Osofsky. Finally, weee meet. Actually, I saw you one night at the Chartres Cathedral, at the lecture on antique books. I know yeeeur friend, Caterina, who speaks so hhhighly of you."

Victor chews silently, turning to face him again. Yes, maybe he does remember. He'll never find Catty in this crowd. Damn! His eyes sweep the room.

"Maybe you'd like a glass of wine?" Oleg asks.

"No! First a glass of water, then wine."

"How about a proper Bordeaux? I believe dat they're serving the Garraud Lalande de Pomerol. Does dat suit you?"

Victor's eyebrows rise. Clearly, this Russian knows his French wines. Oleg speaks to the waiter behind the bar in Russian, and a slim glass of water and a very full goblet of hearty Bordeaux red are handed over.

Oleg steps closer to Victor and speaks quietly, almost conspiratorially. "I hhhear dat you are buying French artifacts, some maisons traditionelles, and businesses?"

Victor answers monosyllabically. "Hmmm." He wonders what chatty Catty has been telling these Russian dogs.

Oleg continues. "I think dat thees ees a veeery important market. Or I should say dat you, my friend, are onto a veeery important market. You hhhave ways to resell these artifacts, no?"

Victor is silent but stays engaged.

"I would like to know theees market, myself. Some of these ancient French towns and villages are ready for redevelopment. I know theees business, those iconic villages, particularly near the coasts. I think dat many old people live eeen these villages and dat new life needs to be brought eeen."

Victor remains silent but sizes up Oleg. Damn! He shouldn't have tuned Catty out when she spoke about him.

Oleg pulls his card from his pocket and extends it to Victor. "Maybe we could hhhelp each other, yes? I may hhhave a favorable proposition for you. Call me if you are interested."

Victor puts the card into his pocket and looks around for Catty.

"Don't worry about Catty. I know dat she weeell find me, and I weeell see that she gets hhhome safely tonight."

Victor stumbles over his words. "Oh, I couldn't. She'll be looking for me, and it would be a—"

"Don't worry, my friend. She eees with my friends now, as we speak. Don't worry. I weeell see dat she ees delivered safely."

**

JP sits at his desk, trying to find invoices from the car-parking company. In this pile of files is a multitude of records, some handwritten on paper scraps and some machine printed: candy vendors, sign makers, dry cleaners, special garbage collectors, antique car-wheel vendors. Where are the damn car parker's documents? Something feels off about this parking problem.

He lifts his head, and Iris, in her all-knowing way, walks over to his desk. He has a peculiar feeling that Iris's dealings with the car parkers have more complications than he can identify. The dog sits, and JP pulls a treat from his pocket. Dolly has perfect manners. Iris winks knowingly at JP. He opens his desk drawer, pulls out a small gold-foil-wrapped dark chocolate square, and hands it to her.

She smiles. "OK, you've buttered up both of us—what do you need?"

He reaches to the far corner of his desk, lifting a pile of files, and flops them front and center. "I can't find any documents on what we pay those damn car hoppers."

She shakes her head. "Yeah, that son of a bitch would only take cash."

JP wrinkles his brow and lips. "Damn! I know that we keep cash on hand to address needs as necessary, but I can't stand doing that shit! We need a record of it, regardless if it's cash or not."

Iris shakes her head. "I didn't review the details with you. I struck a monthly deal with him, but then, after that, he cornered me one night and insisted on weekly cash payments. And I mean insisted! I mentioned it to you in passing, but I didn't emphasize it. I knew that you'd be angry."

"Cornered you? Where was Dolly?"

"I guess she was inside already. He must have been watching me. He's a real snake."

"Can't we use a different company?"

"Believe me, I tried. He's bought up all the competitors in Lower Manhattan. Do not turn your back on him. He's trouble."

He looks up at her for approval. "We need a valet, right? How much do we spend with that creep annually?"

"We'd lose a huge percentage of our business if we axed it. All those Connecticut and Jersey plates you see parked out there . . . They drive in because they know that we'll park 'em."

"What do you know about that guy? I mean, where's he from? And is his business properly licensed? And can we cause him some grief?"

"Sure. I mean, I guess we could. Why, though? It'd only cause us problems. What's got your goat?"

"I'm not altogether sure, but he's talking trash about me, and I don't even know the guy. So how much are we paying him, in cash?"

"I'll have to go back into my records. I can't remember. I don't know much about the guy. I heard that he's from Venezuela, but I don't even know if that's true."

"Don't remember? That's not like you. Well, it doesn't matter. When you find those records, lemme know, eh?"

"I hear that he's got a beautiful wife, if that's of any value."

"Yeah, I heard that too," JP says.

JP and Dolly walk outside. The Highline, the repurposed train line that's become New York's hot spot for landscape design and outdoor fitness and relaxation, has become the spine of this newly hip community. The Highline path is off to the left in his peripheral vision, and the newest restaurants and hotels are kitty-corner from LBC. Dress stores and eyeglass boutiques, coffee shops, and an exotic ice cream store keep the daylight street traffic humming. He sees a lectern out on the sidewalk. A slim Hispanic man with a faint mustache leans on it. His matching red track jacket and hat are emblazoned with bold white writing that reads "Marty's Parking."

As JP watches, a white Rolls convertible with Connecticut license plates pulls up. A blonde with long bedhead tresses and Balenciaga-labeled joggers gets out. She hands the carhop money and cracks some joke with him. He laughs and shakes his head in agreement with her. JP can smell an acrid perfume wafting by. The blonde heads into the ice cream shop and then out and into LBC.

JP watches the young carhop turn on the flashers of the Rolls and put the key into a cabinet that holds dozens of others. He secures the rinky-dink lock on the flimsy door. Dolly sits perfectly still at his heel. JP doesn't know what he's looking for, but there's lots of commotion on the street. Iris is absolutely correct—few if any suburban shoppers would be here were it not for the free parking that he provides. They park with him, stroll through his store, maybe buy something, maybe not, and then go to shop and eat in the neighborhood's newest hot spots. Knowing more about Marty's car parkers wouldn't take much investigation, but as he prioritizes what's next, he lets this parking question default to Iris's bailiwick.

He's thinking about Victor lugging all these heavy artifacts himself from remote hamlets and dragging them to the crating company. It's no job for an old man. How can he help make Victor's role easier?

He's lost in thought, and then the subway train rumbles the sidewalk grate below his feet. The screech is loud and unnerving. He turns his head from the sound and sees Rama darting away from the car parker's lectern with the pegboard of keys clenched in her arms.

***

Victor takes a taxi back to Catty's pied-à-terre. It's a dirty, dark building at the end of a lonely street. He has to unbolt multiple locks to get in, and the place throbs with the essence of perfume.

The decor is loud and incongruous, and the furniture doesn't suit the small space. But for good or ill, the style looks like Catty, all bright jewel tones and metallic accents. The couch slopes at an uncomfortable angle for his tired back, and feathers decorate the ottoman, if that isn't the single oddest material to put on an ottoman, a place to rest one's feet. Ugh! He switches on the TV and then goes to hunt for more antacids.

The news blathers on about a record number of tourists in Paris, the Metro strike, and Marine Le Pen protesting in the Bois de Boulogne. Victor isn't really listening; he's frustrated with himself for not bringing a bottle of antacids of his own here. Now he'll have to go out to a pharmacy tonight. Considering that, he might as well go back to Luisant. But he won't leave without checking in with Catty. He'll wait to make sure that she returns safely. How did he get talked into attending this fete with her in the first place?

He takes off his shoes to be able to put his feet up without damaging the ottoman's feathers. He closes his eyes and is almost asleep when he hears on the news that there was gunfire outside the charitable party at the opening of the Louis Vuitton Foundation Museum in the park. The broadcast shows the gilded guests standing outside the giant tent as the police race around. Musicians, caterers, and revelers stand among the trees and on the grass. All the staged hierarchy has melted, and a free-for-all has spread out of the museum and into the park. Victor listens as the broadcaster gives more background and details on the shooting; then urgent knocking pounds on the front door.

Victor opens the door to find Catty, standing disheveled, her shoes in hand. Her feet are filthy and her makeup smeared. "Oh my! How could you leave me by myself? Well, eet's good that you left. Oleg's driver bringed me home. You cannot believe this crazy night."

Victor gestures to the TV, where more footage shows the chaos in the park, a pack of Marine Le Pen's automatons clashing with the hoi polloi of the artsy charitable set. Victor rubs his stomach and looks at her.

She drops her bag and shoes and begins a wall-to-wall rant. "Yes. And some Russians, some people that even I do not know. Imagine! Well, there was a fight, you know, like about some very expensive art that was not paid for, or I don't even know. And then bang, bang, bang! Real guns! And the police, les flic . . . and well, I'm here now."

She reaches out to Victor, wrapping her arms around him and tucking her head under his chin. He pats her like she's a child who has skinned her knee. Two deep breaths, and he pats her once more to signal the end of this commotion. "OK, Catty. How soon till you can be ready to go back to Luisant?"

Catty falls deeply into the ungracious couch, shaking her head no. "Do you not understand that I was in the dangerous party where there were guns? Maybe you don't really love me, Victor."

He stops tying his shoes and reaches out for her hand. "I'm so sorry that you were scared. Those parties are not for me. I'm glad that you're safe now. We'll catch up later in the week, then. Right?"

She looks away in a pout but then perks up. "Oh, Victor! One more ting. Oleg promised to show me his villa that needs re-decor."

Victor drapes his sport jacket over his arm as he tosses and catches his keys. He turns back to face her. "That's great news, Catty! I know that you'll work hard on that project. I'm glad that you have won him."

She smiles at him and then slumps into the couch. He walks out the door.

***

JP strides into LBC late on Wednesday. It was his last day at the Rohingya settlement house. The mothers hosted a small tea ceremony in his honor. Iris is at the door when he arrives. She has several pink message sheets in her hand, never a good start. JP gives Dolly a treat and askes Iris, "What gives?"

Iris sips her coffee and strokes Dolly slowly. This slow petting rhythm helps calm Iris's overcaffeinated anger. "Man, we've got some stuff to navigate."

Walking to his desk, JP says, "OK, let's go! I'm mean, I'm here, so let's get to work."

Iris gives JP a fierce look. "Victor's stuff's *not* clearing customs, and he's angry. I'll note, he's angry at me. And that damn smarmy Venezuelan car hopper took us off his roster. He fired us!"

JP smirks. "Iris, really . . ."

"And don't mansplain anything to me. I recognize the implications of this, and I'll figure out a workable solution."

"OK. OK. I'm not worried. What if we don't have a valet service for our customers?"

"Yup. That's exactly what I said to myself. But then I reconsidered. No valet means far fewer customers. Trust me, there is nowhere to park in this neighborhood, not even five blocks away. We'll lose our momentum. And once lost . . . well, it won't matter when we get our goods through customs 'cause they'll sit here. My beastly mama always said if you're not out sellin', someone's outsellin' you. I'll fix this." Dolly follows Iris back to her desk.

***

That afternoon, Victor and Oleg meet at Jennie's Café. Omelets, baguettes, butter, and coffee.

Oleg lights another cigarette. "I see that you have the good look, I mean the good eye. You know what to buy and what to leave for the . . . the vultures."

Victor sips his café au lait. "I'm no expert. I buy for the beauty . . . Errr, I mean, I buy what my son tells me sells in New York."

"Exactly. But I watch that you are leeefting and hauling and dragging all of dat, all of those sheeelves and statues, bars and fountains, around in yeeeur own truck."

Victor stares straight ahead, willing himself not to show his concern that Oleg watches and knows his comings and goings—his solitary work.

Oleg jumps, ready to pounce. "So, I have an eeedea that you and I will be partners. I'll bring the trucks, I'll bring the strong boys, I'll help you with the money, errr, the euros, and you and I will select the best of the beautiful to sell. I mean you and I will buy at these auctions the very French parts of homes that you know to be valuable. Yes?"

Victor drinks his coffee and leans back. "Nahhh! My son, JP, is my partner."

Oleg leans in. "I don't see him here helping you lift and wrap and haul these heavy, heavy furnitures. He's eeen New York, living the easy life. Do you wait for him to send you money, your son? You and I will make agreements. You will plan yourself more."

"I'm doing fine. JP and I have a strong business. It's not too hard. I can't bring on other partners. Thanks anyway. I have to leave now. Catty's coming home in a few days, and I have to straighten up."

Oleg sits with a cold stare as Victor walks past him without any backward glance or gesture.

*****

Later, at Victor's house in Luisant, Ludmilla, Anya, and a weak and disheveled Catty stand on the threshold. He's surprised when he opens the door for them.

"What's happened?"

"Oh, Victor," Anya says. "We're not sure what's got Catty feeling so poorly." Anya hands Victor Catty's purse and overnight bag. Catty shuffles into his living room and collapses on his well-worn couch.

"What's wrong, Catty, mon petite chou?" he asks.

She puts her foot up on the cocktail table, her big toe oozing a thick chartreuse pus. Her entire foot is red and hot from the ankle to the heel. "Oh, I tink that I stepped on someting in the Bois de Boulogne, and now it's rotten."

Victor steps back, alarmed, and then reaches to touch the arch of her foot with the slightest tip of his index finger. "So it is."

Victor pats the front pocket of his pants to assure himself that his keys are readily available. "Let's go to the clinic in Chartres center. You need an injection of antibiotics. Then you'll be fine."

Catty turns a pale shade of green at his suggestion. With a shrill panic in her voice, she says, "Oh nooo, Victor! I don't have papers. They throw me in with those sicky Muslims."

Victor steps back even farther. "You what?"

"Yes, it's true. I don't have visa to be here. I can't go to clinic. My friend from Odessa, Annamarie, was so sick with a tummy ache and that's what happened to her. Don't put me in with those immigrants!"

"But it's just down the road and . . . Immigrants? But you and your friends . . . Ahhh. I guess that I understand."

"Call Oleg; he has medics. No, I'll call him." Catty lies sweating on the couch. Her color is pale, and her lack of makeup somehow unsettles Victor. He busies himself in the kitchen, making coffee and looking at auction calendars, as Catty sleeps on the couch.

Two hours later, Oleg knocks on the door. A young Latin man is with him. Oleg soon takes command of the room. "Theees ees Dr.

Ramos. Heee's a good doctor. Heee's from Cuba. Heee's secretly left Venezuela, and heee's working here for us."

Victor looks at Oleg with a raised eyebrow. That introduction was nothing less than confusing. He stands in front of Catty, shielding her but silent. Oleg glances at Ramos and nods in the affirmative.

Ramos begins an explanation. "You know that Cuba has very fine medical training, yes? It's true, but we doctors are the government pawns. They send us to Ecuador, Bolivia, Venezuela, even Brazil. The government sends us as payment for raw materials like oil, rubber, copper. The doctors' payments go right to the Cuban government, and we doctors work in poverty.

"All the doctors were pushed to leave Cuba. I was lucky enough to escape Venezuela. Yes, Oleg helped me land here in the West, here in France." He speaks textbook English without any hesitation as he examines Catty's foot.

Victor watches Ramos give Catty an injection and take her temperature.

Victor speaks directly to Ramos, in French. "Êtes-vous vraiment un le médecin? A real medical doctor?"

"My French . . . I understand you, but I must answer you in English. Yes, I am a medical doctor, but Cuba is so corrupt, I am used as payment to crooks in Venezuela from the crooks in Cuba. I had no life, no control over my work, my family, my fate in Cuba or Venezuela. Oleg has helped me."

Catty stands up. "I must leave you all now. I'll go to rest."

Ramos, Oleg, and Victor stand looking at each other in silence. Finally, Ludmilla, who has been silent in the background, breaks the spell. "Ramos, errr, Dr. Ramos. I am returning to Paris now. You'll come too?"

Oleg says something to Ludmilla in Russian, and she and Ramos both leave.

Victor looks around the living room, at a loss for what to do with Oleg.

Oleg stands with authority. With his arms crossed, he says, "So hhhave you lived here eeen dis village for many years?"

Victor doesn't want to answer any of Oleg's questions. He doesn't want to reveal another personal detail about himself to Oleg, but with Catty's condition, both wounded and illegal, he feels cornered. Though he is in his own home, Victor is defensive. He tries to decide how to treat Oleg. "Aren't you driving back to Paris tonight as well?"

Oleg sits down on the couch and spreads his keys and cigarettes on the coffee table, leaving Victor standing. "No. I like the quiet of dis town. I've rented the hhhouse up on the hhhill while my villa ees being redecorated."

Victor's throat is suddenly parched dry. He swallows deeply, displaying his displeasure.

"Hhhave you considered my proposal? Hhhave you consulted weeeth your son, JP? Eeet's time dat we go to work."

Victor looks offended and says, with a high pitch to his voice, "That was only a day or two ago. Why are you rushing this plan? Maybe I'll get back to you after next week, eh? I'll talk to JP and we'll consider, yes? You're offering capital, strong helpers to move fountains, walls, statues, and streamlined access for customs and international shipping. You're promising quite a lot. I don't know your terms, and I don't know you. I don't want another partner. I don't need another partner. I'm . . ."

Oleg scoops his cigarettes and phone from the table in a single movement. He gestures, signaling to Victor that he is leaving. "Meeester Victor, you may get back to me after neeext week, but my offer weeell hhhave expired. There are others whhho want my partnership. Hhhave you considered dat if I am not your partner, I weeell be your competition? I have eeedeas for big developments. Whole towns, whole more money. I have de proper documents to live and work hhhere in France. Remember the first rule of war, 'Keep your friends close and your enemies closer.' I could be veeery dangerous to you, meeester. Victor. There are others who would value my partnership."

Victor tries to keep his focus on Catty's health, but he can't ignore the cold sweat that chills him as Oleg crosses the room to leave.

***

"Yes, that's right. I said that his name is Fargo," Iris says to JP. "He's my sister's son. She had a crackerjack catering gig going, but her community kitchen, they call them ghost kitchens, was closed, or somethin' like that. Fargo was helping her, mostly with the accounting, the books, but also with carting stuff around when he wasn't in school. He goes to City College."

JP watches Dolly slink back and forth between Fargo and Iris. He remembers that she has a sister nearby, but she hasn't mentioned her in a long time. He knows that Iris is serious about this project—she has a clipboard in hand with color-coded papers. Parking, she says repeatedly, is the cost of doing business. JP doesn't trust his own ambivalence on the subject, and there is no doubt that most of their customers drive in.

Fargo looks kind of strange. He's tall, gangly, with long, pale fingers and an oddly jutting, sharp jaw. He doesn't meet JP's eyes, and his pants are hitched up tightly over his waist by a tattered would-be belt.

JP turns to Fargo. "And you can park the cars on that far lot with the provisional permit that Iris got? You have a valid New York driver's license? Iris, will our insurance cover him?"

Iris steps in immediately. "He's quiet but very focused. Give him a week or two to prove himself. You'll see. I've already situated the insurance. He's bonded."

JP nods. "In that case, it can't be any worse than it is now with no valet. I just hope that Venezuelan gangster doesn't kill him."

Fargo's eyes shine with worry.

Iris chimes in. "Don't worry, Fargo and Dolly will be great partners. I think that gangster's quieted down for a bit. He may have some legal problems, though I'm not certain about all of that. And, oh! I got the scoop on his wife, in case you're interested."

JP breathes deeply. "No, I'm not interested in the wife, but tell me anyway."

Iris answers, "She's the ex-wife now, but she still works for him part-time, in between several other situations."

JP shrugs. "Yeah, I'm not really interested." He turns to face her more directly. "That reminds me, where are we with all that stuff sitting in the customs storage, racking up fees, and no capable broker expediting the process? I've been dodging Victor's calls, as usual, but he'll find me sooner or later. I'm scared to even ask what our late-storage fees have accrued to now. Do you know?"

Iris walks away, shaking her clipboard. "Yes, of course I know. You don't have to ask. I've been speaking with Steppens, who owns the French part of that company, Atlantic. I'm still working on that one."

As she walks away, JP calls out, "Hey, I saw that the big French fountain is gone. Did you sell it to that White Plains guy? Looks kinda empty and dark over on the north wall. Any ideas what we should put there?"

Iris turns around, and Dolly dashes to her side. "Yep. There are bakeries and shelving and ancient stone fireplace mantels that would fit beautifully in that space. I just gotta get 'em outta Sing Sing. Oh, and the fountain guy. Easiest sale I've ever made. I sent him pictures on Monday, and two days later, he was here with check in hand, no wrangling. Boom! I can't imagine what that guy's spread is like. He collects French fountains. I guess collecting is like exotic shopping. Victor does send us some really beautiful stuff!"

⁎

The hot weather is finally breaking. Victor turns off the AC and opens the windows in the living room and kitchen. The breeze clears out the sick-patient aura that has been hanging low in the house. Catty is up and bathed, with her requisite makeup carefully applied. Victor tries to remember if Frida wore so much makeup. But he can't focus.

Oleg has been sending trays of Russian and French delicacies to aid in Catty's recovery. Beet and other vegetable salads, smoked sturgeon, rye breads, cheeses, delicate onion pancakes with pickled veggies stuffed inside, and a roast chicken, duck, and ham. When the care packages first arrived, Victor couldn't decide whether to eat the goodies or not. Obviously, Oleg is bribing him.

Catty stands in her platform shoes in the kitchen, cleaning out the fridge, throwing away the uneaten portions of ham and chicken. Victor hasn't eaten a bite, not of the local Camembert or pickled onions—not one bite! Catty's choice, the rye bread, is gone, but she tosses the stale baguettes. Victor hasn't discussed Oleg's offer of partnership with JP. Oleg's assets—big capital for his and JP's scale of projects—aren't needed. Victor is still holding out hope that at this week's auction in Cevennes, he'll find some hungry young buck willing to haul these big artifacts and installations for cash.

Regarding the "assistance" with customs clearance, Victor doesn't believe for a minute that a Russian gangster type can fix his problems with French and American duties and restrictions. That, he surmises, is pure bullshit. And heaven help France if the damn Russian mobsters have infiltrated French customs.

Is Catty mostly mended? He isn't sure. Made up and fully dressed signal normalcy. Victor begins mapping his foray to the next string of auctions and bank repossessions. He lays out his auction flyers and maps. Marty Roberts, from Victor's old firm in Paris, sends him the latest Sotheby's catalogs, with the current sold prices marked in red for the items Marty is interested in. Victor records these prices carefully. The second-rate limestone fountain without the original copper and zinc plumbing fittings sold for five times what he hopes to spend on buying a truly fine fountain this week.

He's had his eye on the fountain in the town square of Cevennes, and it's finally up for auction. The picture on the flyer doesn't do it justice. There will be few buyers at this Wednesday's sale. He is ready. Once he finds a young man or two to help him wrap and load the items, he won't have to think of Oleg again. Nahhh! They definitely don't need a partner like Oleg.

Very early the next morning, Victor kisses Catty goodbye, slips his toothbrush into his small overnight bag, and drives toward the autoroute and out of town.

***

Fargo and Dolly are a great success with the suburban shoppers. Dolly nuzzles the dog-loving customers, and Fargo is raking in the tips. Along with his car-parking skills, Fargo has been an asset inside the store as well. There's another trough filled with odd, mismatched crystals from hundreds of chandeliers, all swimming loosely in the monstrously large corrugated bin. Some of the glass pieces are large, some not. Some have mates or are strung together with many mates, and some are crystal widows, drowning alone in the giant vat. When not parking cars, Fargo has spent his time sorting through the hundreds of crystals to find a match for many of the light fixtures with missing or broken glass. No matter how beautiful or well proportioned a chandelier is, without its full complement of winking crystal droplets, its value is fractionalized. Fargo has restored several lights to their full beauty, value, and sale price. Iris watches to ensure that he uses his time in the store wisely.

Business at Les Beaux Châteaux moves at a fevered pace. The stock market is up, up, up, and New Yorkers, rich Wall Street New Yorkers, are flush. Sinks and statuary, partners desks and occasional lamps, restaurant bars, and early medical equipment sell and sell. There is even a strange collection of antique puppets from a nineteenth-century fraternal order. The fifteen marionettes are lavishly dressed in velvets and lace, with tinkling jewelry and miniature eyeglasses and feathered hats. The characters have creepy faces and a mothball odor. Though the puppets are priced individually, a tiny stooped man with a birdlike voice buys them all—no quibbling about the price. Anything old and quirky and expensive is selling. Shoppers are in LBC every hour that it is open, never any lulls in traffic or sales. This is a very new pattern, and Iris has hired two new salespeople to keep up with the demand.

Unfortunately, the new inventory that Victor has been sending regularly is still stuck in customs purgatory, and the store is beginning to look sparse. Iris is well aware of the empty corners, and Jenna and Rodrigo, the new employees, have been mumbling about the lack of goods to sell.

No longer are JP's Wednesdays rushed from his morning visits with the Rohingya. Still, he walks into LBC later than anyone else. He knows that this isn't good for team morale and that, sometime soon, Iris will remind him of the value of shared efforts. JP just isn't feeling it. Nothing feels complete. Nothing seems worth extra effort, and nothing is especially attractive. His life feels uncomfortably mediocre; food tastes bland, and wine doesn't intoxicate him. Blue or gray skies mean little to him, and he might as well throw away his phone—he doesn't answer any calls, especially from Victor. There are easily a dozen unanswered calls and texts from him. JP knows that this is no way to run a business, no way to live a life—with fractional engagement and no vibrancy—and yet he can't find his interest in the nearby environs.

Later that night, when he returns to his apartment building, he feels a neighbor's eyes scrutinizing him as he collects his mail from the mail room. He thinks he recognizes her as an LBC shopper and doesn't feel particularly charming or neighborly at the moment. He quickly collects the catalogs and bills that have spilled from his postbox into his arms, looks down, and scoots out into the elevator.

In his apartment, he smells Gosha's cleaning products. Funny, though she's been working for him—cleaning his apartment and doing his laundry—for three years, he's never actually met her. He read her offer for a secure cleaning service in the mail room and hired her through the building concierge. Every week, he leaves her a check, and that's the extent of their interaction. This remote engagement feels decadently American. Merde! He can do his own laundry! Why doesn't he? Maybe it's this nitty-gritty city living. Was he happier scrappy and living in LBC? No, he wouldn't live that lean again by choice. Maybe life in a greener setting, or at least a calmer retreat, would help him regain his verve?

He owns a beautiful home, Ocean Manor, on the ocean in the Hamptons. He visited it once, the day he closed on its purchase. He has rented it to a vegan makeup artist, Layla, and her wife for all these years. They fix and manage everything and send him all the receipts. The house and setting are beautiful. He paid $2.7 million for it. There was a micro real estate slump the year he bought it. JP and Victor share their baritone voice, as well as a drive for finding great values. Although JP and Victor aren't close anymore, they are both known for hunting down and bargaining for good deals.

Ocean Manor is the high end of great. The house could likely now sell for close to five million. But he doesn't need to sell it. Would he feel better living there? Ugh! He'd have to kick Layla out, and up to now, they'd lived happily with the month-to-month contract. Could his happiness be linked to a more bucolic setting? Is it worth the pain of unsettling his tenant? Would living there even fix his malaise?

JP has a restless night but arrives at LBC early to shake off his blue slump. Of course, Iris and Dolly are in ahead of him. Paperwork is on her desk, but she's in the storage area with one of the new hires. JP listens outside as she gives him thoughtful but stern instructions.

"Rodrigo, you gotta slow down, man. Clean this chandelier carefully. And move the zinc bar with Joey and Alfred; please don't just drag it across the floor alone. Neither the floor nor the bar can take that sort of abuse. Sometime, your back will thank me."

JP walks the aisles and listens to Iris's lecture in the distant background. She knows the inventory so well. She knows the provenance of the chandeliers, the bakeries, the bank vault—why did Victor send them a bank vault? When it arrived, JP ran his fingers over the cool steel, spin-dial lock, and sharp corners, but it's so damn heavy! However, JP never thought that they'd sell the puppets. Maybe someone out there wants an old French bank vault?

How can he structure the business going forward so that it will be good for Iris? What will benefit them both? Iris's mother was an antiques dealer in Savannah, Georgia. In the seventies and eighties, she was successful in selling American brown furniture exclusively. Man! The bottom of that market dropped out of the bottom of the world some years ago and never recovered. Before Iris's mother died, she sold a Philadelphia broken-bonnet, ball-in-claw highboy for five thousand dollars, a piece that the high priest of period furniture, Israel Sack, had sold years earlier for forty-five grand. Those simple lines, the robust grains, the elemental functionality—as American as apple pie.

Whether it be functional American furniture or weathered limestone fountains from ancient villages, Iris has an eye for proportion, patina, and pizazz. Inherently, she knows what will sell, and she loves to set up the two-part sale. She nurtures customers. JP knows technological changes and influences that affected the form and function of furniture, architecture, and statuary, but he doesn't know the vogues and trends of American consumers the way that Iris does. Sure, he knows beauty and history, but Iris's knowledge of American geography, marketing, and salability far surpasses his own. He often goes out of his way to compliment her managerial style, but he wants to recognize her aesthetic as well. Maybe this shortage in inventory could give her the opportunity to wholesale a new product line, American artifacts . . . JP thinks on these possible changes.

One thing is certain: though he really stretched his cash to buy this condo, its monotone coldness no longer feels good; it just doesn't feel like home. He's got to change his living arrangement, and soon.

He calls Layla that afternoon.

She answers the phone brightly. "Hey, JP! How are you? Long time, eh? Hold on one minute while I turn down the music. Have you heard this song, 'Winning with the Bulls'?"

"No. I don't know rap music so much. It's good, hunh?" He small-talks for a bit, reporting on his business and querying about hers. And then the bombshell. He says, "Hey, I'm thinkin' about making some changes."

She quickly interrupts. "Finally, you're getting married?"

"No," he says, "nothing so sweet as that, I'm afraid. I need to get out of the city for a stretch. I need some green and calm and, I dunno, peace. I need to . . . Layla, I have to . . . I'm sorry, but I have to ask you guys to leave. It's . . ."

"You have to ask us what? You mean, our house? You want us to leave our house? There's no way! Our business is really taking off, and I have to devote my . . . and our fulfillment is . . ."

JP knew that the neighbors were a very testy bunch. Any zoning violations would be met with swift censure and likely expensive fines. The tone of his voice was much more aggressive than he intended it to be. "Your fulfillment, what? You're not running your business from Ocean Manor? No, please assure me that's not what you've been doing."

Layla backtracked immediately. "Of course not! But this is just the worst time for us to look for appropriate housing. I'm traveling with a new salesperson, and Vicki's been jiggering the scent of new skin serum formulas. Our place smells amazing."

JP is more adamant now. "Please, Layla, tell me that you're not running your business there! There'll be hell to pay."

Layla softens her stance. "JP, please make this change next year or in the fall. I just can't move now. You've always been so understanding and supportive of our label. I just can't do this . . ."

JP breathes deeply, crystallizing his resolve. "Layla, I'll always be supportive of your label and all your entrepreneurial instincts, but that's got nothing to do with our month-to-month agreement for your exclusively residential activities. Month to month. We've always kept our contract that way in case I needed that place. And it's time. And I do!"

***

Later that afternoon, JP walks the aisles of LBC. *Sparse* is a generous description. They haven't received a container from Victor in six weeks. Damn! A single supplier, even if it's your dad, is a *bad* business model. JP knows that this won't be easily fixed.

He sits down at his desk and spreads out the paperwork for all the containers that Victor has sent in the last three months. Pictures with descriptions and his expenses for each item promise a rosy haul for LBC, if only they can get the goods through customs. JP realizes that he doesn't even know why the items are being held up. Victor, for his part, has documented each parcel in plain language, not one frill or enhancement. These goods, if not seen, appear on paper as mainstream and plain: shelves, clocks, fountains, wood, stone, plaster. But if the images and individual histories that Victor included only for JP's edification are understood, the items' uniquely French and antique value will be fully comprehended. In the past, customs agents on both sides of the Atlantic have accepted Victor's simple narrative as gospel, and commerce has commenced. Money is made by all governments, shipping agents, haulers, lawyers, truckers, craters, and more. Now the future of this business may be in peril.

France's newest antagonist, Marine Le Pen, is using a bullhorn to spread her outrage that French culture is being diluted, including the sale of uniquely French artifacts that are leaving the country in large shipping containers. JP realizes that not only is their business model of just one supplier unsustainable, but it might now be over.

He dials the number for that smarmy Johnny, the customs broker, but it's not Johnny who answers.

"Worldwide," a gravely, tobacco-tainted voice answers instead.

"Yes, this is JP from Les Beaux Châteaux, here in New York. Is Johnny available?"

The gravel voice answers, "No, he ain't here no more."

JP can feel the tip of his ears growing hot and red as his blood pressure rises. "Right. Whom shall I speak with regarding four containers that I believe are sitting at Newark holding, awaiting clearance?"

"*Whom* do you wish to speak with? I mean, *shall* I help you?"

JP feels the mocking tone through the ether of their phone connection. This is not the best way to begin with a new, yet absolutely necessary, agent. "Great! What's your name? Are you aware of the cargo that's being held up that I'm waiting for?"

"Yeah. I know who you are. Johnny and your Iris were pretty tight. I canned his ass, just so you know."

JP deferred these logistical complications to Iris years ago. Here's one more aspect of his business, his life, that he's outsourced. So American. Merde!

The unnamed broker continues. "I'm trying to get your goods in, but maybe there's not much truth in these here descriptions. I mean, it says here wood, marble, and plaster. These are antiques, man! The magistrate from France thinks that these may be national treasures, and they may have to sail back home. Dat's what I heard. Did *you* buy these shelves and mantels and doors?"

"What does it matter who bought them? It's your job—you've been paid to move them from Le Havre to New York. I need to know when you will do your job."

"Look, Mac, or Jack, or whatever your name is. I'm warning you about Iris. She and Johnny was workin' some kinda fraud. I couldn't get it outta him exactly what the scam was, but I'm tellin' you to watch out. OK. Enough o' dat. These containers are trouble, and I don't know when or if I'll get them outta Newark holding. You'll hafta—"

JP hangs up the phone, angry at himself as much as at the broker. He takes the folder that Iris marked with color-coded tabs back to her desk. "Iris, I'll have to call that lawyer—what's his name?" He looks at her, and just as she's about to answer, he says, "Oh, right, Bernie. Would you find out if we can hire a different customs broker in the middle of a transaction? That company is inept!"

JP hoped to talk to Iris about what that creep Johnny said—and what the best way to rent out his West Village apartment would be— but the store is so busy with paying customers that they don't have a chance to talk further. At 6:00 p.m., after she locks the front door, he hears her whistle for Dolly, which signals that she's in a hurry to close everything up and scoot out.

JP realizes that he hasn't even one confidant in the world. He can't talk to Victor about the direction of the store, and there seems to be no one else with whom he can share this lonely uncertainty. He's cultivated his solitary self and persona. Is he up to commuting to have a greener, calmer lifestyle in the Hamptons? Should he go to France to talk to Victor and plan for the next iteration of their business? Maybe he should turn the store over to Iris for an extended hiatus. He can afford to pay her more if necessary, and maybe she can figure out a product mix of French *and* American salvage and antiques. JP feels like he's failing—not just passively making mistakes, but like every decision he makes is a poor one, and he doesn't have one lifeline to help him gain some traction.

He feels guilty for having to ask Layla and Vicki to leave Ocean Manor. He watches as Fargo nimbly maneuvers the truck into the loading dock to pick up Iris and Dolly. The street seems so different at night. There is a grittier element on the sidewalks. The hedge-fund mamas with Birkin bags and shiny Mercedeses are long gone. As the sun goes down, out come the guys with bomber jackets and low-hanging jeans, fancy athletic shoes, and geographically labeled base-ball caps. The life of the city that once spoke of mystery and adventure now seems cold and dangerous to JP.

He sees Marty's car hoppers on the other side of the street, watch-ing him and laughing. The ice cream shop is closing. He smiles sweetly at the clerk, who is about to lock the door, and then pushes himself in and orders two scoops in a dish. This place is commonly known in the neighborhood as Groovy Ice Cream. He thinks carefully and realizes that he doesn't even know the correct name. But the name doesn't mat-ter to him, only that this is the best ice cream he's ever had. The rich, brown-black chocolate gelato is sublime. It's almost a brownie, and the sensation of cool and silky chocolate melting down his throat distracts him.

Back outside after his indulgence, he stands and watches the street, the ice cream calming his anxious tongue with comfort. He's been here, in the States, for a long time, but this isn't the home that he imagined. Exactly where home is is another question altogether. JP admonishes himself for missing Frida. *She's not here and cannot cool your hot head. Figure it out yourself, idiot!* He's about to turn and head for his car when out of the corner of his eye, he sees Rama. Again, she is holding the pegboard with all the car hopper's keys wired onto it. Clearly, she's still involved with Marty the snake. He waves at her and she stops, pegboard in hand.

"Hey! You're busy," he says.

Breathless, she nods her head in the affirmative. "I told you that I'm working several jobs. I'm working my ambitious American dream.

This is just one more job that pays my bills. But I won't be here much longer. I've got some big projects popping. I'm moving to the suburbs. Who knows who I'll meet out there, eh?" Without a wave or an adieu, she quickly turns and disappears down the block.

He stands alone on the street, wondering what Victor would think of his lonely life. Would Victor tell him to get in gear and get the containers passed through customs, and the rest of his life will fall into place? JP knows that he should reach out to speak plainly with Victor, but he doesn't want to endure his judgment. JP imagines Layla and Vicki packing boxes in Ocean Manor. Then he tries to unimagine that. It's unfortunate that Layla is taking his move personally. Should he feel guilty? He's losing all sense of right and wrong.

He needs a real estate agent to handle this dirty work. Initially, he thought he'd try to rent out the West Village apartment himself. There are always messages near the mail room requesting sublets and tenancy. Now he's reminded that professionals cost money, but what they save you in personal untidiness is very valuable. He wants a tenant who can pay the rent on time, and that's all. He doesn't care if they're blue or white or a twin or pregnant. He doesn't want to know anyone's life story. Can they pay? Will they pay? Nothing else matters. He'll hire an agent. This is yet one more step to a remote life, the American way of disconnection. Screw it! He needs protection.

He is first to open LBC the following day. Iris is surprised to find him at his desk, alarms off, lights and office machinery up and running, when she arrives. JP is casually thumbing through auction catalogs, *Yankee Peddler* and *New England Heritage Auctioneers*.

Iris gives him a quizzical look. "What gives? Why are you looking at those catalogs?"

"I'm thinking about widening our product mix. We can't get our French goods in, at least not for a while. Maybe we should be reselling what's here, like 'Merican stuff."

In her most sarcastic tone, Iris answers, "Do you mean to say 'American'? Sure!"

She and Dolly walk back into the tool aisle to grab a rubber mallet. JP follows her.

"No, I mean it. You know what'll sell. Why don't you scout a few of these sales? Pick some easy sellers and take a risk on a few great-quality items that will tickle discerning buyers. Go this weekend. Here's two great sales in Connecticut." He shakes the catalogs in his hand.

"Hey, fella! Did you notice that the name of the store is Les Beaux Châteaux? *Yankee* cannot be pronounced properly here. Nahhh! Weather vanes or old duck decoys aren't vogue enough for the Wall Street crowd this year. Philadelphia highboys and ball-in-claw legs are out. Tiffany's the single American brand that sells for top dollar: lighting, glass, silver. Anyway, I gotta be here. My mom constantly reminded me, 'If you're not—'"

JP interrupts her. "Wait! I know it! If you're not out sellin', you're bein' outsold."

"OK, I get your point. My mother's ghost speaks too frequently. Trust me. Victor's stuff will get through eventually, and when it does, we'll make money."

Her sarcasm is confusing to JP when she adds, "Besides, some-one might recognize me from my old auction days." His brow knits together in confusion, not understanding why she wouldn't want to see old colleagues.

"Right. Don't buy anything. Just go to scout. I'll be here sellin'."

He hands her the catalogs and walks back to his desk. Before she can challenge him, he's on the phone with the Boardman Group, New York City's biggest real estate agency.

***

Victor knows most of the rural auctioneers. He's been doing this for enough years to become familiar with the quirks of the various guys. Some are on the take with banks or other tricky dealers, but most are straight buyers and resellers. He tries to stay away from the cheaters, but that would exclude him from a percentage of the best sales. Loud and bold is his best counter to those who hope to go unnoticed quietly in the shadows. He's watched buyers collaborate with cheating sellers, and he's seen auctioneers cheat sellers too. Victor attributes auctions to the three *D*s: death, debt, and/or divorce. Usually people in the desperate straits of liquidation aren't in positions of strength to question subtle signals between buyers, or buyers and auctioneers, in cahoots. Just last month in the village of Spycker, he watched an agricultural equipment auction go down with a preplanned strategy. Two dairy farmers agreed before the sale not to bid each other up. Cheaters.

The fields are vividly green in spite of the hot summer. Travel deep into the heart of France is what he likes best about his life. He occasionally imagines Frida exploring with him. Pity that he wasn't more flexible with her. Would JP enjoy pickin' with him? Nahhh. JP is in New York. Victor's mind wanders back to Frida, her creamy white skin. She was eager to explore. He was the anxious worrier. His focus was always the firm, the clients, the deadlines. Frida was wise to France being wide open. He can't fix his past, but he promises himself that he'll treat Catty as a treasured companion.

The wide meadows and weathered barns give him comfort. Similarly, he's confident traversing the complex currency laws to protect against money laundering. It's the unpredictable political landscape and Russians or piranhas like Oleg that force ancient villagers to make rash decisions and sell their livelihoods during inopportune market changes. He and JP make money during these volatile swings, but he worries for France's future. What happens to a culture that abandons tradition?

He focuses on the auction. No small sinks or statues that he could load himself, but the flyer advertises a tavern room with worn porcelain taps and ancient chestnut wall paneling, and of course, the limestone fountain that he's had his eye on for years. Surely he'll find a young boy or two who can help him load his truck. He pulls into a petrol station, and a grizzled old man with bulbous knuckles pumps the fuel. Once this man is gone, they'll replace his job with a computer. Victor can smell the hysteria; the once-simple French countryside is growing very complex.

The sun is finally up as his pickup barrels over the ancient stone bridge of Vittel. He recognizes several of his competitors' moving vans parked around a food vending truck. Have they been selling to the Russians? The plastic food odor from those roving trucks is vile. He parks and looks at the fountain in the town's square. The bronze plaque next to it is surrounded by blood-red roses. It is a sturdy rectangle divided into two sections, covered in names of those who died in World Wars I and II. He shakes off a chill as he imagines so many men from this village with the same family name who died—so much devastation.

The fountain's good condition hasn't changed from when he drove through months ago. The bronze fittings, cast in the early twentieth century, have a classic three-dolphin nautical theme. Its well-patinaed metallic elements and vanilla-colored limestone base harmonize with beautiful proportions. This won't fit in his truck, and he cannot move it himself. Other arrangements will have to be made, and vandals make quick work of property that's been sold but is unclaimed and unprotected. He'll hire a moving company if there are no strong bucks around.

He's already preregistered his bank check and buyer's ID. Still, he wanders over to the registration desk. There is a printed catalog. Very unusual for a country sale. He picks it up to examine it closely. It isn't a catalog of goods at this sale but rather some crazy list of ancient homes in three neighboring towns, a real estate sales booklet. This is a listing of homes that are complete, not cannibalized, and will only be sold to those who'll commit to preserving them that way. The business is named Whole France. A stunning, tall blonde woman is handing out the brochures. Victor knows that she's not local; she's wearing a black leather jacket and slim-fitting jeans. He notes the out-of-vogue steel-toed work boots. Both the locals and the buyers look away from her.

Foolish! Victor thinks. *Those old houses'll never sell. Their sole worth is in the value of their parts. C'est stupide!*

The auctioneer is about to begin. The small crowd of buyers walks over to the bakery. It closed more than a year before this sale, but the family held out for this long in the hope of finding a buyer for the business, not just the broken-up elements. No such luck.

Victor doesn't go in. He's sent several bakeries to JP recently, and he doesn't know if they've yet been rescued from customs purgatory. The sale is going slowly. There isn't a single buyer for all the assets, so each shelving unit, trolley, and marble rolling slab is selling individually to slow bidders. Victor is getting anxious. How much longer will the breakup take?

He walks inside, and the auctioneer is holding up the clock, removed from the ceiling above the cash wrap. Like the village center, this bakery has a three-dolphin (or are those fish?) bronze clock. The bronze scales on the fish are elegantly wrought, shimmering the light as water droplets of crystal hang around the triumvirate. The clock face has a thick convex glass curvature broadcasting the time to every angle. An unsigned masterpiece. Victor falls hard.

"And we're opening bid, do I hear one hundred?" the auctioneer babbles.

The bakery is silent. Victor looks around. All of the likely bidders are there for other items, such as mixers and ovens, and their funds are marked for those. Victor gestures with his chin to the auctioneer, who answers, "I have a hundred; do I hear one fifty?"

The quiet crowd shuffles their feet. This poor widow's sale won't reap enough to live on.

In his head, he hears the cardinal rule: don't bid against yourself. Victor jerks his chin again at the auctioneer. "I'll give you two fifty."

The auctioneer shakes his head no. "The bid's one hundred à vous, monsieur."

"I'm well aware," Victor barks out in a clear, assertive voice.

"Sold," squawks the auctioneer.

Finally, the crowd moves outside to the central fountain. Victor thinks that he sees the auctioneer wink or make a knowing gesture to someone he doesn't recognize. He tries not to grind his teeth.

The auctioneer begins. "Let's start the bidding at two fifty; do I hear two seventy-five?"

Victor watches the action move around the crowd. He won't bid until the others have played out.

"Nine fifty, est-ce que j'entends a thousand?"

The crowd is quiet. Victor knows that he can sell this in Paris for ten grand, likely twenty-five in New York. He juts his chin at the auctioneer. "One thousand fifty," he says, expecting the sale to conclude there.

But a slim Slavic man steps forward and makes an offer. "Twelve hundred."

The auctioneer regains his energy. "This is a unique piece rendered by a great fer forgé craftsman. What am I bid? Do I hear fifteen hundred?"

The Slav gestures yes.

Victor rubs his temple. "Two thousand!" he belts out.

The tension and bidding last almost ten minutes, with Victor finally triumphant at €5,500. He doesn't regret the purchase, but he didn't expect to pay so much.

He holds the clock, wrapped in a furniture blanket, under his arm as he looks around for a few young men hoping to make a buck. No one in that demographic is anywhere in sight. Victor shakes the bronze and iron fleur-de-lis fence that surrounds the fountain—plenty sturdy, but not tall enough to keep out those who intend to do harm. Damn! These are the moments when he curses JP's absence. He walks back to his truck to settle the clock and retrieve a few tools.

And there is Oleg, in his slick blue suit, the collar wide open. "Victor! Hhheello, friend! How are you? And more importantly, hhhow is dear Catty? Did you all enjoy de food trays that I sent last week? I didn't hhhear?"

Victor smiles in response. He doesn't say a word.

Oleg continues. "You know, Victor, we shouldn't be bidding against de other. That was my associate against you. We should be partners. My offer stands."

Victor closes his eyes for a second and breathes deeply. "I'll keep that in mind."

Oleg walks away.

Victor places the tool bags on the ground for a second and dials JP. No answer. Damn him! He looks back on his calls to JP and realizes that it has been more than a week of multiple calls a day to JP without one return call. What kind of business partner—what kind of son, for that matter—won't return regular calls?

Victor has made enough money to retire now, and JP likely has too. What would he do if he weren't in a partnership with JP? Would he marry Catty? That wouldn't influence his business with JP. In spite of JP's petulance and difficult nature, Victor values his damaged yet important bond with his son. And what of Catty? If he married her, she could be treated as a French person and have access to the medical services that he's contributed to for all these years. Does he want to get married? Is Catty a good choice? Will there be others to choose from in the future? Not very likely. Should he expand his business with

Oleg? Damn! Why doesn't JP call back? Will JP be able to help Victor with these personal decisions? Probably not. JP is cold and businesslike when Victor does actually speak to him. Marrying Catty would add a level of convenience for dealing with Oleg. But Oleg is not a consideration, he admonishes himself. He knows he should be asking himself if he'll be happy with Catty. Can he make her happy? With all her peccadilloes . . . And yet she's kind. But the whole Russian Mafia and Oleg, too, they certainly come with the package.

He tries to remember marriage to Frida, but right now, that's clouded by his anger at JP. How did he and Frida decide to get married? Victor concentrates hard and can't remember when he asked her to marry him. He knew right when they met that he'd marry her, when her father hired Victor's firm to design a headquarters for their truck parts business. Why is there such a gap in his memory? He remembers well their small and elegant wedding in Normandy, his family all gone in the war. Frida's face from their honeymoon in Aix-en-Provence is clear in his mind's eye. She picked him. Yes! That's how they got married; she asked him! He went along with all of her directives. She was smart and creative, and she wore the pants. Is that why JP is so disrespectful now? Frida's family always showed Victor respect and supported his architectural work, but her family's money financed their biggest expenses. No one in her family knew that he remortgaged their apartment. Well, likely little of that chapter of his life would inform this one ahead.

Catty is childish at times, but overall, she is sweet and accommodating. Can he be plain enough to criticize her perfume? He doesn't really care about her terrible French pronunciations. As long as she speaks English with him, they are similarly matched. There will always be the Russian Mafia—both her girlfriends, which they joke about as being Mafia, and the real hustlers and bosses. He cringes at the thought of bringing them into his life in a meaningful way. As much as he hates Marine Le Pen, she has a point about keeping France French. He can hear Frida admonishing him for his conservative, xenophobic tendencies. Well, the horses are out of the barn on that. French culture is changing, with or without his PC views or Marine Le Pen's movement.

After JP left, Victor felt that Paris had become one giant tourist accommodation. When did the community anchors slip away? There wasn't an avenue or alleyway that didn't have hordes of Chinese, Russians, or Americans taking selfies in front of flower boxes, doorways, or even graffiti. Victor saw that the clueless tourists were blind to the rats running by as the selfie photographers scraped dog shit off their shoes.

All his favorite unstarred restaurants and bistros have monthslong reservation lists now. Even though he's known Frederick L'Antoine for years, as things were now, he'd never be able to walk into Aux Bons Cru at 9:00 p.m. without a reservation. OK. OK. But what about Catty? She's never said one word about marriage, but he knows that she intends to live in France for the rest of her life. Couldn't they be secure and happy together?

Victor hadn't even thought of marriage until this very minute; has Catty? Oh, of course, women seek security. Would marriage to Catty give him a more secure partnership with Oleg? No, not very likely. Oleg doesn't show all his cards, even if he is pretending to. Knowing what little he does about Oleg, could he be comfortable with a partnership with him? He hasn't really imagined it until now. With Oleg, he could be free to roam the authentic France that he finds so comforting. The same with JP. He could continue picking and choosing the best bits of French homes and businesses and not have to haul this heavy shit anymore. Oleg could give him just the support that he wants. Ugh! He's a dog, a damn Russian!

Victor wonders, *Would this business be easy if I partnered with Oleg?* In every new direction, there will be unknown hazards, and Oleg is himself a Russian hazard. Slippery and maybe unsavory . . . Russians. He would have liked to speak with Catty in an objective way, but could she be objective? No, her worry about being tossed in with the Muslim immigrants revealed her most vulnerable and xenophobic side. He loves her; he'll talk to her when he gets home. Would marrying Catty be the same as partnering with Oleg? Not exactly, but he should anticipate them being bundled. He looks back and counts how many unanswered calls to JP. Twenty-six! Damn him! Victor needs to speak with Catty as soon as possible. He picks up the tool bags, places them in the truck, and drives off.

By the time he merges onto the autoroute, he is cursing himself for getting distracted by Oleg. He should have taken a few pictures of the fountain and at least told the auction company that he'd have movers back in a few days to collect his purchase. Damn! Why had he let Oleg mess with his head?

Should he turn around? His stomach burns, and though he'd told Oleg that Catty was mostly recovered, Ramos is coming to the house in Luisant later to examine her progress. Likely, that'll mean that Oleg will know her progress anyway. Still, he wants to be with her, to comfort her.

He tries to hold the clock steady and reattach the seat belt while driving, but he just can't get it anchored securely. Traffic is slow on the autoroute, stop and go. The clock is wrapped in a furniture blanket and strapped down with the seat belt, but it rolled out of its security. Victor pulls off the highway into a rest stop and buys several candy bars from the vending machines. He eats two quickly to try to stave off the growls of his angry stomach. The clock is too big and round to be held by the bottom strap of the seat belt and too narrow to be held by the cross-body strap.

There's even a backup at the rest stop, so it takes careful maneuvering to get back onto the autoroute. The traffic jam is unexpected. Both his stomach and head hurt, and JP still hasn't called. Victor's phone rings. *Finally!* he thinks. He doesn't look to see who is calling, as he is watching the road.

"Hello, Victor," Oleg sings across the ether. "I have so many ideas for de future, Victor. I have identified two villages with many, many old people. We can buy the houses, block by block, and you can sell the tasty bits, and then we'll clean them and sell them for big profits. I already hhhave the buyers lined up; trust me. I know dat weee'll be veery successful. Two money streams from different customers. I promise we'll make lots of money weeeth leettle risk. I need your good eye so that we can sell the antiques to de Yanks. What do you say, Victor? We can do dis!"

"Errr, well, it sounds good, but I, errr, will we include JP? I'm just wondering, and . . ."

"No, JP not in theees partnership. Right?"

Victor's hours-long drive, holding Oleg's offer and the clock securely, takes concentrated effort. He puts thoughts of Oleg away for the time being. In order to ensure that the crystal "water droplets" remain attached, he steadies the clock delicately, taking his hands off the steering wheel.

Finally, both exhausted and wired, he arrives in Luisant. Sure enough, Ramos's car is blocking his access to the porte cochere. He bends down into the passenger footwell to collect the candy wrappers and feels a sharp twinge in his back. For a few seconds, he sees stars, but it passes quickly. The narrow gravel path wedged between the garden tile edging and the car makes walking into the side door area precarious. He sank those beautiful green roof tiles along the edge himself to create a garden area. He is rushing and wants to get inside to hear what Ramos has to say about Catty's foot. He opens the car door and sees that in order to keep his balance, he'll have to step on the garden side of the tile edging. He leans back inside the truck cab to unlatch the seat belt and grab the clock. He has candy wrappers in his left hand, and he is rolling the clock into the crook of his right arm and stepping out of the truck, trying to avoid stepping on the tiles. In an unbalanced, uncoordinated move, he tilts backward, and the clock goes flying over his head and out of the truck door, landing in smithereens on the tiles.

Victor turns toward the door to see the damage and slips, falling back and sideways and landing on his right arm on several of the raised tiles. *Ugh! Damn! Merde!* He rolls to his side and then pulls himself upright. The clock face has been smashed head-on by the tiles. He closes his eyes, willing that last move to rewind, just reverse and start again. *Damn!* The clock is garbage now. *Damn it!* He tries to be careful in collecting the clock pieces, but its beauty was the uniquely hand-blown glass face. Without that, the fishes appear flat and static. *Merde!* He loses patience and sweeps the loose pieces onto the furniture blanket that flops to the side. He looks at his right arm and sees that his shirt sleeve is ripped, but he doesn't have time to worry about that now. Hastily grabbing the blanket and its loose contents, he goes inside.

Catty is on the couch with her foot in Ramos's hands. Somehow, Victor feels a hot blast behind his eyes and searing jealousy in his stomach. Nothing is going right. Ramos is softly touching her toes and the arch of her foot. Catty looks up at Victor. She is pale and childlike as she says, "Dr. Ramos doesn't like my foot. I mean, my foot isn't good. It's just that . . ."

Ramos looks up at Victor with a guilty grin, or what Victor perceives as such. "She needs another injection. I don't like the heat, the color, the lack of progress."

Victor loses all rationality. "You're no doctor. Catty, let's go! You have to go to the proper clinic! Enough of this crazy witch doctor."

Catty begins to cry. "Oh no, Victor! They'll report me, and they'll send me back. I can't do it, Victor. No! I'll be better. I will."

Victor pushes Ramos out of the way and leans over the couch to grab Catty's shoulder to lift her up. He sees stars for a second and then nothing.

***

Ocean Manor is clean and perfectly empty when JP arrives. He'd slipped the keys from his West Village apartment into the impersonal key drop in the real estate agent's office before he left the city. He started early to be ahead of the moving van. Layla's cold, businesslike message detailing where the keys and cable connections were left him hollow. He knew better than to expect kindness from her, but he did regret losing her previously friendly manner. They had history. He pushed those worries aside.

In spite of the stiff ocean breeze, he opened all the windows on the water side of the house. He connected his phone to a miniature speaker and selected a playlist of traditional French ditties, musettes, that are played in French cafés. This music reminded him of his mother, and her aesthetic guided him in setting up house. Still, Ocean Manor needed filling up if he was to feel anything but lonely. He had listed the apartment in the city as fully furnished, so the van had only a few items in it: a persimmon-colored fauteuil, a bed, two unopened cartons of vintage photographs that he bought at an auction, Turkish rugs from the old apartment in Paris that had been rolled up the whole time he'd lived in the States, and a huge chandelier with descending-size Austrian crystals from the ballroom of the Waldorf Astoria before low-ceilinged, modern additions were brought in. Where would he hang that monster? Oh, and the *irreverent* India Mahdavi bubble-gum-pink chairs. Those would go in the entrance hall!

The van is nowhere in sight, so he goes around back. The waves are high and splashing up almost onto the lawn. *Climate change in action,* he thinks. Of course, Layla had taken her outside furniture with her. He should have anticipated that and offered to buy it. *C'est la vie.* He can hear lawn mowers operating on both sides of his property, one more service that he'd have to subscribe to. Suddenly, the idea of a wife—or at the very least, an administrator like Iris—seems an urgent necessity.

The air is clean, and he breathes deeply. He lets his eyes relax and enjoy the deep blue of the ocean. The grass is a vibrant green, and the red-brown brick of Ocean Manor entices him to indulge in color. Memories of Parisian life in full Technicolor float through his mind: the honey yellow of the old apartment, the greens, reds, and oranges of the greengrocers' goods out on the streets. Even the gray limestone of so many nineteenth-century buildings holds a vibrancy in his mind. The monotone of his New York City existence will be in his past. Going forward, JP will construct a world of color and warmth.

He hears the van rumbling down the drive. It takes less than thirty minutes for the moving company to empty the truck of JP's boxes. The generous entrance hall opens out on the lawn and the ocean. To the left is the living room, and to the right, the dining room. It's a grand house designed for a big family that hosts lavish parties. Not exactly JP's lifestyle. Still, the warm glow of the book-matched walnut walls, the plaster mermaids dancing on the ceiling, and the allover lived-in patina give him comfort.

He quickly changes into swimming trunks and heads down the cliffside stairs. Layla had hired the best (in her words) carpenter to stabilize the stairs last season. The top of the structure is solidly attached to the cliff, but the high water clearly messed with the lower steps. He reaches the water's edge and is surprised to see rocks but not a grain of the sandy beach that was present in the years before when he visited. That old mindset, absentee landlord, was easy, very American, and maybe not so wise. He'd lost track of the important developments here. He carefully pads across the stones, flings himself into the deeper depths, and dives under the cold Atlantic blanket. He swims some twenty yards out and, catching his breath, looks back at Ocean Manor—stately and homey. He can be calm here. He'll furnish it beautifully and cherry out the landscaping. It should be a Hamptons star attraction. He heard that Calvin Klein had demolished a historical property a few doors down to build a modern, monotone monster.

He'll care for this property in a way that shames those demolitions and modern McMansions. The brisk swim is invigorating. How long since he last swam in the ocean? Maybe when he and Victor took Frida to Aix-en-Provence when she was sick. Too long ago to precisely remember. He dashes that memory—too debilitating.

Out here, yards from shore, he reaches down, and his feet find a surprising sandbar. The sand is smooth and uniform. He digs his toes in deeply, feeling the cool below. His gaze drifts up and down the shoreline. There are new revetments and seawalls protecting the upper bluffs of houses on both sides of Ocean Manor. *More expenses,* he notes. He can manage this. He'll restore Ocean Manor to its former, maybe better-than-former, glory.

Over the next several weeks, JP is consumed with furnishing Ocean Manor and fixing many problems that Layla had not addressed. He begins with an electrical upgrade. He needs this immediately. Sadly, Jimmy, the union electrician from Layla's list of trades, is incredibly slow. On Jimmy's third day of work at Ocean Manor, JP follows him around the house until he says, "Hey, man! I can't work with you breathing down my neck."

JP drives into the city early the next day. He isn't surprised to see Iris at her desk, even though it is 6:45 a.m. She looks up to see him walking in. "Hey, guy! It's about time! We've missed you."

JP is coy. Slowly, he walks around the office. He pulls out the sales drawer files. Sales were flat, almost nothing, until a week ago, when the ledger shows that sales turned around. Then, twenty- and thirty-thousand-dollar days. He looks more carefully at the numbers. "What's up with . . . everything?"

Iris smiles smugly. "Yup, as I predicted, once Victor's stuff got through customs, everything turned around. I was going to call you, but you seemed happily busy out there."

"How . . . I mean, who . . . I mean, when did the stuff get through?"

"Well, first, that jerky guy, the New York manager of Atlantic, Johnny, called, talkin' trash. And then he abandoned that conversation. He said that everything was fixed and that I should anticipate several full containers to be delivered. You've got to see the bakeries he's sent! I'll say, Victor, your dad, he can pick 'em! I mean, he's sent us garden stuff and big old bank vaults and movie theater seats. The theater seats were hot! Those were bought as they were coming off the truck. I hadn't even priced 'em. Well, I mean, I hadn't even called you. We've been so busy. Oh! Sorry, man. How are you? You look well and rested, if a little thin."

JP smiles. "Let's go see those bakeries."

As they walk through Les Beaux Châteaux, JP feels like it is somehow unfamiliar, like he is a guest in someone else's place. New pieces lead to different aisles, and though he recognizes some desks—and the troughs with ceramic hands, printers' type blocks, and crystals, which would probably always be there—so much is new. Iris leads the way, with Dolly at her heel. Damn! He'd forgotten a cookie for Dolly. He was really off his game. Breaking those old and numb routines felt good, all except forgetting Dolly's cookie. He liked having her loyalty.

He could hear a great excitement in Iris's voice. "So, I wasn't sure how to price 'em because they're so unusual. They'll be expensive to move and stuff, but . . ."

For a few seconds, JP couldn't hear the details of what she was saying. Was this vertigo or an out-of-body something or other? He held on to the bench at his side. She was looking away, and he steadied his voice to sound nonchalant. "Hey, how are things working out with Fargo? I mean, can you spare him for a few months?"

Iris turned around. Her face had darkened, looking incredulous. "What? No! He's everywhere. Look how well this is all laid out. He's my right-hand guy, and he hardly says a word. Spare him? What are you talking about? No way!"

"Sorry, Iris. Sorry. I need an administrator, and I can't spare you. You are amazing here!"

"Well, yeah, this is my job."

"I'm gonna fix up Ocean Manor in real style. It's really beautiful, but it needs big work. And I need a really smart, reliable contractor/ manager to be there riding the tradespeople hard while I'm out here or, errr, shopping."

Iris rolls her eyes. "Well, why didn'tcha say so! Franny, my sister, you know, Fargo's mom, has been out of her kitchen for months now. I don't think she makes any money drivin' Uber, and there's no catering jobs without a kitchen. I've wanted to hire her, but I was concerned that you wouldn't like it, and having all of us workin' for you might set us up to be in a bad position. I mean, if you got in a snit or some-thin', my whole family'd be fucked, if you know what I mean? But when you're in need? Well . . ."

***

Franny and her Mary Poppins bottomless bag arrive at Ocean Manor on a busy day. *Trial by fire,* JP thinks. Delivery trucks from Sotheby's auction house in New York were blocking the entrance when the plumbers arrived. They needed their truck as close to the basement access as possible, so the Sotheby's delivery truck had to back all the way down the drive without yet disgorging its goods.

Three different plasterers—all old Italian artisans with diva reputations—a drapery measurer, and a landscape designer are sched-uled to pitch their services within thirty minutes of each other. JP does not suffer competitors passing each other in his hallways or driveways.

The walnut-walled bakery that JP selected for his own kitchen is the richest of Victor's recent shipments. He designs a modern island clad in veiny Calacatta Viola marble to complement the bakery's clas-sic wood and thick cooling slabs for the side counters in his modern-meets-antique kitchen creation. The new cork floor was put in only yesterday. Slick commercial appliances sit in their boxes in the garage, awaiting installation. And several wildly modern light fixtures line the periphery of the kitchen, ready to be placed.

JP doesn't keep a color-coded clipboard as per Iris's style; he keeps details of tradespeople and their appointed schedules in his head. Not surprisingly, he has a headache every night as he goes to sleep. Franny doesn't keep a clipboard either. She arrives in loose cotton cooks' togs in a Mini Cooper, not ideal for hauling furniture from house sales. Briefly interrupting his interview, he shakes her hand, introducing her to the wizened Italian Luca Giocomo, who is in spattered painters' clothes. She stands behind JP silently as he explains to the first plasterer what needs repair and the detailed bas-relief he wants created for the ceilings. Instead of concentrating on the plasterer's questions and feedback, JP's worried whether Franny can do a fraction of all that Iris is capable of.

Mr. Giocomo leaves, and JP turns to Franny. "I need you to explain to these tradespeople the scale of each job. I need you to assess their ability to finish in a reasonable time frame, and then tell me their fees and what you think of their abilities."

She nods. "I've been working in kitchens for the last ten years, but I know lots about building tradespeople. There are Russian plumbers, Hungarian roofers, Bangladeshi stone carvers. One can track the world's conflicts by the origin of the workers here in New York."

JP smiles in agreement. "Sorry, there won't be much cooking here for a while. I mean, I like food, but I've been a basic-nourishment guy for a while. Living alone, I suppose."

Franny nods. "These are my work clothes. I figured that the cooking might come later. I'll teach you to be a gourmand after the house is put together."

"Keeping the tradespeople to a rigorous schedule isn't easy. You'll have to be two thoughts ahead of me in readying the house for these

incremental steps. You have to know that plasterers come before painters, and electricians come before plasterers. And keeping a well-trained
plumber on the payroll at all times is essential. Also, could you find out
what permits and limitations I'll have to work around when I put in a
private dock, sort of a marina, at the shoreline?"

"Iris and I work a little differently, in that I like computer spread-
sheets. I brought my little tablet"—she shakes the small device like it's
a beach shovel, when only a backhoe can do the job—"but I think that
we need a bigger desktop computer so that both you and I can know
exactly what's happening, when. Is there a landline here? If not, I'll get
one. How's about a security system?"

JP points to an antiquated wired window catch that Layla installed
years ago.

"We'll have to pay big for a good monitoring service, as well as a
wireless installation, but it'll pay off when the insurance bids come in.
I'll set myself up in the kitchen—that's my natural home, no matter
what's up. Who is next to arrive? I don't mean to be pushy, but getting
everything shipshape means that I'll need a credit card and a checking account to make all this magic happen. Should I get the info from
Iris, or do you wanna have a local bank? I'll order us an office setup,
including a big computer, today. Is it OK with you that I work here late
into the night?"

JP realized that he shouldn't have doubted Iris or her sister. He can
already tell that this is going to go so much smoother with Franny at
the helm. "I . . . ughhh . . . didn't . . . it's a difficult . . . you and Iris are
so much . . ."

Franny reaches into her bag and lifts out a giant thermos, cup
attached. "I brought this for today, but we'll need to get the kitchen
sorted out ASAP. I don't work well on an empty stomach."

JP wants to present himself as fully in command of all the goings-on,
but clearly, he didn't think of the dozens of things that Franny knows

about setting up a house as a business. "So how much will I pay you, err, I mean, what's your salary history?"

"I spoke to Iris about what she makes. You pay her fairly."

"Right, but she and I have been together for so many—"

"So, I asked her if she'd be bothered if I earned the same salary, and she would be pleased as punch."

"But I don't know you, and that's more than I—"

"That's fair. How's about for six weeks, you pay me minimum wage. I'll keep track of my hours, and you can pay me twelve dollars an hour. If I do as well as Iris, or maybe even better, at setting this up and keeping it humming along, then we can jump to Iris's salary? OK, I'm glad that's settled. I was nervous."

***

JP drives into East Hampton, en route to the Connecticut auction. There are several nationally branded real estate agents with elegant offices on Main Street. His curiosity about comparable values for both the purchase and rental of mansions draws him. He'll fix Ocean Manor to his liking, regardless of the market trends, but the cautious side of his personality needs certainty and knowledge of good value and its cousin, sheer indulgence. He parks in the middle of the block and stops in at Mary's Marvelous. The buttery smell of homey croissants and baguettes fills his soul (perhaps he has recovered from when these aromas made him ill). He slowly sips a café au lait and nibbles a croissant, then leaves a big tip so that he'll be remembered. Dropping a baguette and a second croissant into his car, he scans the block for a local real estate company rather than a national brand. He spent nearly an hour in Mary's Marvelous doing nothing, but he's back to completing his mission.

Cowbells ring as he pushes open the real estate agent's door. A coiffed and chic receptionist sits behind a large desk and smiles.

"Would you like some coffee and a roll?" She gestures to the groaning board full of goodies.

He needn't have gone to Mary's; their goods are here for free. *Note to self.* He sees several middle-aged women in leggings and walking shoes chatting quietly. There is a bank of smaller, glass-enclosed offices lining the back wall. A large wooden table in the center of the room has a fantastic collection of European design magazines intermixed with beautiful listing flyers. He picks one up that advertises a house not unlike Ocean Manor—but several blocks off the water—for sale for a cool fifteen million. *OK, that feels good,* he thinks.

"Do you have questions? Is there someone in particular that you'd like to see?"

"No. I'm just driving through, and I'm curious about the sale and rental market in the area."

The receptionist wheels her chair back behind her desk and collects several flyers and white papers and assembles them into a folder with "Hampton Elegance Realtors" emblazoned across the front. She hands it to him, and as he is thumbing through it, the cowbells sound again. Several people push through, led by none other than Rama. JP raises his head and catches her eye. She hesitates for a fraction of a second as she passes by him. Did she raise her hand in a wave? He can't tell. She leads several people through to one of the glass-enclosed offices in the back. In his surprise, he drops and scatters all the papers on the floor and has to get on his knees to collect them. By the time he looks up again, Rama's group has assembled, and her back is to the larger office. He stands and hesitates. Should he leave a message for her with the receptionist? In the end, he silently nods to her as he leaves, pushing thoughts of Rama out of his mind.

Back in his car, he lowers the canvas convertible top, drives toward the slower coastal road, and heads north. He is glad to be away from LBC, glad to have his own agenda, and he wrestles with a bit of guilt that he's not at the store, making sales and readying the artifacts for the next customers. He should be checking in with Victor, but it seems that Iris has everything under control. Out and about, contemplating fantastic design—this feels great. Or does it? Seeing Rama out here, away from the Meatpacking District, is a bit unsettling. He can't exactly identify why. Nothing ever came of their earlier date, or was it even a date? What does he care where she works? Still, he has a feeling that this is not the last that he'll see of her. The road stretches out in front of him. Franny is in control at Ocean Manor, and he has a reservation at a well-reviewed B&B and a big auction to preview.

Even with JP's time in the States, he hasn't traveled much in the Northeast or in the rest of this gigantic country. Occasionally, he imagines closing up everything and just hitting the road to see the sights. There's the Grand Canyon and Bryce, Joshua Tree, and the Blue Ridge Mountains, and so many other national parks that he's flirted with visiting. He could. Part of him is curious, but for all of his cool reserve and stylish creativity, he hasn't found someone to love or to love him, and he knows that his constant hollowness comes from that ache. He'd love to travel, but not alone. He wants partnership.

The afternoon becomes a blur, and soon enough, he arrives at the Nathan Hale Inn. JP knows little of the American Revolutionary War. Of course, there were a few well-known Frenchmen who became heroes to the Americans, including Lafayette. JP knows basic French history and a little anecdotal New York history. The American revolutionaries, beyond Paul Revere, have little traction in his thoughts. There are plaques and statues all along the roads, and occasionally, he reads them. Oddly, he characterizes the names and faces as so . . . so American. JP knows Thomas Jefferson and that he was constantly in debt, and he treated his slave/lover, Sally Hemmings, with less respect than she deserved. He doesn't know timelines or who, what, where. He knows only odd bits and pieces.

Here he is in the land of the Puritans and early settlers. Iris's disparaging comments about Yankee peddlers and simple functionality, rather than elegance and high style, ring in his memory. Tomorrow he'll preview one of the country's most anticipated auctions. He's always known of it, but he's never even reviewed the catalog before. Now he feels free and open to purchase with purpose. Ocean Manor needs to be filled with important, beautiful furniture, regardless of its ancestry.

He eats dinner in the local spot, a Betsy Ross–themed tavern and grill with several versions of the American flag hanging behind the bar. The roast chicken with mashed potatoes—simple and sturdy—fills him but does not inspire his joy or even well-being. He has two glasses of Napa's finest cabernet at the bar after his meal and feels refreshed. Truly, American winemakers have caught up to the French! His hotel room is small, dark, and musty, but he sleeps well.

The following morning, he checks out and drives the few miles to the auction house, a Yankee-inspired behemoth of architecture with a huge adjacent parking lot. Every space is filled. Navigating through the lot isn't easy. Lolling every which way around are well-coiffed prize hunters who, once they leave their cars, forget that other cars need to pass. Headstrong pedestrians swarm. JP parks a long way down a country lane. Once inside, he finishes his registration and receives a paddle with the number fifty-five emblazoned on it. Intending to leave before the live bidding, he'll follow his usual method of making his choices and leaving absentee bids with the administrators at the front desk. The bidding excitement, some call it hysteria, is difficult for him to resist. Always following the same pattern, he sets his price and lets the values fall where they might.

The place is crawling with dealers and well-heeled auction mavens, with their large handbags across arms brandished with Cartier watches and Van Cleef & Arpels rings and bracelets. Several women have boldly colored Hermès scarves draped across their necklines. Each scarf and neckline is colored differently, and yet to JP, they all look the same.

American brown furniture and English silver dominate the offerings. Portraiture in oil, daguerreotypes, imported china, French porcelain, and decorative items, including umbrella stands and coat trees, silent butlers, and painted blanket chests, are spread across the showroom. He walks the aisles, smiling and watching the auction hawks, some with loupes verifying hallmarks, some with measuring tapes, and most with phone cameras. JP finds the shoppers more interesting than the goods. The stuff is all so functional, so plain, so sensible and unstylish . . . so un-French. How odd that he craves French styling.

The staff members of the auction house, evenly placed throughout the exhibit, are all white, young, and dressed in contemporary but very conservative clothes—navy knee-length skirts and chino pants with matching blazers. It is preppy and early American and boring all at the same time. After JP's third time around the room without even one item catching his interest, he hands back his paddle to the front desk, gets into his car, lowers the top, and drives the hours straight through to Ocean Manor.

Franny has fashioned a desk from the crating material that the chandelier was shipped in. The vintage monster light now hangs in the modern kitchen. It is smashingly wonderful! And not at all what he planned. Finally, some efficiency and serendipity. She sits in an Aeron chair (exactly the same that Iris selected for him at LBC) with office equipment framing her. JP walks in after 9:00 p.m., and she is still typing away. There are fabric samples laid out on the kitchen island and paint samples, applied in ascending order of depth of hue, on the wall. The velvet fauteuil sits invitingly across from her desk. The place is taking shape!

Franny looks up from the computer. "So, how many stupendous treasures did you buy?"

JP shakes his head with a small sense of pride. "Not one thing. There wasn't a single piece that was outstandingly beautiful or uniquely exotic enough to reside here. That's the standard for Ocean Manor."

"Right. You should only buy the best for this house. Though we won't have a road map, per se, I'm glad that you don't have big architectural plans for the refurbishment of this place. In my experience, drawings are never complete, or they pretend to achieve impossible solutions. Let's you and I work this out. I've seen architects compromise and contractors underbid, which sends off an avalanche of change orders, putting entire projects way over budget."

This sounds rehearsed to JP, but no matter. "I, ahh, I haven't set a budget yet for the work here." If she was thinking this while he was away, all the better. Ocean Manor is beautiful regardless of what he adds. He's confident in his own good instincts, and she seems to have reliable execution abilities.

"Excellent!" she exclaims.

There is a pile of the day's mail, not yet sorted or opened. He picks it up and riffles through it, feeling Franny watching him with a specific focus as he flips quickly through the pile. A thick and official-looking letter from the State of Oklahoma, addressed to Frances Lofton, catches his eye.

"What's the State of Oklahoma want with you? And how did they track you down here so quickly?" he asks.

With an emotionless face, she stares straight at her computer and shrugs. "Fargo told me that someone called, and he must have given this address. Some bureaucratic mistake, I'm sure. I don't have a clue. Maybe it's some phishing scam?"

JP nods. "Gosh, those thieves sure look legit, and they never quit, right? You'll lock up? Good night." He goes upstairs to put away his overnight bag and go to sleep.

Chapter Four

The next weeks are busy and focused. This productive, immediate-results kind of work satisfies him. He and Franny make a great team. She is quieter than Iris but direct in execution. She synthesizes his brainstorming into actionable steps. The mudroom across the breeze-way from the garage has a beautiful early-twentieth-century mosaic floor that is badly broken, with swaths of tile missing. JP is torn between replacing it with new tiles or indoor-outdoor carpet. Within a few days, samples of the carpeting and like-colored tiles arrive so that JP can visualize the possibilities. Franny's suggestion of replacing the damaged mosaics with modern tiles but keeping the best of the origi-nals so that they sit side by side in an artistic assemblage wins the day.

JP gives up on early American–influenced styling. Its utility bores him. He selects the choicest and very Frenchest morsels from Les Beaux Châteaux: a limestone fountain and garden urns; fleur-de-lis iron railings for the cliffside walk; iron fer forgé sconces, banisters, and consoles. He combines these vintage specimens with radically mod-ern furniture made by French auteur Joseph Dirand, whose geometric chairs and sofa give a complex spin to Ocean Manor. His scheme is blending with the ocean's cool shades of blue, silver, gray, green, and purple.

JP works two days a week at LBC. Occasionally, he selects and crates up items for his own use from their stock. Carefully managing the accounting of this matter, JP pays the store back at Victor's cost, plus 10 percent for administrative fees.

Occasionally bristling at his potential loss of control of the store's direction, he can act uncharacteristically sharp and impatient with Iris. This change is only between them, and Iris never calls it out. He can't exactly define what has changed, but he can feel her dominance shaping the store's culture. There are days when he embraces her assertive decision-making and days when he admonishes himself for this surrender of the store's destiny. Shouldn't he be here, in the store, more often? *If you have to ask the question,* he says to himself, *the answer is obvious!* And yet, working at Ocean Manor has given him new confidence. He buries away his worries about Iris's power grab.

The commute between Ocean Manor and LBC is tedious, and rather than concentrating on an agenda for work with Iris, JP loses himself in French music and a few French books on tape. He notes that Franny never complains about her commute. Maybe she's bunking in with some cooking friends not far from Ocean Manor. He's sure, however, that she returns home to Alphabet City in Lower Manhattan to check up on Fargo a few times per week.

The spring and summer meld into a blur. Creating a personality for Ocean Manor becomes JP's goal and focus. He populates the huge house with storied fixtures and rare art and artifacts, mixing classic and contemporary styles. He's pleased living here, except that there are no visitors, save tradespeople. It isn't the hollow existence of living in New York in a modern cube, but JP longs for a community or an intimate family. This hollowness chills him, especially at night, when his only companion is the sound of the waves. Regardless of this lonely ache, he doesn't change his patterns. He doesn't join clubs or invite locals to tour or dine. Does he think that worthy relationships will fall out of the sky? No, he knows that family and friends take cultivation, effort, and most difficult for him, openness. He is unknown even to himself. How can he connect with satisfying endeavors when he doesn't or can't identify what or whom he longs for? Sporadically, he allows himself to indulge in these questions. Rather than wallow without answers, he pushes these worries aside. He imagines unsympathetic conversations, with Victor saying things like, "Find a family! Are you even a complete person without children and a partner?" JP doesn't reveal this sensitivity to Victor. Instead, he redoubles his energy into making Ocean Manor elegant and livable.

The perennial garden is tired and sparse, but some of the old wisteria vines and heirloom roses are as beautiful as any that he remembers from historical châteaux in France. He cuts back the ancient vines and rigs up supports for the new green shoots. Spending considerable time on the beach, he drinks his morning coffee out in the yard, assessing the progress, and goes swimming nightly as the sun sets. He regards the shoreline protection that his neighbors installed—from gigantic piles of granite rocks barged in (at huge expense) to rebar supports clawing the top of the sand bluffs to slow their retreat. Assessing that each type of system is very expensive and ugly, he regards both methods of shoreline protection as failures. Beach erosion is the victor. And these man-made scars will look far worse when the water level eventually recedes and the beaches extend their sand once again. Ocean Manor's old (though he has no idea exactly how old) seawall is cracked and worn around the edges, but it's stable. He has no scientific or engineering assessments, but he believes that it will protect the house and the yard for decades to come.

JP has gone back to town in East Hampton a few times to look around at the shops and the crowd. Would he eagerly greet Rama if she was around the corner? There are a few wine bars with soft lighting and softer music to suit the forty-and-older set, along with a few loud

Hamptons bars with eighties summer music blaring. He prefers browsing the home decor shops during the day.

One sunny Wednesday, he is in the hardware store, just cruising around. He needs deer repellent and some outside light bulbs, and he notices that the street is draped with flags, red-white-and-blue bunting, and banners. Ahhh, yes. The Fourth of July. Another of the days, like Thanksgiving, that he always forgets about until it's too late and he is alone, again. Today is only July 1, though, so he has some time to address this before it's too late. He buys a few boxes of sparklers along with the rest of the items on his list. He dashes back to Ocean Manor.

"Hey, Franny! Franny!"

He watches her as she looks up. She seems alarmed that he's flushed and speaking quickly. Hasn't she seen him excited before? Maybe not . . .

"Hey, Franny. How about you and Fargo and Iris and Dolly all come out here for the Fourth? I mean, we could have dinner and swim and . . ."

"I've heard that East Hampton has the best fireworks show in all of Long Island. Do you wanna call Iris, or should I?"

JP is so excited. "You plan the menu, and I'll call Iris."

***

On the Fourth, the weather is beautiful. Soft, billowy clouds drift in the azure sky. The ocean is warm, and neighbors try to play volleyball in the shallows, but the oceanside waves are too rough for organized play. Individual swimmers and boaters dot the shoreline.

Franny hasn't been working on household chores for two days. She's been foraging for special foods from every farmers market within fifty miles. There is so much food on the counters of the kitchen, one might think that the party is planned for thirty people rather than ten. The kitchen smells amazingly delicious. JP has set up badminton, horseshoes, and a game where you try to grab a greased watermelon.

In the afternoon, after the guests arrive, they all go to town to watch the parade, which is colorful and fun. Marching bands from local high schools, floats from different community clubs, a crew of riders on antique bicycles, several antique cars, and Boy and Girl Scouts—Iris's seal of approval says, "It's very all-American."

After the parade, everyone swims and plays keep-away from Dolly with a ball. The sun is bright, and everyone is relaxed and cheerful.

The smell of charcoal barbecues lingers from afternoon till after sunset. The pink glow of the setting sun gives way to darkness and the arbitrary flight patterns of lightning bugs. Ocean Manor's symmetrical windows shimmer a golden light from the waterside perspective. JP is pleased with the lighting scheme that he and Franny devised. He's used all vintage mismatched fixtures, inside and out, with the most current electrical sophistication in their wiring. Franny found a Guyanese electrician, Alfred, with great know-how. The depth of Alfred's expertise enables JP to control the quality of the light—either very bright or cool and moody. He creates different values of nighttime mystery. True artistry!

Franny, Fargo, and Franny's catering friends go up early to start assembling dinner. Iris is as relaxed as JP has ever seen her. "It's all good at LBC," she says. "Now that Victor's stuff is coming in regularly, our traffic in and sales out are hot."

JP is content that Iris is managing well and doesn't delve any deeper. He isn't ready to return to regular hours or pressures or any responsible retail role-playing. He still wants to build a dock and marina at the water's edge, if he can wrangle a permit from the officials in charge. And there are other unfinished projects at Ocean Manor, enough, he deems, for him to be full-time here through the end of the year.

Franny and Fargo have invited a few catering friends to dinner, so the kitchen is full of folks in starched white toques with many tattoos. Dinner is resplendent—green gazpacho, lobsters and clams, salads, breads, corn, and tomatoes six different ways. There are pitchers of margaritas, white wines, rosé wines, and a rosé-and-watermelon frozen cocktail. Strawberry and peach pie with homemade ice cream round out the menu. Franny is so happy and proud.

Franny and JP have made the beds in all the bedrooms, and JP expects that everyone will stay overnight. Franny's catering friends are working at a visiting rapper's rented house a few miles down the beach. He's a TikTok star JP has never heard of called Prized Troofi. Franny's friends speak about him in glowing terms, but JP doesn't have a clue about his music. The cooks say that he's a social media whiz, and it's rumored that he's away for the holiday, actually on Martha's Vineyard with the Obamas. Anyway, Franny's friends decide to stay at the rapper's rented house in his absence.

After so much sun and water play and the huge dinner, JP isn't excited for the fireworks. He tells Franny, "I'll stay up here and finish the dishes. The blankets are sitting on the second landing on the staircase down to the beach."

"Are you kidding?" Franny asks rhetorically. "You're coming down to watch. What are you, un-American? Wait, don't answer that."

They both giggle.

"I'm tired. I've seen fireworks. I'll see you guys in the morning."

Franny leaves the kitchen. Dolly walks in as JP is sudsing up the dishes. She brushes against his knees and then sits next to him, her nose nudging him to hurry up. JP rolls his eyes. "OK! All right! I get the message. I'm coming!"

The others are out back, and they all join JP and walk down to the rocky patch at the shoreline. The neighbors on both sides have wedged folding chairs into the rock gaps. JP and Roger, Franny's pastry chef friend, go up to the garage and bring down more chairs. It is finally getting dark. They watch the fireworks barge motor out farther into the sea. Someone's stereo blares the 1812 Overture just as the fireworks begin. The margarita pitcher is being passed around. JP feels a sweet contentedness as he listens to the music and watches the light show. For a minute, he closes his eyes, softening into the joy of the evening. A familiar smell that isn't barbecue or suntan oil rouses him from his stupor. Someone bumps him, and he slowly opens his eyes. Rama sits on the rocks next to him, looking out at the fireworks. He breathes her in, deeply. Dolly comes over and sniffs Rama, then tentatively walks away, looking over her shoulder several times at her.

JP isn't alarmed; he's mellow. Did she seek him out, or is this a chance meeting? How can this be happenstance? How did she just walk across all those adjacent private properties? It's dark out. She seems to be on her own; no others are following her into his party. Both Franny and Iris shine their flashlights over at JP. He imagines their quizzical expressions, but it's dark, and he can't see their faces clearly. They don't get up or turn to introduce themselves. Rama has just sort of slid in. The fireworks display ends with a flourish, and the music switches to beachy, loud summer tunes. Franny, Fargo, Iris, and the catering crew collect most of the blankets and chairs and begin heading up the stairs.

Iris stops and asks, "See you for coffee in the morning?"

"Of course!" JP calls out confidently.

The last of the fireworks smoke clears off the beach, but the music continues.

"Let's swim!" Rama says as she drops her loose caftan into the sand. The outline of her naked body is vague in the darkness.

JP checks in with himself; he is fairly drunk. He hops a bit as he takes off his shorts and shoes, enjoying the relative cover of darkness. He can't see exactly, but he thinks that she is in the water. He traverses the rocks carefully and dives under tentatively; he knows that the water is shallow here. A few short underwater strokes, and he comes up to look for her. She is right in front of him. She swims over and smooths her body across his. Wow! No one else is nearby in the water. They swim to a shallower area where they can stand, and she pulls herself right up to him. She reaches her long, slim arm around his neck and kisses him slowly and passionately. Their kisses are salty, the seawater dripping from their heads. He reaches out and touches her ass, firm and smooth. He drops a bit lower and sucks her nipples. She arches back, indulging in his sexuality. Their kiss becomes energized and hungry. His hands are all over her. She pulls his cock up and sandwiches it between them, the cool water keeping their goose bumps up and alert. She wraps herself around him, not quite letting him inside but urging his interest. She nibbles his ear and neck. He reaches down and gently puts his fingers in her. She tightens slightly. He can't tell if she is wet; they are both slick with seawater. She kisses him vigorously, signaling him to continue.

He stops and holds her face. "Is this what you want? Do you want to fuck?"

"Yes," she whispers.

"It's been a long time since I've done this. Be kind to me."

"Just like riding a bicycle, only lots better."

He looks at the shoreline and notices that all the neighbors have left. He and Rama are alone in the darkness. He pulls her shallower so that he can keep his balance, reaches down, and slides inside of her. Warm and cold. Her kiss encourages him. Her vigor and strength urge him on. He bends his head again and bites her nipple, hard this time, and she growls. He disengages and carries her up to the shallow area, where a small patch of sand protects them from the rocks. He lays her down. He can feel that they are both cold, but he nibbles her stomach, her pubic hair, the inside of her thighs. She is so dark he can really only see the whites of her eyes and her teeth. But he can feel her enthusiasm. Gently, he touches her labia and touches the tip of his tongue to her clit. She yelps in excitement. More and more, his tongue explores her. She holds herself open. It is so dark he can see little, but her hospitality shows him where to go. He mounts her and slides inside with ease. Their kisses slow, and her breathing deepens. *Oh, this feels good,* he thinks. She feels good. She holds his sides and arches and curls away and then toward him, seawater splashing between them.

He stops and turns her over, lifting her onto her hands and knees. He wonders if the neighbors are watching from above, but it's much too dark to see anything. He enters her slowly from behind, holding her sides firmly. They are both cold and shaking a bit, but neither dares to break the spell. In and out as slowly as he can manage. He lifts a big scoop of wet sand and puts it on her back. Whoops! A mistake. It makes her colder still, and her shaking gets vigorous. But the wet sand dripping down her flanks is so sexy. He pulls out one last time and comes on her back, mixing his hot stuff with the wet sand on her.

They get up, and she follows him, grabbing her caftan as they stop on the first landing of his stairs, where the blankets have been folded and left and privacy prevails. Still, they hardly say a word to each other. He wonders again where she came from. He pulls her in front of him, and she lies down on the stair landing, making a pillow of her caftan and warming herself with a blanket. He returns to her pubic hair, licking and nibbling. She puts her hands to block him, saying, "It's OK." He doesn't say a word but gently pushes her hands away. Slowly and tenderly, he touches the tip of her clit with the tip of his tongue. He feels her lie back. He reaches inside and strokes as his tongue finds the wettest soft spots. Pleasuring her feels strangely not intimate. He hardly knows her. Still, following her signals, he slows his movements. He is persistent yet tender. He doesn't rush, making each stroke a fireworks explosion of sensuality. He slows even more when her surrender becomes imminent. Her orgasm is silent as her muscles lock in a rigid tension, centering in her vagina. He reaches out and feels her clenched jaw first, then her outstretched fingers. She breathes deeply, and her sweetness floods his mouth. He feels her melt into the blanket, and the tension throughout her body folds into herself. As she turns inward, he isn't surprised that she doesn't trust him enough to show her satisfaction. Rama turns away from him on her side, and he assumes that she closes her eyes.

JP stands up and whispers to her, "Where have you come from?"

He aches to be loved, to have something meaty with someone who is worth heartache and a complex connection. Rama isn't forthcoming. She doesn't say anything as she stretches on her back like a cat. She looks around at the stairs going up and collects her sandals from the blanket on the rocks. She hardly acknowledges JP. In the dark, he can't see her clearly.

She waves. "See ya." And she walks off into the night.

JP is at once sated and unsettled. He believes that this sort of pleasure demands a presence, and Rama was present, or was she? Her remoteness is disturbing. Is she messing with him or just vapid and empty? Neither option feels good.

***

Victor comes to consciousness in a hospital bed in the emergency ward at the hospital in Chartres. Catty and Ramos sit beside the bed.

"Oh, Victor, here we are." She leans over him and kisses his cheek.

Victor concentrates a minute more and realizes that he fell and hurt his arm while he was unloading the truck, but the trauma of that didn't register until he blacked out.

Ramos speaks up. "Mr. Victor, I think that you fainted from shock. Your arm is broken in two places. The doctors here are contacting a surgeon." He points to X-rays glowing on the wall. Victor lies back, closing his eyes in surrender.

Several hours later, Victor wakes up while several health professionals in white coats mill around, speaking in hushed tones. The pain in his arm is now searing, and he has no patience for all these strangers lingering near his bed.

"Yes! It's me! And my arm is killing me! What's going on? Ramos, why are you still here? What are you and Catty up to?"

Quickly, Catty hobbles to his side. "Oh, darling, they're going to fix your arm in a few days. Ramos will make sure dat the best procedures feex you."

A younger doctor in a stiffly starched lab coat introduces himself. "I'm Dr. Gevreney. I must inform you that you've had a severe injury to your arm in two places. You have a displaced humeral shaft fracture, and these bones need stabilization and immobilization. Our hand and finger surgeon is in Lille right now on an emergency. As soon as he returns, we will bring you in for this corrective surgery. In the meantime, we will manage your pain. I've already requested medication, and it should be here momentarily. I can explain these X-rays when you are ready to examine the damage."

***

Father Allard walks into Victor's hospital room quietly, without fanfare. Normally right-handed, Victor is clumsily shaving left-handed with an electric razor. Father Allard rolls his white sleeves up under his black overshirt and, after gently pushing Victor back, finishes shaving him.

"Thank you, Father. I was thinking of you the other day. I saw a beautifully bound book of the writings of Thomas Aquinas. I was in the bidding, but it got away from me. Have you been reading anything good lately?"

The priest rolls his eyes as if someone from above could remind him of what he's read recently. "Mostly the newspaper. I haven't had much time for pleasure reading." A static pause with unaccounted friction lingers. "This wedding, this marriage, Victor, seems very rushed. I know that you are a cautious man, so I am hesitant to question you. Why must we do this here, today? Why don't we wait till you are returned to good health and you can stand in the beautiful light of our Chartres Cathedral and pledge your love to Ms. Caterina, is it? I haven't even met her, Ms. Caterina. Does she share your love of quality? Does she understand handmade and artisanal culture?"

Victor is not a believer, and his relationship with Father Allard is as a customer and fine-book dealer, but the priest consistently alludes to Victor's time in the church. Momentarily, Victor feels an urge to raise his voice and scream this truth to Father Allard, but he's not really angry, and the urge passes. He smiles and plays along with the churchgoing game. "My Catty may not have my discerning eye, but I know that art has no value unless you can share it. She's not from our church, Father. She's a Russian Jew. She knows oppression from her history there. I'm sure that she'll enjoy your sermons now that we'll be married."

Catty and Ramos come into the small hospital room, followed by an older man holding an accordion. He begins to play a French tune, even before Catty says a word. Without any control, Victor tears up. *This is music that Frida loved.* He wipes his nose and eyes quickly with his good hand.

Ramos chimes in. "This is a very emotional moment, and Monsieur Victor is on lots of medications right now."

"Hunh?" Catty asks, confused.

Victor shimmies to sit up straighter and takes a deep breath while answering, "It's OK, Catty. This is wonderful."

She pulls back a beautifully tasteful lace veil. Victor is relieved that her makeup is normal and that although she's in a medical boot, she's elegantly dressed in a slim ivory blouse and a matching straight skirt.

Ramos introduces himself to Father Allard. "Good afternoon, Father. I'm a friend of Victor's. We have one more guest coming. I know that he'll be here very soon. Could you wait just a few minutes?" Father Allard nods in agreement, but Victor looks at Catty with a question on his brow. "Oh, darling, Oleg is giving me away."

Victor closes his eyes and breathes deeply, reluctantly nodding in agreement.

***

JP and Franny find a similar rhythm that JP had with Iris. Iris is generally more creative. If JP doesn't give her specific direction on how to grow the business at LBC, she goes ahead and creates promotional events, advertising programs, and merchandise presentations. Franny is working in JP's house. And though he treats it like an extension of his LBC business, it isn't a public store; he lives here. Franny is careful to follow his directives very meticulously.

"Let's paint the back stairs shiny black and have the banister polished to a high gloss," JP says.

Franny, who works very specifically, asks, "And the landings between the stairs and out to the mudroom door, also high-gloss black?"

"Good question. I'd better go and look at that again. I know that it'd be crazy expensive, but would you just look into the cost of plating that banister in a high-gloss chrome, or even nickel?" JP is exact too.

JP spends very little time at LBC, though he and Iris speak every morning about the direction of the store and the goods that Victor is sending. JP doesn't miss speaking to Victor. Iris takes care of everything. He remembers that Victor moved, but he isn't even sure where he lives now. He tries to imagine Victor living in France but away from Paris. That question begins to irritate him. Where would Victor live if not Paris?

Iris speaks to him if there are problems or specific pricing details about fixtures or customs support. She says that she and Victor get along well but that they don't speak about anything but resolving logistical complications. As JP settles into his life in the Hamptons, still personally lonely, he tries to imagine Victor visiting. What would they discuss beyond the store?

Ocean Manor is getting talked about. JP knows that the tradespeople gossip with different designers, and they to magazines and social media types. He doesn't direct her specifically, but Franny knows to brush off the few calls for interviews. Ocean Manor isn't a store.

The summer rhythm blends the days and nights into a blur. As is their late-morning process, Franny hands him his edited pile of mail. Today, it's topped with a particularly beautiful invitation with a mill embossed onto rich, creamy card stock. A handwritten note on floral stationery is attached to the invitation with an exotic paper clip. Can there be exotic paper clips? He holds one in his hand. Mini Vert, a design writer for the *New York Times*, has written this note, he reads on her letterhead. The note asks him to be the celebrity auctioneer for the annual Millerworks soiree and fundraising event next month. JP reads the note and examines the invitation carefully.

Franny looks up from the computer. "Yeah, I noticed that one too. That's *the* event of the season. They raise hundreds of thousands of dollars at that fancy party and auction. All the biggest artists donate works for the Millerworks Academy to sell at auction. It's a big deal, ya know."

JP hands the invitation back to Franny. "I'll think about it."

Franny shakes her head in acknowledgment. "Yup. I guess the secret's out that you're living here."

"Why would I need to keep myself a secret?"

Franny looks back to her computer. "I don't know, but it's not a secret anymore."

JP drives back into town to Mary's Marvelous and then to the hardware store. He is standing in line at the cash wrap when Iris calls. "Hey, I gotta guy who's bargaining hard for this desk. He's walking toward me, so just go with my act, huh?"

JP agrees, not thinking much of Iris's sales game. They've done this playacting for years, making purchasers feel like they've worked hard, driven hard bargains. JP pushes the package of sponges, wood soap, scrapers, and paintbrushes along on the conveyer belt. He is listening to Iris go on with her act, and he turns to see Rama right behind him in line. "Hey, Iris, I gotta go. Sorry."

Iris isn't pleased. "No, wait, it'll just take a few—"

He hangs up and turns to Rama. "Good afternoon, mademoiselle. I haven't seen you since, hmmm, since July Fourth. How are you? Do you live here or in the city these days?"

Rama smiles and extends her hand to shake his. This is odd but OK. "Yes, it has been awhile. You know, I have several jobs. I'm here and there."

JP feels his cheeks getting hot and red. He pays the cashier and looks back at Rama. He waits outside on the sidewalk for her to finish her purchase. He is about to ask her for her number and if she'll come to Ocean Manor for dinner.

He has just opened his mouth to ask when she says, "I hear that you're going to be the guest auctioneer for the Millerworks Auction this year."

JP shakes his head in surprise, then lowers his brow and asks, "You heard what?"

She begins to repeat herself when he interrupts her. "Yes. No. I can't imagine that you heard that. Who are you talking to? I haven't decided about that yet; I've only just been asked. Where did you . . . ?"

Cloaked in a veneer of ambivalence, she walks past him on the sidewalk, turns back, and says over her shoulder, "I have my sources," as she turns the corner and strides into the real estate office.

Rama's mystery was initially compelling, but now her goofy, adolescent shenanigans irritate him. Romantic games are fun to an extent, but this is more frustrating than exciting. Still, he doesn't want to go to the auction alone. He follows her inside the real estate office and asks, "Rama? Gotta minute? Please, come outside to chat for just a sec."

She slowly saunters back out of the office and asks, "How are you?" She smiles, looking down.

"I'm fine. Can't you see?"

She mumbles.

OK! She wants games, but he will play it straight and see where they land. He asks, "Would you accompany me to the Millerworks party? You know, I'm a foreigner, and this is all new to me. I need a reliable guide."

Rama smiles. "Yes, of course, monsieur. I can show you the ropes. It's not for several weeks, but we can plan to attend together. You can reach me at Lark's Lane. I'll be there all summer."

"Where? I mean, how do I reach you?"

"You can always leave a message here at the office for me. But I'm staying at Lark's Lane—house-sitting while Prized Troofi is out on tour. It's not half a mile from you. I'll see you for the Millerworks." She hands him her business card, turns on her heel, and goes inside.

Back at Ocean Manor, JP asks Franny, "Would you find out a little more about . . ."

"The Millerworks auction? I'm on it. I'll type it up later tonight. Right now, I've gotta run to the bank and then take Fargo to pick up his new truck."

"New truck? Wow. He must be making excellent tips over there."

"I guess the dealer offered him great terms or something like that."

"Glad that he's making his own credit instead of you having to sign for him."

"It's cash, so it's not complicated."

JP leans against the kitchen threshold as Franny finishes printing the news clips about Millerworks. He adds, "Well, yeah, cash makes for good terms."

Franny reaches over the desk and hands him a folder full of news clippings and the mission statement and roster of the Millerworks board. He reads the listed board members. There are big names, including the disgraced multibillionaire Steven Cohen, as well as the Gagosian Gallery and other well-known celebrities who spend their summers in the Hamptons. He doesn't know any of these people personally, only by reputation. He wonders why they've chosen him to be their guest auctioneer, but he considers that it would be great publicity for Les Beaux Châteaux. It would even add to Ocean Manor's value, too, in a triangulated way. But something inside him knows that he won't live here too long.

He asks Franny to call the Millerworks group to accept their invitation and find out exactly what will be expected of him that night. Then he walks to the back stairs to contemplate the color scheme and banister. He loves this view of the ocean from the back door—simple framing of the vista, unlike the elaborately framed windows at the front of the house. He is pleased with the lush, tiered hedges that famed landscape designer Elana Romo devised and installed. They look like they've been here forever. Ocean Manor is the opposite of those monotone, austere, modern McMansions. *Patinaed, luxe detail in all its glory, thy embodiment is here at Ocean Manor,* he smugly thinks to himself.

JP has done several guest auctioneer appearances for charitable causes in the Meatpacking District. Connections for the Homeless, Love for All—an LGBTQ group—and the Rohingya Literacy Project have all asked, and he has delivered, in successive years. All of those groups netted healthy profits relative to his largesse. He is glad to support them. He'd probably have helped more groups had they asked. Well, the Rohingya didn't ask; he set up the entire event for them, but they had no idea about American philanthropy. Now, here is the Millerworks. The social scene in the Hamptons is fussier and even more cliquey than in the city. Instinctively, he's known that he shouldn't disregard invitations to country clubs or coffee klatches if he really wants to find his community or a partner, but he's never warmed to any of these groups. The marketing expert in him, however, considers that his generosity reflects favorably on Ocean Manor and LBC too.

JP imagines the evening: the elegantly coiffed partners of the hedge-fund set paired with the widened waists of the champions of financial markets. He is impressed with the caliber of the artists donating their works. There will be a silent auction and twenty-five lots for a live auction. Phew! He knows that'll be a long night. Will there be anyone to catch his romantic attention? Well, obviously, Rama will be his plus-one. Does she fit the romantic bill? No! Emphatically, no. No doubt she is sexy, really sexy, but she is also opaque and nonsensical. He feels cauterized to her sharp edge. She doesn't cut him anymore. He won't chase her for so little feedback.

Franny has done more research on the Millerworks Academy and its fundraisers of the past. She's printed pictures of JP from his other guest-auctioneering events and gossip pages from wrap-ups. Gossip columnists regard him as efficient but remote and disinterested. JP doesn't mind that characterization. He is interested in the various groups' success but not in their internal politics. He thinks about himself. If not a specific cause, what is he truly interested in? New York? Antiques? Ocean Manor? He cares about these things, but they don't burn a fire in his gut. He hasn't let his mind wander like this in eons ... Victor's warning about the fascistic popularity of Marine Le Pen ... What? Is that what really worries him? It has been years since he read a French paper or googled a lead about French politics or culture. He's shut down almost everything French about himself, not wanting to remember how much he misses his mother. He recalls his acceptance to the Sorbonne and the mindless years in between. He and Victor created tall towers protecting themselves from each other. He left France without regrets. Home? New York is home; well, it's as comfortable a center of gravity as he expects to find for now.

The summer continues, and Ocean Manor is almost fully furnished. He and Franny, with Iris and Fargo, host a small barbecue for all the hands-on tradespeople. Iris sticks to his side the entire evening, reminding him of the work that each tradesperson did. Remarkable that she knows it all, when it was Franny who had hired them. The fete is much more fun than he'd anticipated. The old Italian plasterers are real characters, singing and dancing after a few bottles of wine. The party was Franny's idea. He wouldn't have dreamed it up. In France, tradespeople and managers never mix it up this way.

The landscaping is filling in, and the window washers are finally finished. JP is poking around for projects to occupy himself. He is biding his time till the Millerworks party is over this Saturday. Will he go back to working at LBC more regularly? Why fix a thing if it isn't broken? LBC is humming along with Iris at the helm. She needs a break or a vacation, but that isn't permanent.

His phone rings, breaking his dreaming spell. Iris has a particular urgency in her voice, though they had talked at length earlier that morning. "Hey, guy. When was the last time you spoke with Victor?"

"I dunno. It's been some time. Why? What's up?"

"You need to call him ASAP," she says, hanging up.

Victor's influence is the last thing JP wants to shape his future. He has been somewhat relaxed about the mystery of what might lie ahead. Now, though, the thought of including Victor in his plans twists his guts. He also knows that if Iris is so emphatic that he should call, it has to be for a good reason.

He dials Victor, hoping that he won't answer. His father picks up on the first ring.

"Hello! Long time! How are you?"

This lighthearted tone isn't what JP expects. He is tentative in his response. "I'm OK. The summer weather here is nice. And you?"

"I'm not so well, well . . . I'm OK, but I've been hurt. I've broken my arm very severely, and I need you to come here as soon as possible to collect a number of these projects that I've bought at auction but not retrieved yet."

"Oh no! Are you in pain? I mean, do you need medical help? What's happened? You need me there? Aren't there . . . ?"

"Well, I'm all right. Catty, my wife . . ."

"Wife? What?"

"Just get here, and I'll explain it all to you. I've bought four or five important rooms. A gymnasium, fountains, and bakeries, and these damn Russians are robbing me blind. You have to come here to disassemble these—"

"Russians? What? I have to do a thing this weekend. Do you really need me there? Can't you hire someone to help? I mean, this isn't—"

"I said that I need you. My damn partners are thugs, and I can't trust them. I need—"

"Partners? What? I'm your partner."

"Oh, you idiot! You haven't acted like a partner in months. Really, you act like a ten-year-old boy. I wouldn't call you if I didn't have to. I have bought several installations that I cannot retrieve and remove. I'm hurt; I can't do it. The Russians don't know about these items, and I intend to keep it that way. You have to come here as soon as possible before these are lost, stolen, or damaged."

"OK. I can leave here Tuesday and be in Paris on Wednesday morning."

"No! You've got to . . . I guess that'll have to suffice. Rent a car . . . No, just take an Uber here to Luisant, and you can drive my—"

"Luisant?"

"Yes. Just outside of Chartres. I've been living here for a few years already."

JP hangs up and feels doom closing around his head. The lightness of remaking Ocean Manor vanishes. He hasn't been in France for a long time. Memories of his mother won't haunt him much, but taking orders from Victor? With new freaking partners and a wife? JP wonders if Victor has been too sly for his own good.

He calls Iris to explain that he'll be going to France on Tuesday. Iris is concerned that Victor is angry at her. JP assures her that's not the case. He says, "No, no. That customs thing caught us flat-footed. Nothing like that had held up our goods before. And I wasn't there to unravel that mystery. You've been great. You and Franny have been terrific!"

"Why, what's up with Victor? Is he OK?"

"No, no, he's not. He's injured himself. He has a broken arm, and I need to go to France to help him with some stuff so that his Russian partners don't rob him blind."

"What?"

"Exactly! I don't know who these Russian partners are, but it sounds like Victor is in over his head. Some kind of Mafia. I'm not sure what I can do or learn. Speaking of that, did you know that he got married?"

***

Franny prepares a folder of information about the Millerworks auction. Directions, the invitation, pictures with the names and titles of a few of the members of the board of directors, several news clips from social pages from past auctions, and a dozen thumbnail descriptions of the art that he will be auctioning.

JP knows that Franny will keep Ocean Manor in good stead for the few days that he will be gone. She knows as well as he does which tradespeople need a push to finish and which need payment. There are adequate funds in the neighborhood bank to cover all that. And Iris Fed-Exed him his green card and passport, both of which he keeps in the safe at LBC.

He thumbs through the folder, but it is difficult to think about the Millerworks auction instead of the questions buzzing in his head about what to expect in France. He dresses carefully and is pleased with the trim the local barber gave him. Frankie, originally from New Orleans, likes to practice his French with JP. He chats and chats, cutting and chatting. If JP didn't stop him, he'd have no hair left. This French persona is a bit of a conundrum. JP needs to be French—all the fancy folks love his exoticism—but all that he has mastered in his American self gives him pride. He feels like an imposter, though not entirely in a bad way.

The six-car garage at Ocean Manor is a great bonus. He's been on a binge, buying vintage cars. Tonight, a cool summer night, is perfect to drive the burgundy MG convertible. It smells a bit of wax, but the chrome glitters. He just had it all replated. He thinks for a minute that he hasn't once missed living in the city, in that impersonal monotone box. Still, Ocean Manor, beautiful as it is, doesn't fit him exactly either. There is no one he shares this beauty with here. Franny and Iris are as close as he's gotten. He trusts them, maybe even loves them, but he keeps the slimmest of professional walls between himself and their kind hearts. They, for their part, reveal very little of themselves. Maybe someday they'll share more of their past?

This old MG does not have a GPS, so he uses his phone and the map that Franny has printed to navigate to the auction. Franny doesn't know that he is taking Rama as his date. He figures that she'll read about it in the gossip press in a few days. The roads are so dark compared with the busy, brightly lit streets of New York City. He drives next to tall hedges and weathered stone walls, as well as high entrance gates that say *stay out* and *welcome* simultaneously. There is a cultivated charm to these homes that have names instead of addresses, but the practicality is another thing entirely. He is pleased with himself for having asked Rama for the street name and number. Her text revealed nothing save for the relevant information and the hour that she'll be ready.

He turns onto the road to a dark, foreboding property with a tiny sign reading "Lark's Lane." He'd never have found it without the numeric information. The wide circular driveway encompasses a huge fountain with carved birds, presumably larks, landing on Zeus. No lights shine on the sculpture, and there are none on inside the house either. Dim walkway lights guide him to the front door, where a small glow surrounds the door handle, mailbox, and doorbell. He rings. Rama emerges immediately, quickly closing the door behind her.

He smiles, greeting her. He can barely see her in the dark. Her sheer black dress is dappled with tiny crystals, and he smells, even before he realizes, that the full ripe white flowers bursting from her bosom are fresh gardenias. Her teeth flash bright white, and fashion-forward bright-purple-pink lipstick emphasizes her wide, sensuous lips.

He quickly shines his business smile, no added allure. In his mind, this is a business night, and her presence is a business addition. "Hey! Thanks for helping me out tonight. I don't know many people out here."

Rama smiles coyly. He isn't going to fuel her mystery games.

"Have you been to the Millerworks Academy before?" she asks.

"No. I haven't had time to explore very much and no time for classes. How is it that you're staying at this estate, Lark's Lane? Is it a pretty property?"

Looking straight ahead and not at him, she answers, "I rented it to my friend Prized Troofi, and well, likely you know that he's the hottest rapper since Kanye. He's renting this place, but he's hardly been here. He's touring, and he goes back to Michigan lots to see his mom."

"Your friends with Prized Troofi? I'm a bit shy to admit that I don't know his music, but I hear lots about him. He must be a social media phenom."

"Yes, don't be so surprised. I have lots of friends. I've had lots of jobs. I meet lots of interesting people. Anyway, while he's in Berrien Springs with his mom, I've been house-sitting for him. It's a pretty property, but it lacks the up-to-date amenities that an expensive rental should have. I think that he really likes it here. Maybe he'll look for something nearby that's more modern?"

They approach the Millerworks property. Even though they are an hour late, the car line to get into the parking lot is long. A small army of valets stands at attention. He doesn't recognize the group, EZ-Car, or any of the workers, thankfully. He looks at Rama to see if she shows any signs of recognizing anyone. If she does, she doesn't let on.

A tall, middle-aged blonde he recognizes from Franny's cheat sheets rushes to them. "Oh, JP! We're so glad that you've agreed to be our auctioneer! I'm Goldie Weaver, chair of tonight's soiree. So nice to meet you!"

"Nice to meet you, Goldie." He pivots to face Rama. "Allow me to introduce my friend, Ms. Rama Gueye."

Rama extends her hand, and Goldie turns away to lead them to the party, no handshake. He is put off. They follow her through an older building attached to the mill. There is an exhibition space, along with several classroom openings across from that. Beautifully dressed patrons meander in and out of the classrooms, adding their bids on the hanging clipboards next to the artwork for sale.

Once through the building, they emerge onto a giant meadow with three huge tents. Goldie brings them to a small circle of people. Rama stands very close to JP. Goldie pivots and points to an older, hunched, and gray-haired man with a wide girth and a Breguet watch (JP can't help but notice the brand).

"This is my husband, Norman," she says.

They all smile and shake hands. Norman quickly remarks on Rama's scent. "Ms. Gueye, those gardenias are intoxicating. I'll follow you all night."

Rama looks down at her bust, plucks a small bloom from it, and hands it to Norman. "Enjoy!"

Norman is quick to retort. "Thank you, but I'm sure that it smells so much better on you. Let me follow anyway."

JP is put off again but chuckles to ease the tension, following Goldie's haughty laugh.

Goldie quickly diverts the conversation, pointing to the tents ahead. "That's food and drink, that's the art for the live auction, and that's the cash wrap. Come find me a few minutes before ten in that area just on the side of the auction tent—that area that's closed off. Then we'll start the auction. And thank you again for your generosity."

JP is a bit tense to be on his own with Rama, but he's asked her to join him so that he won't be alone in this swarm of chic bigwigs. He has his remarks memorized, so no need to duck away for that. He opts to peruse the silent auction area to maybe buy some goodies for Ocean Manor. They return to the building and stroll through the maze of plexiglass tripods holding different pieces. *Ah! Here is a Pablo Vargas Lugo, wow! Spectacular abstract . . .*

Disapprovingly, Rama says, "This is very old-school. Most auctions of this caliber have people bidding on their phones."

"I imagine that they have their reasons. I hate it when everyone has their nose in their phone. Maybe Ms. Goldie feels similarly?" He looks to see where the bidding is. He lifts up the attached clipboard and shows Rama: $20,000. "Oh là là! This stuff is way fancier than I'd anticipated. Here's another that I like. An Amoako Boafo painting, seventy-five hundred dollars. That's somewhat better, but I don't think that I'll be buying anything tonight. Well, that's bad form, I suppose. I should buy *something*, don't you think?"

She looks at him with a jaded scowl. "What do you care, good form? You're doing these people a favor. You don't owe them anything. Maybe they should give you a painting?"

They both chuckle, and he answers, "You and I do business differently, I think."

He'll have to find something. They keep walking and come upon a Shara Hughes piece. He looks at it carefully close-up, then stands a few paces back. He looks at his watch—still plenty of time to browse. His quiet contemplation is interrupted.

"Funny that you would like that one. I like it, too, and I thought our taste was very different," Rama says.

He looks at her more carefully in the light now. Her beautiful gauzy, see-through dress shows everything and nothing. A mystery. And the fresh gardenias bursting out, not only is the white contrast striking against her black skin, but as Norman said, she smells so good. Regardless of her smell, JP is weary of her cultivated mystery, and he does not trust her.

She smiles, showing her bright white teeth. "Come on—let's go get a drink!"

He follows her through the building and into the very crowded food tent. She holds his hand as they slither through the crowd. She greets people all along their route like a local ambassador. They find a relatively quiet bar in a far corner.

"You certainly know lots of people here. I didn't realize that you're a celebrity," he says.

She smiles. "Yeah, right. You're our celebrity auctioneer! I have made lots of friends this summer. You know, I'm a Realtor; I have to be out and about. I never see you in town. I mean out here. Are you watchin' Netflix? Where have you been?"

In a nearby tent, loud music begins radiating out to the far reaches of the party. Rama's face lights up. "That's him! That's Prized Troofi. Well, his real name is Carter Melrose. I'd heard that he might play this gig, but I wasn't sure. Funny, I didn't see him at Lark's Lane." The party buzzes on, with hardly any notice of the music. This is an integrally connected crowd, and everyone is eager to see and be seen by everyone else. Rama's brow furrows. "This crowd is too old and stuffed to really get his great music. It's a waste."

JP looks at his watch. "I've gotta go find Goldie in a few minutes. What can I get you to drink?"

"I always like champagne," Rama says. "I think that they do have real French champagne. Is it Veuve?"

He turns to the bartender. "May I have a glass of red wine and a glass of champagne?"

The bartender nods his head in the affirmative.

"Don't worry—I know exactly where Goldie will be waiting for you," Rama says. "We don't have to rush. Let's go listen to Troofi." She directs him to follow her through the crowd again. But he hesitates. She tries to engage him. "I hear that Ocean Manor is beautiful. Tell me about what you've created."

JP looks down, still sorting out how he should treat Rama. Is he attracted to her, or are her antics unappealing? The pause hangs heavily between them as the buzz of the party sizzles and the music from outside throbs. She does not fill the empty space with easy chatter. He looks up and out, across the glamorous crowd.

He snaps back to the conversation with a business-minded determination. "Oh yeah! Ocean Manor is a knockout! I love living on the water. If you don't mind, I'm just gonna go rehearse my remarks a minute or two. I'll meet you in that area near where the live auction'll be. OK?"

Rama utters a disparaging growl and slithers off into the crowd. JP slips out through a break in the tent's wall. He isn't thinking much about the auction; rather, his anxious focus is on what he will find once he gets to France. How will Victor present his new situation? He watches the catering crew loading and unloading crates of glasses and wines. He feels lucky that he has become the celebrity auctioneer rather than the caterer's lackey. He reflects on his path here in the States. Luckily, things worked well at LBC, but the business could just as easily have slipped through his fingers; otherwise, he could be hauling those heavy crates.

He walks around the food tent and back onto the path to the auction tent. Inside is a maze of drapery and holding areas: benches, boxes, easels, clipboards, and well-dressed young women, all buzzing around in high-heeled shoes. He doesn't see Goldie or Rama. He pulls back the big drapes that form the proscenium. The security detail still hasn't let auction-eager patrons in. He stands to the side as dozens of attractive support people dash around, holding clipboards, canvases, and electronic cords.

His phone pings. Maybe Rama is looking for him. Nope, only a message from the airline that his first-class upgrade request has been denied—all first-class passengers have checked in. *Drat!*

Goldie quietly comes up next to him and links her arm in his. "Looks like you don't have a drink. Shall I show you our greenroom, as it were, and we can get a drink in there? I asked Norman to keep people out so that you could have some quiet. I told him we would be there later, but hopefully, the bartender's there now. Shall we?"

She leads him through a maze of ever-more drapery and stanchions to an area cooled by loud-blowing mobile air conditioners. Goldie is speaking to him, but he can't make out exactly what she is saying over the din of the air handlers. It is surprisingly dark. Ah yes, he can hear her remarking on that: "I thought that Norman would have blah, blah, blah." No, he can't quite hear.

She disappears into the darkness and turns on the bright lights. JP's vision is blinded for a second. While his eyes are adjusting, he hears Goldie scream, "What the hell is going on? I mean, what the hell is happening? Norman, you sophomoric idiot, what are you doing to me?"

JP finally focuses to see Rama crouched between Norman's knees on the ground. He's leaning up against cardboard boxes. She is giving him a blow job. Purple-pink lipstick is smeared all over his white shirt as well as her white gardenias, which are smashed and dangling from the top of her cleavage.

Norman straightens up and zips his pants while Rama turns toward JP, smiling, and then bursts into peals of loud laughter. Norman backs away, disappearing into the drapery. Goldie dashes over to Rama and slaps her across the face with gargantuan power. Still, Rama is cracking up. Goldie stops and takes an inventory of the room. Amazingly, there's no one else around.

She screams, "Get out of here, you slut! JP, how could you bring a witch like this to my party? OK, OK! We'll deal with this. This is *the* Millerworks auction!"

Music begins in the auditorium, and Goldie retreats into the drapery maze. JP looks at Rama. Her gardenias are smashed, but beyond that, she doesn't look any worse for wear.

"You'd better disappear before she comes back and does something really horrible to you," he says.

JP hears Goldie on the stage with her bouncy voice welcoming the Millerworks patrons. A tall, long-haired volunteer brings JP out to another holding area next to the stage. He stands and quietly admires the art lined up on the plexiglass tripods while his thoughts are racing about Rama and what a wild, reckless fiend she is. The crowd fills up the auditorium seats. JP wonders if this is high American elegance. *Is this your crowd, man?* Quickly, the lights break his self-reflective meditation as Goldie, in a moment of irrefutable suavity, concludes her introduction of him. He helps her get down from the stage and ascends himself . . . Up on the stage alone with several lights making him glow like . . . like some kind of celebrity. A strange, out-of-body experience. Where did Rama disappear to?

"Thank you, Goldie, and the Millerworks community. I am in awe of your fine mission. Beauty and art have been the driving forces in my life. Thank you for giving me this honor to be on stage with this extraordinary art!" The crowd applauds. "Let's get down to business. Item number one is a . . ."

The twenty-five art pieces sell high and to enthusiastic purchasers. JP has no idea how long the sale is taking; he is in a bubble of glowing light and in a rhythm with bidders and world-class art. "Fair warning," he says as each piece is sold. Goldie, Rama, and Norman are nowhere to be seen. Two young women bring each art piece to the front of the stage after the conclusion of the previous piece's sale. For the last item, number twenty-five, a huge painting by Kerry James Marshall is brought to the stage. The audience quiets down unexpectedly.

JP knows vaguely about Marshall's work, but he didn't expect such reverence. The bidding starts vigorously and escalates from there. He watches as the crescendo builds to a final sale of $570,000. "Fair warning!" He likes to hit the gavel to its bottom. A great success for the Millerworks, Marshall, and Stuart Cohen, the purchaser. The volunteer art managers take the painting down to the cash wrap. JP feels the snap of flashes circling him. Stuart Cohen walks up to him and shakes his hand as the flashes continue.

Goldie approaches him. "Oh, JP! I'm so pleased! You smashed all of our past records for prices paid. This is a great success!" She raises her empty glass, and more flashes snap around them. *Wow, she's a show-must-go-on kind of woman,* he thinks.

JP nods his appreciation. "Thank you for this wonderful opportunity to learn about your art and the Millerworks. You've built a terrific organization. You all must be so proud."

He backs out, trying to extricate himself from the lingering louche Hamptons crowd. Goldie is still clapping as he slips out of the tent and into the dark of the night. He approaches the valet circle and hands his ticket to the manager. He moves back into the shadows as others come out of the tent. He has ten dollars in his pocket to give to the attendant. He is watching as people get into their cars and drive off. From the darkened area of the meadow, Rama creeps up behind him, surprising him as she tugs at his jacket. He is startled and turns around quickly.

"I've got your key," she says. "Let's go!"

He laughs, catching his breath. "Right. Of course! You know all the car parkers."

Her smug smile suggests she'd rigged this from the beginning. They walk into the darkened night. Just walking, eyes straight ahead, not talking, not touching.

Rama finally breaks the silence. "Why haven't you called me? I have been thinking about you."

"I could say the same to you."

She chuckles. He smells the gardenias' perfume wafting from her bosom. "We fucked so nicely. I've wanted to do it again. Maybe tonight is your lucky night?"

JP marches ahead, carefully not looking at her. "Look, tonight was really crazy. But this is not my style. I mean, your show with Norman was absurd! I think what you did tonight was horrible!"

They arrive at his car.

She raises an eyebrow and almost growls her response. "That old geezer was hounding me, following me, begging me. Who are you to judge—"

"I don't care who you fuck, but don't hurt other people, and quit with the high school antics—get a room! There was no reason for you to embarrass everyone. And *hounding* you, really? You were only gone from my side for twenty minutes. Hounding? Really? I'll take you home. Let's go!"

Rama pivots to face him, takes a step back, and slaps him across the face. She turns and walks away, throwing her gardenias on the ground. "No, thanks. I'm going home with Norman."

***

JP is sitting at the gate, waiting to board the flight to Paris, when Iris calls.

"So, I heard you scored big at the auction. Record sales and all that, eh?"

He explains the disaster Rama invoked and that he was ultimately responsible for.

"Well, if Franny and, by extension, I haven't heard about it, maybe Goldie will keep her reputation as a champion fundraiser host intact and you won't have to face that? Oh, and Victor sent me his address for you to take an Uber to in Luisant. I'll text it to you."

"Iris, I just don't know where I belong. I'm not looking forward to spending time with Victor and his new Russian wife. And I really bombed my Hamptons existence."

"You'll have a great time in France, and I suspect that there'll be big surprises when you return to Ocean Manor on the other side."

"What surprises?"

"Oh, nothing. I was looking at your itinerary. You're coming back to New York on Monday? Really? Is that enough time?"

"Please! That will be all that I can handle. I'll figure out how to hire some muscle. God knows why Victor hasn't been able to do that, and then I'll be home . . . Home, that's a funny word. Ah, they're calling my group. Gotta go. Talk to you soon!"

His mind drifts as he boards the plane and settles in. Iris is his most trusted confidant. He has no one closer or more knowledgeable of his comings and goings. Has he shared his intimate thoughts too much? He didn't intend to both be her boss and also make her his confessor, but that's how their arrangement has evolved. He hasn't offered much room for her to share her private thoughts. That unloading, he realizes, is all one-way. As he analyzes that from this removed perspective, the inequality of it seems out of balance. Iris and Franny have added to LBC's success. They don't have his aesthetic roots, his French vision. They're logistics people, even process experts. But once he got his footing, it's been his concept that's made LBC a unique success. He'll give them or sell (with advantageous terms) them some equity. The processes are valuable. He'll concern himself with this when he gets back. He wants Iris to trust him. He'll tell her that as soon as they are together again at LBC.

Chapter Five

JP clears customs and shakes off his travel "dust." He notes that the people in the immigration lines in Paris are much quieter than those at Kennedy Airport. *French people operate at a lower decibel level.*

He sits in the back of an Uber, watching the French countryside pass. He's allotted himself no time in Paris, not even a quick trip to his favorite coffee shop or the patisserie near La Place des Vosges. Maybe he should come back here to Paris after a few days to just settle down a little. Well, first things first. The driver turns off the autoroute and onto a Chartres frontage road. JP's annoyed at the low-slung light manufacturing buildings with giant loading docks and zero architectural character that greet visitors to this world-renowned city. He admonishes himself for his snooty opinion, but he is put off. Slowly, the car winds around to the city center. The giant medieval cathedral towers over the whole city, the blue from the ancient stained-glass windows radiating across the central square.

It is nice to listen to the driver's radio. Even the grocery store and auto sales advertising in French is enjoyable and soothing. A few minutes past Chartres into Luisant, the car pulls into the driveway of a small, tasteful stone home with a welcoming walkway and classic

French lanterns adorning the front door. Yes, he has surely arrived at Victor's home. As he gets out, he notices the beautiful green roof tiles lining the walkway.

He rings the bell, and a delicate Latin man answers the door. "You've arrived! You must be JP! I'm Ramos, Dr. Ramos. Victor will be relieved that you're here!"

JP walks in. The shell of the house is nondescript, but Victor's arrangements and antiques create a subtly sophisticated atmosphere. Windows look out of the main parlor toward the street and, at the kitchen window, out over the sink onto the small *potager*, the kitchen garden. Ancient copper cooking implements hang over the stove, and Turkish rugs bring color and pedigree to the house. Vintage lighting fixtures adorn the walls. An old pharmacist's cabinet graces the entrance area. Ironically, there are lots of current pharmaceutical bottles atop the old cabinet, an incontrovertible sign that sick people live here.

JP hears muffled steps as Victor emerges from a distant hallway. JP recognizes his slippers, the same soft leather style and cut that he's always worn. Victor's right side is bandaged to brace his injured arm. He walks carefully and slowly. He is watching his own feet step upon the rug, passing Ramos and glancing up at JP as he approaches him.

JP stares in shock, no hug or kiss—no touch of any kind.

"So, you made it. You haven't been here, à chez moi, have you? I've been here for a few years, but I guess that you've been gone à nombreuses années now. I like it. There isn't the terrible traffic of Paris, yet the cathedral radiates its beauté ancienne, so I am not out of place. I'm sorry that Catty cannot come here just now. Elle est malade. That's why Ramos is still here. He's her doctor, though maybe soon she'll go to the clinic in town."

"Right, ta femme? Are you both injured? What happened?"

"Well, yes, we are both injured, but it happened separately. I slipped and fell just getting out of my truck. I think I landed on those damn roof tiles that I edged the walking path with. And Catty was at a party in the Bois de Boulogne and her shoes hurt her, so she had them in her hand, and then there was a fight, a fistfight that turned into a gunfight, and she had to leave the party quickly and cut herself in the park. I've had surgery on these old bones by France's best hand and wrist specialist, so I will eventually be fully healed. Catty's citizenship is still in question, and her access to the national health services is not yet assured. Dr. Ramos here is our black-market doctor."

Ramos smiles. "I'll just go back to talk with her one more time before I leave."

JP follows Victor into the kitchen. It's small but orderly.

"Catty's friend, Anya, brought some fruit, cheese, and a baguette. You know that there aren't any fucking bakeries in this village? Chartres has several, but in many areas of the whole country, there are no bakeries for kilometers. La France va en enfer. There, can you take the coffee and that tray outside? We can't talk until Ramos leaves. He works for the damn Russians."

"Right. C'est quoi le Russians? I don't . . ."

"Shhh! Wait till he leaves!"

JP pushes through the carved Dutch door, clearly not original to the house but a fitting addition. With its half cut, one can open the top door for air and ensure safety with the bottom door securely closed. The kitchen's quiet beauty reveals itself slowly. An old nickel butler's sink accommodates dirty dishes and some washed peaches. Mismatched Limoges, Rouen, and Saint-Cloud patterned porcelain cups and saucers show Victor's continued homage to timeless French quality.

JP watches Victor sit down with care to avoid pain to his arm. "I've talked to my guy at the trailer rental garage in Chartres. They'll be waiting for you tomorrow. You'll see the hitch is very easy to use."

JP smells the rich coffee. *Is coffee better in France?* At home, JP is something of a coffee snob, buying boutique-roasted beans that he carefully pours water over in his prized handblown glass vessel. Victor, surprisingly, uses the exact brand of carafe in the same size.

In the tiny garden, iron bistro chairs sit beside a large iron and stone table. It is too big for the space but striking in its mass. JP puts the tray and coffee down. Ramos comes out into the garden, his brow knotted as he looks at Victor.

"She won't go to the visitors' clinic. I don't blame her for not wanting to go there, but I don't like what I see. She's had a low fever for days, and that toe isn't draining well. I've given her the antibiotics that I have, but clearly, this is not what she needs. I think that tomorrow, if she's not better, we'll have to bring her to one clinic or another. I'll be here about ten tomorrow." Victor's face darkens, though he is silent. He remains seated as Ramos lets himself out. Victor breathes an anguished sigh.

JP wants to comfort him, but it's been so long, he doesn't know where to begin. "What's up?"

"Ramos is only part of the problem. I didn't know that she didn't have papers to be here. We've been together for about a year, and I didn't know her status until this happened and she wouldn't go to the clinic. That damn Oleg has everyone dancing to his tune. Ramos is a Cuban doctor who was working slave wages in Venezuela when Oleg picked him up and somehow got him papers to be here. He's Oleg's healer for his army of black-market slime buckets. It's complicated, but Catty is afraid that if she goes to the regular clinic, she'll be put in with Muslims and catch some disease from them. It's irrational, I know. She'd rather be treated by Ramos, our witch doctor. No, no, he's a real doc, but he's definitely in over his head with Catty's infection."

Unable to offer something definitive, JP looks around. The house and garden are sweet, with a small iron fountain (currently dry) and ferns and bromeliads swaying in the light breeze. JP is shocked to see Victor with such dramatic injuries, but it is surprisingly comforting to sit with him. All the static that's kept them from speaking regularly (even if it was only about business matters), as they always had, melts away in this minute. They'll work together.

"I'm sorry that she's sick and can't be treated properly. I can see why you're frustrated with that Ramos guy and the system. I'm sorry that you've met with such a bad accident too. You look stable—no more pain?" Victor shakes his head no. "So who are these partners of yours?"

Victor looks down sheepishly. He wiggles against his bandages and almost loses his balance on the chair.

"It's such a long story, and I don't even understand all of it myself, but these Russians are all over France. And France? Ugh! Nothing is great here. The unions are strong. Productivity is low. Morale is shit. Our traditions are being disrespected and disappearing. I hardly know the place. These guys, these Russian dogs, they studied me. They watched me pickin' all over the country. They watched me sending stuff to you, and they saw me struggling to get it to the port. Or I suspect that they paid the local muscle to disappear so that I couldn't load and crate away my goods. And Catty? She's a Russian too. She's kind of part of their show, but she doesn't even know it. But she's a good woman. I love her."

"So how can I help? I mean, Iris says that you're sending her great stuff. Why not keep these guys close, and we'll make do with this new situation? Why don't we show them our cards and say that I'm in on the partnership?"

"No! No! What does Iris know? Does she talk to these people? Sometimes I think that she knows more about our business than you do. Anyway, that's for later. We can't talk to these guys like that. These Russians play for keeps. They make people disappear and break people's kneecaps—these are dangerous people. I need you to pretend that you came here only to check up on me and my accident."

JP is so riveted by Victor's story that neither of them notices Catty standing just inside the Dutch door, listening to them, until JP looks up and spots her. He jumps to his feet and extends his hand across the opening.

"Oh! Hi! I'm JP. You must be Catty. I'm so sorry that you aren't well, but I hear that Dr. Ramos is fixing you up. He said that he'd be here to look in on you in the morning. Oh, and congratulations on your marriage to my dad . . . Victor."

She turns to Victor and says, "Who is dangerous persons and makes people disappear and breaks their knees?"

Victor strains in his bandages to turn around to speak to her. "Oh, some people that JP knows in Brooklyn. You know how crazy it is in the States."

Catty hobbles over in her medical boot to sit with them. She is flushed and unsteady. She looks up at JP, trying to focus on him.

"You two don't look so same, err, I mean, so like a family, but you hhhave Victor's voice. I hear dat," she says.

Victor wiggles himself to standing. He squares his shoulders and walks to Catty's side.

In his deepest voice, which resonates with pride, he says, "JP, this is my wife, Catty, Caterina. Catty, this is my only child, my son, Jean Paul." JP sees a Victor that he doesn't recognize. Victor's gestures are both respectful and tender with Catty. JP doesn't recall this patience that Victor now displays. His own anxiety melts. Could Victor be proud of his work too? He shakes off his own needy notions, intending to show Catty appropriate respect.

JP smiles his brightest greeting and offers her his hand. She responds with a dead-fish handshake.

Victor jumps in. "My Catty's not feeling herself. Give her a day or two, and she'll be glad to welcome you into our home."

Catty looks up at JP with a vague, faraway look and smiles.

Jet-lagged and anxious about the artifacts that he needs to collect and transport, JP goes out walking after Victor goes to sleep. Luisant's clean streets and flower displays all around seem, to JP, out of storybook

France. The village square, anchored by the majestic cathedral, isn't totally quiet. The tavern is open, but inside, he doesn't find anyone to talk to. The clusters of townspeople seem to be either young mothers in athleisure wear or groups of slickly dressed bodybuilders speaking Russian. JP drinks his familiar burgundy quickly, without interruption.

***

"You were right. I'll be here for about two more weeks. Would you change my return flight to the fifteenth? If I finish sooner than that, I'll go to Paris to relax for a bit," JP says on the phone to Iris.

"Hey, guy! What's going on? Is Victor OK? Are you guys getting along?" Iris asks.

JP is short and businesslike. He knows that Iris will understand that he can't elaborate. "Yeah. France is very beautiful, and I'll send you photos."

"Sure, I'll change your ticket. Remind me of our United Airlines password so that I can get your miles accounted for and all that stuff."

After coffee in the garden again, JP and Victor sit together at Victor's desk. There, a folder with maps, receipts, descriptions, door lock codes, and other logistically important documents is organized by village location and artifact name. It isn't quite Iris's color-coded tabs, but Victor has prepared every detail so that JP can complete this mission with as little friction and confusion as possible. "All my tools are clean and bundled. There's a small tripod with one battery-operated light, which should be adequate for the work." JP isn't concentrating on Victor's instructions. The entire job seems beyond his scope, but Victor expects completion. JP notes their familiar miscommunication, but he cannot reconcile that now.

In addition to Victor's pickup truck, JP rents a trailer to attach to it. He intends to hire local kids to work with him to load the big artifacts.

The first on Victor's list, the gymnasium, is in a tiny medieval town, Argentan. JP's mind returns to Victor and Catty as the kilometers speed by. He was glad to see Victor adoringly at her side as he officially introduced her. Is Catty one to demand such reverence, or has Victor changed on his own? Maybe he and Victor will spend some time together, fully examining the business and future goals, as well as for them as a family. He hasn't thought of Victor as family in a long time.

The GPS announces his exit in one kilometer. He hasn't done this removal work in many years. Suddenly, he wishes that he'd spent more time reviewing the full scope of the task, what needs to be collected, and how it should be done. He and Victor used to do this retrieval labor together, but that was a lifetime ago. This isn't work for rough and sloppy construction hicks . . . *bouseux*. He knows how detailed and fastidious one needs to be to do the job well.

This school has been closed for a long time. Likely, there haven't been school-aged kids living in this village for decades. Most residential areas are uninhabited—two or three houses on each block are empty of everything, their doors hanging open like a woman unexpectedly undressed in public, open for all to see. Just driving through, JP squirms uncomfortably. This is a ghost town. The school is on the village periphery, with a meadow and a dusty football field attached. He turns off the truck and sits for several minutes, coaxing himself to get out and do the job. Where is this apprehension coming from? He knows this work. Victor's many lessons play in his imagination. *There are no shortcuts. Just get out of the truck and do the job!*

There are chains draped and anchored haphazardly across the school door entrance, but as JP approaches, a bent old janitor meets him and unlocks the chains, opening metal gates. The old man tells him to move the truck next to the gym entrance, pointing around the corner, then hobbles away. With each stride, the heavy bag of tools clanks at JP's shins. The custodian has left JP alone to disassemble the smooth and mellowed gymnasium floor as well as the mural of classical Greek athletes painted on the wall. The old caretaker didn't offer to help, and there aren't any locals standing anywhere nearby looking for work. In fact, there is no one looking on at all. He's in the gym alone.

Rather than an extension of his hand, the hammer feels clumsy and heavy, slipping through his sweaty fingers. The cleft breaks nails rather than removing them. His hands and heart aren't into this; he breathes in clarifying oxygen and takes a few minutes to rethink this challenge. His eyes skip around the gym, from corner to corner. The beauty that attracted Victor is subtle, but the mellowed floorboards tell of generations of French kids. Kids grown and gone. He wonders how he might display these for those who would buy a gym floor. He forces himself to concentrate!

After multiple breaks and cracks of nails and boards, he finally gets a rhythm and properly removes a single board from the edge of the gym floor. Then a whole row lifts like a set of dominoes; the entire floor has been set tongue and groove, with no nails or glue, perfect craftsmanship, likely from the early twentieth century. Each board fits tightly into its mate's ridges on either side. Oh yeah! He knows how to do this. His hands operate without a narrative. The floorboards are uniform in size and texture, and they're easy to load into the trailer. Easy as the technique is, JP works for hours, removing the boards and carefully covering and loading them.

The sun is lower in the sky by the time he looks carefully at the frescoed painting of athletes. This will not be so easy. This piece is painted right on the original stucco. There is no removing it unless he can remove and take the entire ten-foot-long wall. Victor's notes specify that he purchased the mural too. It would be worthwhile to remove the whole thing if JP had help and a huge transport vehicle. Not today. Amazingly, not one person comes to watch or question him for the seven or so hours that he is in the gym working. No one. He imagines

Victor doing this work alone, all the time. Today, he can understand Victor's dedication to beauty more intimately.

It is dark by the time he finishes loading everything into the trailer. As soon as he is done, as if by magic, the old janitor appears and slowly winds the heavy chains, and secures the lock behind them. JP asks the old man where the nearest restaurant is. He checks his phone, but the signal is so weak, he can't identify much. The old janitor mumbles something, and JP drives according to where he thinks the old man had directed him. Sure enough, La Belle Rose, positioned near the junction of multiple national roads, is open.

Outside, old and empty newspaper vending machines line the pathway into the restaurant. There is one open basket of magazines that look like real estate listings. It has a bright-yellow banner that shouts *Whole France* across the top. JP takes one in with him to read as he eats. The smell inside is so French, he nearly swoons with nostalgia as he follows the young hostess to his seat. Is it the onions, the mushrooms, or the cognac butter sauce that he smells? He is very hungry after working without a meal or a break all day.

JP thumbs through the *Whole France* magazine. He reads the mission statement on the inside page: to keep France French. To resist selling broken-up homes to salvage dealers. He hasn't even thought of his salvage work as unwhole. It is a business—his business. This Whole France movement also keeps a data bank of homes or businesses that will not sell out to be cannibalized. The properties listed in this sales book are to be sold at reduced prices, only to committed individuals who will keep the integral elements intact and not sell roof tiles, floorboards, old sinks, or garden planters to odds-and-sods salvage groups.

He eats a roast chicken with thyme sauce heartily and books a room at the adjacent truck stop. He sleeps deeply and wakes in the dark to drive to the next stop on Victor's list. He knows this village. It is on the way to his grand-mère's house on the beach. JP, Victor, and Frida passed through this village many times when he was young.

The red-and-orange sunrise gives this next truck stop a glorious glow. Strong, hot coffee and the warm daylight lift his spirits. Again, he finds the magazines with *Whole France* screaming across the top. He wonders if truck drivers are concerned with Whole France preservation.

The village doesn't look anything like he remembers. Gone are the sparkling windows and busy villagers. Many rooflines sag. The vacant buildings sport filthy, broken doors and cracked stoops; he's distinctly aware that French charm disappears when the boulangeries and the *bouchers* vacate the main streets. The geographical distinctions that once made this town uniquely French have been erased by abandonment and disinvestment. Why wasn't Whole France here when this village was spiraling into oblivion?

The truck radio twangs with sentimental French songs of romance and heartache. The accordion vibes and French beats remind him of his mother. He knows these melodies. Whole France's ideology sings along with the radio. Through a new lens, he recognizes that not cannibalizing a French town or neighborhood is a bedrock. Broken villages and broken buildings stink of a dysfunctional culture. JP can blur his eyes and see accordion musicians playing in the square, but they're gone as he refocuses. The truck door squeaks as it opens, and he steps out into reality.

He walks to the bakery, where there's a lockbox on the front door. Victor gave him the combination for this in his notes. He'll have to dig it out of his backpack. He's forgotten that this is the process to gain entry into abandoned buildings. He turns back to the truck, and walking toward him is a beautiful blonde Amazon. Well, not an Amazon, but a French woman. Her slim-fitting jeans and badass leather jacket give her a strength, a sort of French swagger. She walks toward JP likes she knows him. JP reaches into the cab of the truck, looking for his backpack inside. He glances back up the street, and she's instantly in front of him. She sticks out her hand, American style. "Bonjour, je suis Veronique Dupont." JP thinks for a few seconds. *Should I know her?*

"Good morning. I'm JP Marchand."

"Ahhh. The infamous JP Marchand! I've followed your father's storied salvage works for a few years. I even know a bit about Les Beaux Châteaux and your success in New York."

"Pardon. I'm at a loss. I have no idea who you are. Please help me."

He looks carefully at her hands as she holds the corners of her jacket. Long ivory fingers topped with large, almond-shaped nails fidget with the zippers. A slim gold wedding band glows on her left hand, the continental badge of marriage. Big, blonde curls of varying lengths wave like thick seaweed branches in an ocean current. Her angular jaw and dark brows frame her green eyes. Pink lipstick seems strangely juxtaposed to the boss-lady aura of the leather jacket. She is speaking to him, but he hasn't heard a word, he is so taken with her presence.

"I said, are you here to collect the boulangerie? I know that your dad has been buying them from villages all over the country."

JP shakes himself back to the moment. "Oh! Right. Yes, I just have to get the lockbox code to get into the building."

"Oh, come on over. I know the code. I've been watching over this building for more than a year."

He is puzzled.

She answers as though she can read his thoughts. "Yes, I do have the code. I'm working to keep these old villages whole and not ripped apart and sold off to foreign developers and un-French profiteers."

"Un-French profiteers?"

"Exactly! Your business, knowingly or not, has killed village after village. Without the touchstone, the social meeting place of the boulangerie, or other staples of village life, the soul of these ancient towns shrivels and dies. Of course, our culture has changed. Young people don't want to be bakers, with so little money to be made for so many

long, difficult hours of work. The tradition of handing down this hon-
orable profession to one's following generation has faded."

"But . . . I didn't . . ."

"Of course, you see your slice of the business pie. But here's so
much more."

They stand underneath the iron and glass marquee that once shel-
tered and welcomed bakery patrons. Holding the lockbox, she punches
in the code, fiddles with the keys, and finally opens the bakery door.
Several pigeons fly out above their heads, forcing them to quickly
crouch down together, bumping each other's heads and shoulders. He
can see the deep blue-green of her eyes now up close. Her even, square
teeth match her square jaw. Just as they resume their polite distance
and chuckle at their fright, a bird's nest topples off the rim of the door,
making them jump back in unison as eggs smash on the bakery floor.
They laugh at their combined double surprise.

After stepping back and apart in shock, they walk into the dim and
filthy bakery. A large crystal chandelier hangs from the ceiling. Even
in this forgotten room, it radiates elegance and purpose. It hangs precariously next to a huge hole in the ceiling that is open to the sky. JP's
eyes slowly adjust to see the edges of the gaping hole and the blue sky
poking through. French craftsmanship and authentic materials allow
him to imagine this bakery in its heyday; he can almost see the ladies
with bags full of goods from the greengrocer and the butcher, standing
in line to purchase their baguettes and tarts.

Cobweb drapery hangs thick as velvet. He can't tell exactly what
color the floor tile is for the filth coating it. He has been out of this
deconstruction practice for so long, he's forgotten that the darkness
can add romance to these already elegant masterpieces of functional
beauty. But the dim rooms, even during daylight hours, make removal
of these assets very difficult. He surmises that there's been no electric power in this building for years. He remembers the small tripod

light packed into the truck, puny in this mostly dark bakery without electricity.

The Amazon stands in the middle of the room, admiring it. "Can you smell the bague—Ahh! We can't be sentimental. Let us urgently notice the open ceiling. Lucky for you and Victor, it's been a very dry year." She looks around, taking in the details, but she knows this bakery. She continues. "The truth is that this was a wonderful bakery and a lovely village. And now you own the most beautiful parts of it. This village, Gravelines, is a loss. It's done. I'm trying to preserve and protect other villages from this fate. France is old—I mean, we have an aging population. Young people leave village life for big cities and . . . Well, you know all this. You've lived it. You may not know that I'm trying to preserve some of it."

"Excuse me. I know that you introduced yourself earlier, but could you remind me of your name again, madame?"

"I'm Veronique Dupont. I've organized a group called Whole France. We're trying to preserve some cultural aspects and real brick-and-mortar elements of France's ancient villages."

"Well, that sounds worthy. For some reason, you know me and my business. Am I your boogeyman? I'm simply an independent entrepreneur trying to make the most of business opportunities. I didn't put these bakeries or ancient villages out of business, you know."

"Yes, of course, you are not singulièrement responsable. There're multiple factors forcing the demise of these villages. I'm just trying to slow down the destruction and help some folks who may want to preserve these antique places. Once the bakery is dismantled, there's little promise for a community to regain any traction. Once one house on a street is cannibalized, the value of the other houses falls immediately, and then they, too, are hollowed out. Whole France tries to identify possible buyers of homes or businesses who'll promise to keep the buildings intact, and we help them with bridge loans or low-cost mortgages."

"Oh, so you're Louie XIV reincarnated, or are you related to Christine Lagarde?"

"No, not hardly. My resources are my pen and my wits."

"And who are the boogeymen in this story, aside from Victor and me?"

"Well, no offense, you guys are small potatoes. And we could manage with the likes of you guys. Everyone thinks that Darwinian success depends on competition, yet experience has proven that we could all do better with cooperation. It's the Russian Mafia whose mantra is *all or nothing*. They're buying up whole villages once they've devalued them. They're buying beautiful towns where old people have been weakened. The Russians flush them out with crippling tactics and redevelop the areas to sell to their compatriots who are looking to park their money offshore in lucrative, fairly liquid French real estate."

JP looks away from her. He begins circling the bakery, trying to identify where his first nail removal will start, all the while thinking about Veronique's Whole France. He can't imagine being a baker. Why do people choose such difficult work? He never knew anyone, personally, who was a baker; he never even knew a baker's son, or daughter, or nephew. The world has changed. Technology and market forces wreck things to find more productive solutions. There is nothing new in that. Change is the only constant.

"And why are you here supervising me? I have all the documents that prove my dad bought these assets from a willing seller. And actually, I'm really behind schedule." He turns to examine the doorframe more closely.

"I know that you're French, even though you live in New York. If you speak up, if you resist these unscrupulous tactics, if you help preserve even one village, we could get some notice. I need a revolving bank fund to help identify buyers who need bridge loans."

"Bridge loans? You're very virtuous, Ms. Dupont. No doubt you'll save French culture. Sadly, I'm not your man. I'm just helping my dad for a short time. I'm going back to New York very soon."

"Your business model, sir, could last for a long time, surgically selecting as Victor does. But with the Russians, or whichever group is next, and their ubiquitous suffocation of chains of towns, your supply will dry up sooner than you expect."

He turns on the flashlight of his phone to closely examine the wood trim. He doesn't look at her. Veronique pulls a headlamp out of her small fanny pack and hands it to JP.

"Where is your dad? He's known for doing this work by himself."

"How do you know so much about our work?" JP holds the lamp on the elasticized band in his hand like it is diseased. He hands it back to her.

A long, restless pause hangs between them. Should he be alarmed at her knowledge of their work, their comings and goings? She looks innocent enough. Well, not at all innocent, now that he notices. Her clothes and presentation clearly communicate her badass intentions. Black leather jacket and unruly, beautiful hair. Didn't he call her an Amazon in his mind when he first noticed her? A fighter? Her confident posture and untamed beauty give him pause and shortness of breath.

"Go chase the Russians if they're the bad guys. You said yourself that we're small potatoes. Really, I have this bakery and one more city hall ceiling in Guînes to collect for Victor, and then I'm back across the Atlantic fast as you can say Jack Rabbit."

"Jack rabbit? What does that mean? How long will you be here in France?"

"It's an American expression, I think. Maybe I've misunderstood that?"

"I haven't heard Americans use that expression. That's not the point. I have a crew that's experienced in removing these assets, as you call them. My crew and I could help you. I can get headlamps, klieg lights, cords, and a power source for you . . . Jack Rabbit. Help me and I'll help you."

"You know that I'm taking this apart to ship to New York to sell to an American buyer, right?"

"Yes, I know your business. You're small, specific. You're not buying entire towns and repurposing them to benefit money launderers or criminal heads of state. If you step up to protect and preserve these antique treasures, maybe there'll be a chance to resist the big bad guys."

JP looks around. The filth alone will make this job long and slow. The lack of light will make the meticulous removal of woodwork nearly impossible. Victor should have given him a better understanding of the scope of these jobs, or he should have dialed down to what the real work would be. Well, maybe Victor didn't tell him purposely, hoping that JP wouldn't resist the scale of the jobs.

She asks again, "Where is Victor?"

"He's hurt, injured. He fell and broke his arm, and he's bandaged up for a while."

"So you won't be returning to the States like Jack Rabbit, then?"

"This is the second on a three-stop tour, madame. And then, yes, it will be a brief trip. So what do you want from me in exchange for some help here?"

She pulls a brochure out of her bag, the same *Whole France* one that he's seen at the truck stops. "I need a spokesperson bigger than I am. You would be perfect. More than that, I need help with banks. I've identified three villages that are in a Russian developer's sights right now. These villages have very old residents. They'll tip easily and very soon. I've created a data bank of potential buyers of homes and shops who will honor a commitment to keep them whole if I can help them with financing. Take your pick of which you'd want to do first. I need both—financing and a spokesperson—to happen simultaneously. Simple!"

JP stands up straight and assesses her proposal. She wants him to buy into her movement. To be the face of Whole France. Screw that— he's a New Yorker, a salvage seller!

She continues. "Honestly, you won't have to do much at all. Just be the pretty face. I'll do the work. Help me get this thing rolling, and you can go back to New York, and I'll go back to my family."

Note to self, he thinks, *she's married.* "Where do you live? Has your town been overrun by Russians?"

"I live in touristic Honfleur in Normandy. We still have our bakeries, but there are so many Russians, both renting our most beautiful villas and day-trippers illegally picking apples from our orchards. French is the second language in Honfleur. Russian is now our lingua franca."

"So this is an anti-Russian movement? Whole France positions itself as a victim, I think." He hesitates and quickly changes the subject. "Actually, I know Honfleur well. My cousins used to live in Pennedepie."

"Maybe your cousins' house is lived in by Russians now. And, no! This isn't anti-Russian. This is a pro-French protection, resistance. Did you live in Normandy?"

"No, no. I've always lived in big cities. Melting pots with Russians, Algerians, Indians, even some Germans, but very few Germans in Paris. We're getting off the point here. I've got this job to do. You could possibly help me execute it. And in exchange for this help, you want me to make banking arrangements, like guarantee loans, *and* you want me to be a spokesperson against my own livelihood? Pardon, Madame Dupont, I just can't do it."

"Did you know that ten million people visited the Louvre last year? Paris has so many tourists. The largest part of the municipal budget is sanitation, imagine! And Paris is changed. It's Disney-fied. It's beautiful and picturesque and, sadly, has lost so much of its authenticity. I want to keep the rest of France in its real state, if possible. Can you imagine the Russians gold-plating this village? What a nightmare. I can see it already, and it's not pretty. I'm not against tourism, but I know that when real culture is diluted, the very authenticity that tourists travel here to see and feel may be in jeopardy."

Veronique purses her lips so tightly that they are white for a split second. She looks down at her toes as if some answer is available where she hasn't looked earlier. She shakes her head and pulls the zippers of her jacket down and close together. She turns and speaks to JP in English, as if somehow that is more businesslike. "Very well. My loss, monsieur. As you traverse France, I suspect that our paths will cross again. I can help you. Please take my card." From her wallet, she pulls out a thick, square business card with her name, contact information, and *WHOLE FRANCE* printed in bright yellow across the bottom.

JP puts it in his back pocket. "I won't be here long. I've got business in New York. I suspect that soon, you'll catch up with Victor. You'll like him; he's actually much more polite than I am, and of course, he's really French."

Veronique walks out of the dark bakery.

He'll have to find a hardware store or someplace to rent lights, as well as a way to access power. He looks at his phone, but with so few bars of cellular connectivity, he'll have to drive for better reception to figure it out. He waits a few minutes, imagining that she's walked away.

This project is too big. He can't do it alone. He dials Victor.

***

Victor watches Catty sleeping. Her face is slick with sweat, and her color is pasty gray. He looks at the bottles that line the bathroom vanity, his with prescription typing from the clinic in Chartres, hers with Ramos's curlicue handwriting in mismatched bottles. He knows the treatment isn't going well, though Catty doesn't complain. She welcomes Ramos's practice on her. Victor knows that she should be either in the hospital or under the care of the doctors at the main city clinic.

He can intuit all he wants, but he can't drive her there with his arm plastered to his side.

He'll gladly pay for her treatment at the clinic, if he can just get her there. Maybe he'll call Catty's friend Anya? Right! He should have figured this out days ago. He walks from the bedroom to the kitchen, where his phone sits on the table. They could go tonight if Anya can get here soon. Just as he reaches for the phone, JP calls. Victor knows that this will be a complicated call. He's asked too much of out-of-practice JP to collect all these important properties.

Their phone conversation is a mash-up of talking past one another—unheard cues and misunderstood answers. Victor can't follow JP's complaints. He knows the projects are big and detailed, but all he can focus on is calling Anya as soon as possible.

"I'm stuck. I can't do this alone. I'm going to abandon this bakery and go to the city hall and be done. I'm sorry."

Victor listens half-heartedly. "Right. D'accord." He neither gives his blessing nor pushes JP to follow through. He can't worry right now that Oleg and his crew will soon move in and topple the whole village. He hoped to rescue the bakery before they ravaged everything, but with Catty's condition, he can't parse that out now. Their angry sign-off rings with familiar dissatisfaction. Victor dials Anya as soon as JP hangs up.

***

JP walks back into the bakery. He can do this. He's done it dozens of times with Victor years ago. He definitely needs to take down the chandelier. That's obviously worth saving. He touches every light switch—no power anywhere. He remembers the small ladder in the truck but instead pulls a rusted wheeled cart from the corner into the main room under the light fixture. The hole in the ceiling gives him enough light from outside to identify the electrical cap and supporting beams and materials. Carefully, he stands on the cart, and with some effort, he unscrews the bronze cap from the ceiling. The old barnyard-type wiring with cloth covering reminds him of his family apartment in Paris: high engineering in its day and a fire threat as it ages. He looks through the ceiling hole to the sky and sees darkening clouds. He reaches up into the trusses, loosening the braces and wires that hold the fixture. When he hears the shrieking of mice and rats, he immediately withdraws his hand, unintentionally dislodging something important—the whole chandelier sways and creaks and finally stops. *OK, all good.* But then there's the brutal slow-motion sound of old joists splintering. The swinging fixture breaks free from the ceiling, bouncing off the wheeled cart that he is precariously balanced on, and smashes to the ground. The crash is deafening, followed by the seconds-long tinkling of crystals breaking. The cloud of dust reaches all the way to his nose and eyes, temporarily blinding him. He carefully descends from the cart and sneezes four violent blasts.

"Damn it! Damn, damn, damn!"

There must be an easier way to get this done. He examines the injured chandelier, lying on its side like a dying deer hit by a speeding truck.

"Damn it!" He's made a mess of the nicest specimen in the whole place. "Damn it!"

The dust settles. He looks around and inspects the craftsmanship of wooden niches, molding profiles, and matching wood grains mirroring each other on the opposite sides of the room. There is nothing simple about this bakery. This project calls for skilled and experienced work. Damn! He's aggravated! He holds his phone upright and walks around the room, trying to catch a signal. Maybe he'll hire some muscle at a hardware store, more likely a community center, a church?

As he walks, eyes glued to the phone, he feels something drop on his head, then another. Ugh! Are there more damn birds? No, worse, rain! Surely it is a sign to abandon this project. He reaches into his back pocket and pulls out Veronique's card. Should he work with her?

He dials. The signal is faint and sporadic, but she hears his call for help.

"Sure, I can have two guys there in half an hour and two more with lights and power a few hours after that." JP doesn't hear exactly what she offers, but he hopes for useful assistance.

Thirty minutes later, two square-shouldered men with full beards and easy smiles stride into the bakery. Large tool bags, coils of electrical cords, and other kits are strapped to their backs and tucked under their arms. They're wearing marine-grade foul-weather gear. "Bonjour, je suis Alan."

The second, "Je suis Bernard."

The rain is consistently falling, and there is a river inside the bakery, quaintly called Pain et Beurre.

"Oui, nous travaillons con Madame Dupont et Whole France. Nous avons attendu take this building apart for several months."

They spread a heavy canvas on the ground, trying to stay away from the river of rainwater. JP stands to the side in his *walk-in-the-park* slicker that is already soaked. Alan and Bernard snicker quietly about the ruined chandelier.

JP tries casual conversation. "How do you guys know Veronique, errr, Madame Dupont?"

Bernard is very talkative, explaining that Whole France has grassroots support and a patron who trains workers in how to dismantle and preserve historical items and, fortunately, owns hardware stores. Whole France's foundation does free, ongoing training of workers. Mostly, the group boards up historical buildings until Madame Dupont finds the best buyers for the properties.

JP watches as they lay the round canvas out. Attached is an interior parachute-like pouch with dozens of cushioned pockets that protect the crystals. Once the wires are untangled, they tuck the crystals into the ascending pockets. Riveted, JP watches. He hasn't seen a protective apparatus like this. After the chandelier is rolled up and tucked into a dry corner, the guys direct the ever-widening river of rainwater out the door.

Veronique arrives in a heavy-duty yellow slicker over her leather jacket. Her wet hair curls and snakes under the headlamp's wide elastic band.

"You didn't tell me that you had such an expert crew. These guys put Victor and me to shame."

She smiles and nods. "The second crew with lights is a little slow in the rain, but they're coming."

Once the entire team is assembled, Veronique directs them. Obviously, they have practiced such deconstruction many times. A small generator loudly powers the portable floodlights that wash the wood walls with bright bluish light. Each carpenter wears a headlamp and a double tool belt to accommodate the surgically specific tools necessary to remove, yet preserve, the woodwork. JP watches as they bundle like shapes and materials and load them into his trailer, and some into their specially equipped van, outfitted to categorize and store the materials. He works alongside them, but he is out of practice, slow and clumsy. He's already damaged several carved capitals. Hours later, they dry and wrap their tools and reload the lights into the support van.

Veronique is dusty and wet but resolved as she closes the door to their van. "We can't meet you in Guînes tomorrow, but we'll be there in two days to help you with that amazing ceiling in the *mairie*, the city hall. I don't think there's much else there that you'll want, but we'll see when we meet you. We'll keep this stuff in our van, and when it's all collected, we'll help you to the Port of Le Havre."

JP stands in awe. This certainly is the easier and more successful way to get the job done!

The rain hasn't stopped in all these hours, and JP is soaked. The group splits up in all directions. He wonders if he should go back to Chartres or on to Guînes to check out the city hall.

Veronique doubles back and asks him, "Where will you stay? Or what will you do? How about I call my friend who owns a petit inn an hour's drive from here and about three hours from Guînes? The cuisine and boulangerie at her place are incredible. Shall I call her?"

JP hesitates, trying to imagine how much he will owe this woman. "Sure. That sounds . . . errr. That sounds perfect, except that I have lots of phone calls to make and correspondence to handle. Maybe there's a better internet signal at the truck stops? I'll meet you in two days, seven in the morning, at the mairie?"

"Nonsense! I was just at her place last month. She's got a great business setup. You can even send messages from her garden. In fact, she's kept the damn Russians out of her village. She's helped the library and other public institutions, and—well, you'll see. She saved the town, helping them establish a baker's collective that sells bread to several nearby villages that have lost their bakeries. I'll text you the name and address and see you on Friday."

***

JP drives through the dark night. He follows his phone's directives through tiny hamlets, that is, when there's a signal. Some turns and stretches have zero signal, so he guesses which way to go. He's forgotten that so much of France is rural. He drives carefully; the trailer is a whipping, slipping appendage on the back of Victor's big truck. He can't see the sheer cliffs that hang over the river on this moonless night, but he knows that they are steep. He imagines that Veronique likes to drive fast. This is taking much longer than she said it would. He tries to assess what little he knows of her: Is she a badass Amazon or a calculated, trained preservationist? *Don't be such a sexist,* he admonishes himself. *Those qualities don't have to be mutually exclusive.*

He turns and twists down tiny lanes that test the nimbleness of the pickup truck and his own driving confidence. A dense hedge of hydrangea spills into a circular drive with the beautiful Norman-style Hotel Bonnet in front. Its subtly lit sign welcomes him after a long day and an even longer, tense nighttime drive. He grabs his bags, one with clothes and one with his laptop, wires, and tech paraphernalia. The rain is constant, and as he runs inside, he can hear the river rushing nearby.

Madame Christophe, a tall, large-boned Black woman, stands erect behind the bar. She wears stylish jeans and a close-fitting blouse. Très chic. Her wide smile gives him comfort. The *Whole France* magazine is on the corner of the bar, and he picks it up.

Madame Christophe nods in approval. "Veronique has arranged everything. I just need your credit card for an imprint. The room is up one flight of stairs." Madame Christophe urges him to go directly to the dining room because the cook is ready to depart.

He wants to look carefully at the early photos of the hotel on the walls, but instead, he goes directly to the dining room. Chrissy, as she likes to be called, greets him there. The house aperitif, with local honey, champagne, and unidentified botanical bitters, waits for him at the table. The light is low, and the candles' glow makes the room feel settled and safe. This is much better than a truck-stop hotel and diner.

Chrissy doesn't offer any choice for a meal as she begins bringing dishes out to him from the kitchen. First is a mushroom soup, rich in earthy chanterelles, sherry, and butter, a heavenly fragrance that brings back memories of his mother. She also presents a carafe of the local appellation. JP leans back, enjoying this French experience. He drinks deeply and watches quietly as Chrissy serves him grilled white fish with a vegetable medley; a large pat of pale butter; and a warm, paper-wrapped baguette. JP is suddenly very tired. The *Whole France* magazine sits unopened on the table as he eats and drinks, replaying the events of the day. The red-faced, fat cook, now in street clothes, pops his head out of the kitchen, bidding JP and Chrissy good night.

JP checks his phone, and just as Veronique had assured him, he has full bars. Too bad he is too tired and it is too late to call Victor. He refuses the coffee that Chrissy offers. While she is in another room, he clears his plates and cutlery. The kitchen is small but efficiently laid out. Professional steel appliances create an inner horseshoe, with a separate baking corner complete with a cool marble workstation and its own oven. He'll make a keener observation in the morning.

Upstairs, his room has a large window overlooking the garden, on which he pulls the long drapery closed. Thick Turkish rugs soften his stride, and the modern bathroom has a small but deep soaking tub tucked into the corner. He is tempted to relax in it, but the bed has a stronger pull.

He draws the pillow under his neck and tries to list all the calls that he needs to make tomorrow, but after thinking of Iris, he sleeps.

Bright light through a small breach in the window covering wakes him. Leaning over to check the time on his phone, he almost falls off the bed when he realizes that it is 11:30. Still too early to call Iris in New York, but Victor will be anxious to hear from him.

They speak as JP looks out onto the garden below. JP can hear that Victor is distracted. The bakery, the chandelier, the coffered ceiling . . . His flat voice betrays that nothing rings a bell of recall or pride. Catty is now Victor's sole concern. JP is surprised by this care. He can't remember one day of work missed by Victor when Frida was ill. It is unfortunate that Catty isn't well, but JP is pleasantly surprised by Victor's sincere sensitivity and protective instincts.

He washes and dresses. Chrissy is busy in the salon, arranging flowers, when he arrives downstairs. Coffee is in a carafe, and the delicious butter, baguettes, and croissants sit on a small buffet. He heaps the fruit compote onto his plate.

Chrissy advises him to sit in the garden. "But one thing. I got a notice from your bank that the card you gave me is being held for suspected fraud."

JP rolls his eyes and says, "Ugh! I forgot to alert them that I'm traveling here in France, and they're being cautious." He pulls out his wallet and hands her a second card. "Here, this one should work."

He reads emails for a few minutes, after which Chrissy comes out to join him, returning his card. She tells him how she came to France as a child. Her mother was a cook from Guadeloupe who worked in the kitchen of a nearby château. Chrissy knows upstate New York from her student days. She earned a degree in hospitality from Cornell. She believes in Veronique's mission and works with a group of bakers in the region to create and maintain a bakers' collective. This, she tells JP, should be the model for other local regions to save their bakeries and communities. The cook beckons her then, and she leaves JP in the garden.

He thinks again that he should call Iris, but it is still very early at home. Instead, he looks at the bicycle leaning on the garden gate. In all his years in New York, he hasn't ridden once. Today's the day. He pedals into the village. La Toulzanie is the opposite of the village he was in the day before. The streets here are clean, and busy people converse in the commercial square. The town is ancient and mellow, and its stone architecture is well maintained. Busy shops, cafés, and wine-tasting rooms dot the commercial area. Roofs are taut, and the gardens are vibrant. A beautiful library that was a hospital in the seventeenth century now has indoor and outdoor reading areas. Two large bank buildings, kitty-corner from each other, cast their paternal shade over the community.

A long stone building with symmetrical windows and a red tile roof stands at a forty-five-degree angle to the square. The plaque explains that it was a mental hospital in the seventeenth century and has been renewed as the Bakers' Collective of the Lot River Region. Four vans specially outfitted as bread-delivery vehicles are parked behind the building. He looks into the bakery's window to see young people in offices, milling areas, and the large baking center, with a long wall with six or more ovens lined up in a row. The modern setting is bright and clean, with windows to look out onto all the activities. And though he is outside, he can hear the loud, fun music inside. Today's offering is Chicago-style blues twanging throughout the workstations.

He returns to the central square and sits on a bench in the park. He calls Iris.

She answers on the first ring. "Hey, guy! How goes it? How's Victor?"

JP watches the parcel-laden villagers greet one another with patience and sincerity as he listens to Iris's waste-no-time questions. He breathes deeply.

"JP? JP? Are you there? Can you hear me?"

"Yeah, sure. I hear you. It's all OK. Well, Victor's not OK at all, but I'm settling in, you know. Calming down a bit."

"Oh, sure. That's good. Have you figured out the Russian stuff? Can I help you with the shipping articles? I have the guy's name at the Port of Le Havre. I can prep him for your arrival. I'll arrange for the crating folks to meet you—"

"Iris! Slow down. I still have one more big day to collect a ceiling from Guînes's city hall tomorrow. And, well, I've gotten help from a preservation group to collect these assets, and I'm not sure exactly what I'm gonna have to do for them in repayment. I might have to stay here longer than I originally expected."

"Well, sure . . . No problem. Franny and I have it under control here and over at Ocean Manor. Repayment? Will you need money over there? Ya know, there's all these money-laundering restrictions now in the EU with cash payments. Should we work it through Victor's bank? Send me his account numbers and passwords and I'll have it ready for you."

"Well, it might not be money exactly that I have to give them. I mean, well, yes. I do need to renew my relationship with Victor's bank. Is it only in Chartres, or is it in Paris as well?"

"I'll find out. What do you need from a bank?"

"I need a bank partner for a preservation movement."

"A what?"

"Exactly. I'm on the hook for a big job."

He is about to explain that he's gotten a fraud email alert from JPMorgan Chase at home, but just then, he watches Veronique drive through town in a big American pickup truck. Now, he notices that it is similar to Victor's. He guesses that she's heading to the hotel.

"Hey, Iris, I gotta run. I'll call you later."

As he coasts into the driveway of Hotel Bonnet, he watches Veronique and Chrissy laughing.

"Hey," Victor says as he approaches, "I didn't expect to see you until tomorrow at Guînes. I was enjoying this downtime. Tell me that your team isn't expecting to work at the mairie until tomorrow."

"No, of course not. My kids went off to scouting camp, so I thought I'd come down here early to convince you to commit to Whole France. I have some grandes idées that I'm itching to get off the ground. I really think that you're the catalyst we need. Come on—let's go into the village to look at the co-op."

"Oh. Right. I saw that. It's beautiful and modern."

"I want that to be the basic model for other districts. It is expensive to do it well, but why bother if you're not going to do anything expertly and beautifully?"

JP looks at her wild hair blowing in the breeze. Her flushed cheeks radiate vitality, along with confidence. Her squared shoulders and leather jacket contribute to her forthright presentation. She has a plan. For a split second, he envies her knowledge and her life's direction. He isn't young anymore, and still, home and a specific calling are elusive. He's a grown man, yet the yoke of fulfilling his obligations to Victor, and to his mother's memory, and even to France is still unstable and unresolved in his mind.

She calls him back to the conversation. "So, should we go and take a look? JP? Let's go to the co-op, eh? The bike is OK for you?"

Soon, they walk through the front door of the former mental asylum. Loud R & B music thumps. JP wonders, *Is that Keb' Mo'?* American music. People working in all areas of the building seem to be grooving to the beat. An older, hunched man, François, greets Veronique warmly.

Veronique is all business. JP can't concentrate on the facts that she rattles off: the co-op, or the new business launches, or the villages already looted, or the dozens of villages ready to fall prey to Mafia creeps. Or even the price of a good baguette. He is distracted. It is her wild hair, like Medusa, whose snake-covered head mesmerized men's thoughts. So, too, does Veronique captivate JP's fantasy.

They return in the late afternoon to Hotel Bonnet. Chrissy and her brother, Pepper, are in the garden, working in the potager. Pepper has on earphones and is singing Prized Troofi's song "Runnin' with the Bulls" with a full voice.

After they sit to chat, JP learns that Pepper also went to Cornell and then worked in upper management at Starbucks for twenty years. It is his vision that executed the co-op here and his money that seeded the start-up. Pepper's large build and quick smile make him seem like a teddy bear, but he, too, is all business.

"We need an endowment, a foundational cushion, to get a revolving credit line circulating in our group of identified preservationists and borrowers. The co-op has created meaningful jobs; they pay a living wage, sort of. But more than anything, unlike Starbucks, which sends all profits back to headquarters, our workers and consumers spend their money here, in our own region. This strengthens our community for us. From what I observed at Starbucks, very few resources are returned to the community where the shop is. To me, that's ass-backward. My

idea, to get an infusion of the capital that would really make a difference for our future, is that Prized Troofi does a charity concert for us
so that we can build on a five- or ten-million-euro base."

Chrissy, Veronique, and Pepper all laugh. Chrissy gets up to
retrieve the lemonade pitcher and says, "Right. You just call up Prized
Troofi and ask him for this tiny favor, eh?"

"So you've heard of this rapper named Prized Troofi?"

Chrissy and Pepper answer in unison, "Oh, yeah! Great guy!"

JP pushes back from the table a bit and thinks about this idea . . . A
charity concert to build Whole France's foundation.

Chrissy and Pepper are leaving very early in the morning to go to
Paris for a few days. She advises Veronique and JP not to be too late in
asking Archie, the cook, to serve dinner.

JP and Veronique head out on bikes to other villages in the district.
Veronique knows the geography very well, though they are hundreds
of kilometers away from her home. She takes a baguette in her backpack, and they stop at two different farms to purchase a morsel du
fromage and a premier cru wine from the second, very beautiful, farm
and winery. The sun seems to follow them on the small lanes and on to
the forested place she picks to eat. They both drink from the bottle, as
they forgot glasses, which seems very intimate to JP. They sit in a glade
with the bikes close by. JP hopes that he'll learn more about her, but she
buzzes about villages at risk and the people she knows who have lost
their homes and savings.

"For instance, in the village of Aubusson, you remember the his-
torically important tapestries? With modern central heating now-
adays, wall tapestries are not in demand. They're, as you Americans
say, *toast*. I've seen people's household goods sitting out on the curb
like garbage as the new Russian owners waste no time moving in. No
weaving industry there now, but great access to the river Creuse and a
life outdoors. Russian developers squeezed the vitality out of them in
less than a year. The bakery and butcher closed, and then the historical

houses fell fast. Oh, they're so cute: stone with tile roofs and red shutters. The Russians cannibalized one house. They bought the roof tiles, and then the whole street sold out for fear of being the last French household on the block. In a flash, the town could have changed its name to Moscow on the Creuse."

In her animation, she cleverly turns the conversation to JP and his coming of age in France, then life in New York.

"No," he replies to her question, "I've never been married. Commercial life in the States is all-consuming. I've made some time for art and music, but I don't know the rest of the country, and strangely, my best friend is Iris, my employee and store manager."

Veronique listens attentively. They eat the cheese and a box of tiny wild fraises that Chrissy tucked into her pack. And they drink. She doesn't offer a reciprocal explanation of her journey. She lets the silent pauses stretch. Finally, she asks, "Do you have any ideas for Whole France? How we could develop a financial foundation to execute this revolving credit?"

Damn! She is all business.

"I've been thinking about that since Pepper suggested a big concert. I have an idea."

***

Back at Hotel Bonnet, they retreat to their separate rooms. Each has phone calls to make and other work. JP rummages in his planner to find Rama's contact information. No luck. Damn! What is the name of her real estate company? He searches the internet and finally finds the number. After multiple calls, the receptionist says that she will have Rama call him.

She calls right back. "Hello, JP. I thought that you were in France."

"I am indeed. I've got an idea. I need your help. I have a proposition, a business opportunity for you. I can promise you a big fat commission to rent Ocean Manor to your friend, Carter, err, Prized Troofi, for the next year or longer if you can help me get him to do a benefit concert here in France for a preservation organization that I'm working with here."

"A what?"

"Didn't you say that he wants to rent a beautiful and up-to-date home on the water? Ocean Manor is fantastic! I've modernized and decorated it myself. Everything is top shelf, from the fastest Wi-Fi to the professional kitchen and lighting, to the beach access and barbecue area. It's Troofi's dream. His mom'll love it! It's going to be very expensive to rent, so you'll make a boatload of money. I'll give you this exclusive for a short time if you can help me secure one concert here."

"Well, I don't know. I'll have to take lots of—"

"Nope! That's not the answer I'm looking for! I'll arrange for you and Carter to tour it tomorrow or Friday and decide by Monday. After that, the offer will be withdrawn. Take it or not."

"But how much will it be to rent? And . . . I have several other clients who would love to—"

"Nope! This offer is only good with the concert assurance. And I'm not sure yet how much the rent will be. I'll have to get back to you on that. I can promise you that there isn't a more beautiful, perfect place in all Long Island. Mr. Troofi will adore you! I'll call right now to make the arrangements for you to get into the house. Otherwise, the offer's off. He's still in town, isn't he? Still at Lark's Lane?"

"Well, yes, but I'll—"

"Call me right back!"

JP waits for Rama's call. Veronique knocks on his door twice to call him for dinner; he was hoping to have some progress on the concert idea before they sat down. No luck.

The dining room is elegant, with flowers everywhere and glowing with candlelight. Two other sets of diners are finished and leaving the room. JP and Veronique's appetizer is on the table, and Veronique's cheeks are deeply flushed. She's clearly had several glasses of wine while she waited.

Rushing to sit, he blurts out bits of his thoughts. "I'm working on a plan . . . I mean, I don't have anything committed to, errr . . . Could you tell me a bit more about how I am to repay you and Whole France for your expert help?"

She leans back in her chair, open and smiling. He senses that perhaps the quid pro quo isn't foremost on her mind. She shifts her weight, leaning in and looking him in the eye. "I started this project twenty or so years ago when I was an undergraduate. It was a thesis project that my advisor endorsed. He suggested that I create a database of threatened properties and villages, and, well, once I had the database for almost every region of France, I needed to put the damned information to good use!"

They laugh and eat tiny pickled eggplants with watermelon slices, and they drink deeply. "I married that college thesis advisor, Caron. I'm his third wife. He is retired now, happily entrenched in remote Honfleur. We have two young children, whom Caron mostly cares for, along with nannies, while I am traveling across the countryside."

The chef brings out seafood stew with flavors of the sea and a hint of brandy and saffron—ambrosia!

"The shrimp in the States tastes like rubber," JP says. "These taste like the sea."

They eat, suddenly quiet. JP can feel her wanting to ask personal questions of him. He won't hide.

Vivi, as she likes to be called, has a catalog of questions ready. "Why did you move to the States?"

JP explains how he and Victor had to separate after the death of Frida, his mother, or at least that's what he believed at the time. Though he didn't understand back then that selling salvage was his calling, this trip has changed his mind. "Selling these beautiful French artifacts is like second sight to me. I have regular buyers who love these artifacts, a community of aficionados. Victor's selected the most iconic and classic pieces to send to me. Retail in the States is competitively cutthroat, and my long hours are difficult, or they were until Iris slowly accumulated most of the tiresome responsibilities of LBC. Victor is always one step ahead of the design-fickle US market. He sends amazing treasures that somehow become the focus of the decorating and lifestyle press. I can predict these voguish trends as our staff members are uncrating the containers that he sends."

He imagines Victor now, resting at home with Catty. JP's time in France has refocused his respect for Victor's dogged perseverance and hard work. He tries to recall the last time that he told Victor how well he's managed their inventory. He'll make a point of congratulating him on his impeccable selections when he returns to Luisant.

Finally, he and Vivi cannot eat another bite. They sit back in the comfortable chairs, absorbing the romantic atmosphere. They've finished the first carafe of wine and are almost done with the second when she puts her hand on his. "I won't hold your feet to the fire, but I'll be grateful if you help us bring Whole France to the next level, into a strong financial foundation, and to broadcast on both sides of the Atlantic how preservation is elemental to culture and, ultimately, to preserving local financial good health too."

JP had digested Vivi's thesis long ago. He's just filed it so deeply that the principles that guide his and Victor's work have gotten lost in the profits; they both have made lots of money. Is it a doomed and finite enterprise? He really needs to examine these questions with Victor. But right now, at this moment, he can't—won't—focus on business goals. He wants to love Vivi. No! That can't be! She is married, with kids, for God's sake. He watches her settle deeper in her chair as she finishes a glass of wine. Her square jawline hypnotizes him. She brushes her wild locks away from her eyes, only to have them fall back again. What is so appealing about her? Her determination, drive, and confidence that her work is for the greater good. Is that particularly

French? He's met many folks at home who radiate such well-being in themselves, but Veronique is different. Vivi's self-confidence, he notes, is a powerful aphrodisiac!

She puts her hand on his again as she makes a point about the value of her database. He feels a quiver radiate from his sternum to his sex at her touch.

Keeping his voice even, though his body is vibrating in excitement, he says, "So did you try to buy these homes yourself? I mean to protect 'em?" She prattles on about academic exercises turning the corner to fill real-life problems.

JP blurts out, "After my mom died, my dad expected that I would just continue following his vision for my life. Well, that didn't work out so well. I had to leave France."

Again, Vivi directs the conversation and asks about the business end of LBC. He explains their laissez-faire structure of a removed owner and a hands-on manager: "Because Iris manages the logistics drudgery, I'm free to be in France to help Victor or withdraw to the Hamptons to soothe my soul. The big-picture concept and long-term aesthetic have always been mine."

Vivi looks askance. "Mon Dieu!" she responds. "If you're not careful, you'll get your head handed to you. Concept is, of course, important, but you'll be robbed blind if you're not in on the logistics, no?"

He assures her that in the States, this arrangement is de rigueur.

***

She stands up, and he realizes that the evening is ending. How to continue the discussion without being clumsy or foolish? His mind is racing, trying to decide what to comment on, as she slips her arm through his and says, "It'll be an early morning. Shall we go to bed? Your room or mine?"

He looks at her with large eyes as she continues, "I knew from the minute I saw you fumbling with the lockbox back in Gravelines that we'd be lovers."

JP doesn't say a word, holding his breath and holding her close. In tandem, they ascend the stairs. She directs him to her room. Inside, she says, "We have to leave here all packed up in a few hours. Set your alarm too. We need to be on the road by five sharp."

Silently, he sets his alarm for 4:00 a.m. and places his phone on the counter. He moves to her and turns her to face him, putting his hands on her hips. He asks, "Really? Do you really want to do this with your family innocently waiting for you in Honfleur?"

"I am careful, but this is life. It's complicated, and be forewarned. You can't fall for me. Of course, if you don't, I'll hound you till you do. I want you to want me, but don't dare truly desire me. I'll pull you into my life and push you out the minute I sense unchecked passion. Possession is not allowed under any circumstances! There's no winning me."

"Excuse me?"

She pulls her T-shirt up over her head, revealing a delicate lace bra and goose bumps, as she answers, "I am committed to my family, ardently committed, but Caron and I have an understanding. I am traveling, and what I do while away is my business. He does not fuss about it, and I don't either. That makes engaging with me either extraordinarily simple or overbearingly complex. Take your pick."

JP laughs. "How very French of you both."

She stands in front of him in her lace bra and slim jeans. Her skin glows and flushes with drink and excitement. She unbuttons his shirt and pulls his bare chest close to hers. He reaches around to unclasp her bra and bends down to lick her cherrylike nipples. Her skin has a magnetic force, pulling his fingers to explore her every texture. Her audible breath urges him on. He unzips her fly and helps her out of her jeans and underwear.

Kneeling, he touches her pubic hair, then looks up and asks, "May I?"

She laughs and pulls his head into her. The soft fur-line of hair between her belly button and pubic bone stands up, electrically turned on. Gently opening her labia, he touches his tongue to her clit. Hard, hot, and wet, she welcomes him to advance again.

She lifts him up and gently touches his cock, advising, "Slow down. We have until four, and you've not yet kissed me."

He pulls her close. They are the same height. She tucks his penis between her legs as she kisses him and then holds his cheeks.

She pulls him toward the bed, and they lie face to face, kissing. Exactly how long, JP can't measure. He lays his arm over her small waist and then runs his hands roughly through her wild hair. Every part of her is pristinely soft, save her hands. He's watched her carefully work with deerskin gloves, but she and her crew are literally hands-on.

She laughs. "Have you wanted to do that all night?"

A rhetorical question that calms him. He kisses her breasts again, and she lies back, smiling. Her small figure has been disguised by her badass jacket and persona. He touches her clit again, and she shudders. Slowly, she pulls him onto her, guiding his cock inside her.

She looks deeply into his eyes, and a mellow "Ahhh" and a small chuckle emanate from deep in her stomach. He doesn't move, exhilarating in their anticipation and now triumphant fit. Slowly, he rocks her. She lifts her head to kiss him, pulling him down to kiss her more. Their movements are not large or exaggerated, rather, slow and tender. She smiles brightly as his gaze locks onto hers; she is right with him—fully receptive. Slowly, he is building. He recites the ABCs, distracting himself, but her face and thrilling body turn him past the point of no return. It hasn't been so long since he fucked Rama, but this feels so new, so complete. Like every nerve in his body is applauding. She pushes him back and then on top of her to cum, hot and large, and all of his tension seems to empty onto her belly.

She pulls him back onto her, sandwiching his cum between them. Again, he touches her labia, her clit. She smells both clean and animal. *How is that possible?* he wonders.

He licks the inside of her ankles, her calves, her thighs as she laughs. "Don't you tease me!"

He nibbles her pubic hair, the hollows of her waist, her nipples. She feels so French. *What the hell does that mean?* he asks himself. French or not, he is going to give her a slow and agonizingly great orgasm. He reaches around the inside of her thighs, squeezing her muscles tightly. Her strong, articulate hands are in his hair, and he massages his fingers deeply into her and teasingly out. Then his tongue, delicately awakening her every hot spot. Is she singing? Some harmony emanates from her, and he pushes her farther into the bed, spreads her legs, and kisses and pets her until her song stops. She stops moving altogether and then pulls his hair deep at its roots, pushing her hips and pelvis up into his face.

***

They have been asleep for what seems like ten minutes, he at the bottom of the bed and she on her side, when the alarm rings.

Separately, they drive the quiet autoroute. JP doesn't check his GPS; he just stays close to Veronique. He pulls alongside her as the sun rises, shining a deeply hued brilliance on their windshields. A feeling of a new day fills him with excitement. Dozens of new life scenarios float through his wandering mind. Should he stay here in France? Will she come to New York regularly? What exactly is her agreement with her husband? *Husband . . . Don't forget the husband!* he reminds himself.

She signals to pull off at the truck stop ahead. She brushes his lips with hers as she heads inside to get them coffees as he fuels the trucks. He doesn't want this to end tonight, just when it feels so right.

He pulls out his phone and texts Rama: "What's the status of the house rental? I need to know. After today, I will withdraw the offer." He thinks about actually sending it now, the middle of the night in New York. *What the hell?* He pushes "Send."

Rama writes back immediately: "I don't like your terms. I don't like your approach. If I decide to tell Troofi about your offer and he accepts, I'll let you know when I'm ready."

JP writes back: "Whatever's best for you. If you're too busy, I'll find another real estate agent willing to bring my offer to him. I was trying to do you a favor."

Veronique returns with two tall, steaming cups of coffee. JP takes them out of her hands and puts them on the roof. He gently pushes her back against the truck cab and leans into her, kissing her deeply and then running kisses down her neck and clavicle. Her wild hair spreads back against the truck. She looks into his eyes and smiles broadly. They get into their respective trucks and back on the road. Already, he misses her. The green of pastoral France seems more vibrant than he remembered. The cows appear shaggier, and the local radio music sappier, yet more authentic and heartfelt than he's remembered. He loves la belle France.

At last, they exit the autoroute and approach Guînes village. Like many French villages, right at the entrance gate of the town, a commemorative bronze plaque with the names of the men killed in both world wars greets them. These are the grandfathers and great-grandfathers of the people who live here now. But as they drive deeper into town, he realizes that very few people actually do live here. It isn't as dirty or looted as the other dying villages where they were earlier, but the haphazard roofs and ghostly commercial strip signal that the exodus happened awhile back. He follows Veronique to the mairie, majestic and solid, built of limestone, with a slate roof and an iconic French oval window in the center of the doors and other windows. He loves these classic buildings, just as Victor does.

Vivi's team is already unloading, their tools in large canvas and leather bags lined up as if in a military parade next to their pickup trucks. All four of the men hold large coffee cups and brandish eager smiles. They greet Vivi energetically. Again, she must have the lockbox code memorized because she goes right to the front door and opens it. The tall, vaulted ceiling and terrazzo floor ring with the echo of a once-rich municipal authority.

Vivi circles back to link arms with JP. "Wait till you see your ceiling; you'll wet your pants. Your dad buys the best of the best!"

They climb the flying staircase that curves to the second floor, arriving at the now-silent hallways that, for the past two hundred years, overheard the city's business.

Veronique looks up and smiles, asking rhetorically, "Isn't that a sight?" JP turns to gaze at the huge glowing ceiling.

Her team follows up the steep stairs with ladders, tool bags, and scaffolding frames.

The coffered ceiling, a perfect square room, is made up of symmetrical gold-leafed lotus flowers that extend just below the square enclosure, separating it from its neighbor. The room is huge, maybe thirty feet square. JP wonders how it will fit into the transport vehicles to get to Le Havre.

He pulls out a measuring tape and skitters around, saying out loud, "Thirty feet by thirty feet. It's a perfect square."

All heads turn toward him, and Vivi asks, "Feet? When did you go imperial?"

JP smirks. "I work in America and sell big artifacts to American houses."

The team sets up scaffolding and assembles a system to loosen each strip of ten flowers, which in turn will release the contiguous rows. Furniture blankets are open to receive the gold plaster treasures. The team, JP, and Vivi work till late in the afternoon, coaxing, prying, and protecting hundreds of the plaster and gold treasures. At three thirty,

Vivi assesses that a second day and an additional truck will be necessary for the work to be complete. A sigh of relief loosens JP's shoulders. *One more night with her,* he thinks.

He checks his phone for the first time all day. Whoops, he'd given a strict ultimatum to Rama, and yup, there are six texts and two voice mails from her. He reads her last texts first. "Yes, Troofi has heard about Ocean Manor, and he's interested in possibly renting it. What kind of organization wants a concert? Could the concert be next year, as his schedule is very busy?"

***

Veronique and JP decide to stay at the truck stop ten kilometers away. They will start work again early the next morning. After the mairie is carefully locked and her team leaves for the night, Vivi says, "Eh, give me some time on the phone. Let's meet back here in an hour."

JP makes his calls. First, a short and unsatisfying call with a distracted Victor. JP can't quite understand if Catty is in the hospital or going, but Victor has no time or interest in speaking to JP just now.

Next, he calls Iris to check that LBC is humming along as expected. Her quick, upbeat response assures him that he doesn't have to worry. She comments in passing that the bank has called with fraud alerts, but she'll address these minor annoyances. Another quick check with Franny, and he gets a similar report. "Yes, the very handsome rapper, Prized Troofi, visited," she said. "Together with his real estate agent, they poked around the house. A bit too familiar for my taste. Poking in closets and cabinets. But anyway. They sounded very excited. You received a few small deliveries, thank-you flowers from the Millerworks, and the property tax bill arrived at the house rather than being sent to the bank, but I'll get to the bottom of that."

He hardly focuses as he hangs up with her. He is dreaming about fucking Vivi and how he wants to make her happy. Memories of her smell and the feel of her rise in his thoughts. This is here, now. Vivi is here and now. All the details of Franny and taxes and bank frictions seem frivolous in light of the immediacy of Vivi.

Finally, he texts Rama. Her cool responses: "Troofi and I did tour Ocean Manor. How much is the rent and for how long will the contract last? Troofi is keen on Whole France, but the date to perform will be difficult to agree upon." JP writes back: "The entire offer is contingent on a mutually agreeable concert date before the Christmas season of next year. Propose realistic potential dates as soon as possible!"

JP sits on the truck's flatbed, waiting for Veronique. He googles stadiums near Paris, near Chartres, near Marseilles. It has been years since he's gone to stadium concerts. They all look awful to him. How much is the net from a mostly sold-out performance? France is notoriously unionized, so all the labor for said shows is paid at big, set union scales. How much money will put Whole France on solid footing to run a revolving loan fund? No doubt Vivi has thought these questions through. He doesn't want to say no to anything that she proposes. He wants to be in her orbit, to be near her, to learn from her, to please her. *Wow! This is a bit overboard,* he thinks to himself. *She's married—don't forget that—she's married! If you play the side squeeze, you'll always be second. Can you deal with that, man?* He tries to bring himself back to be in the moment.

She finally returns to the trucks, looking deep in thought, not the bright-smiling nymph that adored him earlier that morning.

"Everything as it should be?" he asks.

She responds with a half-hearted harrumph in the affirmative that isn't very convincing.

"Vivi, I can finish up with the team if you need to go home now," he offers.

She purses her lips and hesitates for a minute, then snaps herself out of her funk. "Nope! I'll finish this with you. It's a long drive to

Honfleur. I need to start that journey in the early morning. Not tomorrow. I'll finish your project before I go home."

In his head, JP thanks Cupid, or whoever is in charge of love and romance.

The truck stop is much nicer than American truckers' rendezvous sites. The rooms aren't glamorous, but they are clean, and the Wi-Fi is free. The bathroom is small and lit by irritating blue LED lights, but it has a bathtub, shallow and narrow, but indeed a bathtub. JP has an agenda. They tour local villages, assessing work that Whole France has done in some nearby towns and what is missing in other areas. The tiny truckers' dinner buffet is surprisingly tasty and inexpensive. The local wine by the carafe is delicious. France has many blessings to share.

Back in their room, JP draws a bath.

"Yikes! I haven't taken a bath in eons," she says demurely.

"Let's break that spell."

He describes the deep cast-iron tub he has installed in the master bath of Ocean Manor and the Zen joy he has when looking out on the ocean while relaxing in hot bathwater. This shallow tub is scratched and chipped turquoise porcelain that doesn't really accommodate two grown adults, but JP choreographs Vivi across his chest, and they rest after the day's strenuous work while drinking more of the local vintage from in-room coffee mugs. JP is relaxed and thrilled at the same time. This contentment is buoyed by occasional moments of bracing pleasure. His mind races with reminders that this moment is only a moment. *Enjoy this moment.* They are quietly sated in each other's presence.

That night, and the work the following day, flashes by in, what seems to JP, an instant. Crates and trailers and multiple measurements and geometry somehow align. Each element of the ceiling fits into the trucks destined for Le Havre and then on to LBC in New York.

Rama texts him every hour, it seems. Prized Troofi loves the house, but arranging a date for a concert in France will be almost impossible.

The negotiations stall with the producer/promoter, not with Troofi. No venue seems right, no profit big enough to split advantageously so that Whole France can create a financial foundation. JP knows that his amateurish approach to contract negotiation and concert promotion will likely backfire, but he wants to give Vivi a monumental gift to elevate Whole France before she leaves for home. He wants to mark her forever with his generosity.

JP can hardly get a hammer in his hand when the next texts arrive. His pocket doesn't stop buzzing. Vivi finally suggests that he go out into the square to finish his business.

An hour later, she comes out and asks, "What's up? What's caught your attention?"

JP explains his plans and the excruciating logistical details.

She bursts into a celebratory smile and a little dance. "Wow! That's an amazing idea! That's just fantastic! That's just what we need!"

JP rolls his eyes. "It's not a done deal yet. It's far from done. Not even good odds. You and your team have made this trip across France, this asset collection, this chore for Victor so possible, and you've done it so professionally. I want to hold up my part of the bargain. I'm not sure that I can pull this off, but if not this, we'll figure out a worthy spectacle to make Whole France, well, whole."

Veronique stands back and curtsies deeply. Then she pulls JP in close and kisses him passionately. "You understand this project. You see how important it is, don't you? I love you for that!"

JP nods in sincere agreement. He's found her! She is what he's been searching for all this time. They kiss again, and JP feels like this might be their last embrace. He doesn't want to let go. But of course, she isn't leaving till the next morning. He wants to remember her face exactly, every line and curve, texture, and color. He is suddenly keenly focused so that this memory will not dwindle or fade. Her sweet breath mixes with the faint smell of her leather jacket as he inhales. Will he be able to conjure this smell in his mind tomorrow or next week? Not a chance.

She pulls away and says, "OK. You keep workin' your magic. I'll be inside deconstructing so that we really do finish this afternoon."

JP hesitates for a minute before calling Rama again. Where will he live? Should he ask Rama to find him somewhere suitable? Somehow that seems like an awful choice. Maybe he'll stay in France to be close to Vivi?

Rama texts again, this time with a firm proposal. Can they swing Roland Garros on Valentine's Day next year, and can Troofi sign to rent the house for two years, beginning ASAP? The tension of this unfinished project lifts from his shoulders. He can make this work!

JP sits quietly in his truck as Vivi locks the mairie again. The crew has left, promising to meet him at the Port of Le Havre at seven thirty the next morning. Back at the truck stop, neither he nor Vivi is very hungry; they push their food around their plates before returning to their room. JP isn't straining to make conversation. Their silence is a sanctuary of calm and purposeful romance. They have tender, slow sex and fall asleep in each other's arms.

JP can feel her pragmatic mind already switching gears as they pack up the following morning. Veronique brings coffees out to the dark parking lot.

"We have a million logistical details to work out, not to mention more work for you to do for Whole France. This is not goodbye. Rather, I'll call you next week to confirm the details. My team will be at the Port of Le Havre right on time; please don't keep them waiting."

With that, she swings herself up into the cab of her truck and drives away. JP stands alone in a vacuum of exhilaration and profound sadness. His life has just begun, or was this just a short, passionate detour? There is no denying his happiness. Maybe he is in love. He knows there'd be hell to pay. After all, she is married. But his heart has grown ten sizes in the last two days. He is absolutely in love.

As he drives, he plays back their lovemaking in the movie of his mind. The hours and kilometers fly by, and then he is at the turnoff for the giant port. He drives to the administrative offices, and just as she promised, her crew is waiting for him. They greet him warmly as he goes inside the narrow office between the gigantic hoists loading the even more gigantic cargo ships.

The last step before he returns to Victor's side is to set in motion this administrative work. Then they'll unload the trucks and pack the shipping containers. JP knows exactly what is to be loaded; it's slow work but not complicated. Still, he's a bit on edge. He finds his old friend Guy Steppens and explains that Victor can't be here to drop these artifacts and that he, JP, is on his way back to Victor as soon as the paperwork is finalized. Redheaded and barrel-chested, Guy is jovial and eager to help. He pulls Les Beaux Châteaux's computer file up on the screen. It reads across the top "Fonds Insuffisants NSF."

Guy looks at JP and checks back deeper into the file. Again, he looks at JP, puzzled. "It says that your account is fonds insuffisans. That the last two payments bounced back. What do you know about this?"

JP shakes himself out of his love-drunk bliss. "What? What are you talking about? We've been shipping containers through your line for years. We've never bounced a check in all this time that I'm aware of. There must be some explanation. Iris won't be in the office for another two hours. Errr, I guess I'll wait. I hope it'll be OK that these guys unload, and I'll wait here till I can get Iris and the bank on the phone."

Steppens agrees to the unusual unloading. Nothing is yet crated. There, JP's work sits splayed out, unprotected, just lying out between the crating stations, hoists, and cargo ships. Steppens returns to his office. JP tries to sleep in the flatbed, but with the clanking noise of gigantic machinery, from hoists to forklifts and nail guns, sleep is out of the question.

He doesn't want to call Victor and try to explain the NSF status when he doesn't know the details of it. Instead, he googles Veronique and her husband, Caron, and Honfleur. There are pictures of her graduating with Caron by her side. They obviously were a thing while she was an undergrad. Pictures of them at glamorous Whole France charity events, he in a tuxedo and she in very revealing evening clothes. Announcements of their children's births and a retirement ceremony for Caron from Sorbonne. He looks very old to JP. Caron is now an advisor to the small historical society in Honfleur and teaches continuing education classes in creative writing. JP sees lots of announcements about the creation of Whole France, with calls for construction workers interested in particular training in preservation. The organization even generates its own news regarding threatened villages and the dread of towns totally overtaken by Russian expats, and its Facebook page explains in blunt language the worrisome wave of unchecked Russian suffocation of French village life. JP notes with horror the Russian developers mugging for Facebook posts about wrecking crews and new Russian colonies to be built.

All this time to kill, and JP doesn't investigate the bank's alerts about fraud and the mysterious NSF of payments to Atlantic Shipping Lines. He's confident that these technical snafus will straighten out in a matter of minutes once he speaks to Iris and the bank. He doesn't think twice about any insult to his business or himself. He'll just dream of Vivi and wait till he can reach Iris at the store.

Finally, he calls the business phone at LBC. Strangely, the answering machine kicks in. He checks his watch; it is 8:00 a.m. in New York, and she's likely been at her desk for an hour. He dials her cell next.

"Yeah!" she answers.

"Oh, hey, Iris, have I caught you at a bad time?"

It takes several seconds for her to answer. "No. Right. Sorry, JP. What's up?"

He explains the situation and the NSF status at Atlantic. Surprisingly, she sounds nonchalant, detached, explaining that she hasn't had a chance yet to sort out those problems. Not alarmed but impatient, JP implores that she rectify these difficulties with the bank directly. He senses a reluctance when she agrees to call the bank. "Yeah, right. Sure, I can, ahhh, oh, OK. The bank. OK, I'll call." That's strange. She's not as direct and businesslike as JP expects, but he doesn't want to focus on her compliance or Atlantic Shipping. He's dreaming of Veronique.

JP continues to sit. Waiting. He calls Victor, who answers on the first ring. He is crying. "Dad, what's the matter? My God, what's going on?"

Victor explains that Catty has been in shock and has sepsis, a condition that makes her recovery tenuous at best. She is in the intensive care unit and he can't talk much, but he probably won't be home when JP returns because he is at the Chartres City Hospital. Victor hangs up without saying goodbye.

Steppens comes out to talk to JP. "Sorry, friend, I know that we've done business together for so many years, but my bank is still questioning your bank. We need certified wire transfers." JP knows that there has to be some bureaucratic bungling, a mistake at the bank. Why hasn't Iris rectified this yet?

A bit on edge, he calls her again. With an ambivalent tone, she agrees to call the bank again.

"Really, Iris," he says, "I've got to get back to Victor. He's in a terrible situation. I shouldn't be sitting here at the docks, and these goods need to get crated and loaded before they're damaged. None of that can happen until the bank certifies our credit. Why is this in question?"

With an intolerant, lackadaisical tone that he's never heard from her, she says, "Right! I'll get to the bottom of the confusion as soon as I have a minute."

Demanding that this snafu should be her first priority feels mean and redundant. She's now aware that he needs this fixed directly. Checking his impatience, he waits and waits into the late afternoon, wasting time sunbathing and googling Lark's Lane, Prized Troofi's tour schedule, and the photos from the Millerworks soiree. He'll buy

Lark's Lane and fix it to the height of beauty and tech-savvy readiness to match Ocean Manor. A good project for when he gets home. Vivi will surely come to visit.

Steppens comes out of his office as the sun drops and the temperature cools. "OK. It's finally done. We'll crate and ship these containers. I'm estimating that there are two full boxes, but if there's more, I'll go ahead and make the charges. I'm not sure what's up with your office staff, but it's not the same as it was even a few weeks ago. If I were you, I'd check into that!"

JP's mind is already on what is up with Victor and Catty. He hears Steppens but, jingling his keys, doesn't listen carefully. He's gotta get on the road! He has hours of driving ahead. He signs the bills of lading and is back in the truck's cab before the documents are scanned and filed.

He texts Iris: "Is everything OK with the bank screwup? Call me if you need my help. Just call me so that I know that everything is all secure." He keeps his phone at the ready to see her return message. None comes.

He maps the GPS guidance, tunes into the local music station, and heads to Victor. His mind bounces right back to his and Vivi's love-making, enjoying all that he remembers. Her direct feedback. Her generous way and eager hunger for him. Her soft kisses that could make him weep. He wants to know all her kisses: her greeting kiss, her affirmation kiss, her miss-you kiss, her good-night kiss. He misses her kiss already. He is happy to indulge himself in these "movies."

Victor's crying also plays into his thoughts. He can't remember ever seeing or hearing Victor cry. Not ever before. Catty is clearly very important to him. That, or his very nature has changed. Is the old, gruff, and cold Victor gone for good? Would his mother have liked the more tender Victor?

Another buzz on his phone. The call goes directly to voice mail. The cellular signal must be weak. Again, a banking alert from JPMorgan

Chase. He'll call Iris back when he gets to Victor's to fix these aggravating problems.

Rama forwards an email contract for a Valentine's Day concert with great projections for big profits. He can't see many details, as driving makes reading contract details in an email all but impossible—and dangerous. He thinks more about how he'll set up a special bank account at Victor's Chartres bank to be able to deposit money for Whole France with as few money-laundering restrictions as possible.

Visions of how he and Vivi will stay connected dance in his head. She in New York and he visiting in Paris. He can make this arrangement work if she'll be open-minded about what is possible.

It is after 10:00 p.m. as he pulls into Victor's driveway. He can't tell if Victor is home because he has Victor's truck. The front door is locked. He finds the hidden key, letting himself into the empty house. Victor must be at the hospital, as he had forecast. JP finally has a chance to look around the house. Hardly a sign of Catty's mark here. Victor has a point of view, a specific taste and organizational regimen that doesn't allow for much variation. The place looks almost the same as their old apartment in Paris, except that this house is on the ground floor. The art, rugs, and furniture are placed almost exactly as they were all those years ago.

He snoops in their bedroom. Catty's closet is full to overstuffed with brightly colored clothes and dozens of high-heeled shoes. Her makeup table is crammed with jars and bottles, brushes, and sponges, but it is carefully wedged into a small corner of the bathroom. Bandages and medications line Victor's side of the counter in descending size.

JP goes into the kitchen to make himself an espresso; he drinks it down quickly, washes his face in the kitchen sink, grabs the truck keys, and heads out to find the hospital.

Waiting in the empty corridor after asking a nurse to find Victor, JP is suddenly worried for his dad. Victor creeps toward him, looking like an old man, haggard by time and illness, one with the full awareness of the brevity of life. He hardly looks like the man JP left only a few days before. His bandaged side makes his balance uncertain, and his multiday beard and rheumy eyes give him an unkempt appearance. JP doesn't know if he should hug Victor or not. He stands uncomfortably at a formal distance.

"I'm here now, Victor . . . Dad, let me help you. Should we sit together? Are you hungry? How's she doing?"

Victor turns away from JP; his eyes close. He is holding his breath and holding back tears.

JP pats his hand and says, "It's OK, Dad. It's OK."

To which Victor shoots back, "Oh no, it's not! Elle est en train de mourir. She's dying. She's dying, and there's not a damn thing that I or anyone can do to le répare! I should have taken her to the proper clinic as soon as she was hurt. But I let her terrible immigration and xeno-phobic fears convince me that she'd get good enough treatment from fucking Ramos and Oleg. Ha! Those fuckers. Anya's up there now, but I have to be with her when she dies. She has to know how much I love her."

JP sits on the plastic couch in the blue light of the waiting room, nauseous. He can't remember if Victor was with Frida when she died. JP can't remember exactly what happened or what he was doing on the day his mother died. The funeral and out-of-town family and mourners play in his memory, but he isn't sure if she died alone. Should he go up to Catty's room and comfort Victor? Would that make up for their estrangement after Frida died? No, he thinks, this isn't about selfish reparations. Victor's grief needs to be allowed to fully express itself. *When Victor needs me, I'll be available.*

He returns to Victor's house to sleep. Some hours later, Victor stumbles in, puffy, red, ragged, and exhausted. "Elle est partie!" he bellows.

JP sits beside him, listening. Anya walks in the door at the same time as she rings the bell. Victor looks up and sneers. She begins talking a mile a minute in a high-pitched voice that JP finds to be like nails on a chalkboard. "And Veeector, you must contact our rabbi, Mortgenthau. Of course, heee's in Paris . . . Well, maybe we should hhhave a funeral in Paris? I don't like the synagogue here. Well, we'll have to see what Oleg say. Heee'll want to . . ."

Victor stands up, using JP for balance. "Get out! Get out with your Russian ways! I said, *get out*! And stay away, you and that son of a bitch Oleg. You killed her. You cheating scum, get out of my world! Get out!"

Anya quickly grabs her handbag and turns to Victor. "It eees a fearful ting to love what death can touch." Then she scurries out the front door.

The room is silent. JP sharpens his focus with the impact of Anya's words. Victor begins sobbing deep, breathless sobs. JP tries to calm him, sitting with him quietly. Eventually, JP digs out some sleeping pills from his own Dopp kit and gets Victor to lie down.

As Victor sleeps, JP reads through the auction catalogs that Victor has marked so diligently with sale prices and comparables that he has purchased out in the field, for a fraction of the auction prices. JP thinks about Victor's care and specificity in their business—a man who appreciates value and rarity at the same time. LBC sells the best of the best because of Victor's selective taste and connections with resellers across France. And like Vivi said, not ruining entire villages but surgically purchasing uniquely exceptional artifacts. Can they go on? *Should* they go on, knowing what JP now knows about the mission of Whole France?

JP is deep in thought when there is a knock on the front door, and then whoever is there pushes open the unlocked door. JP thinks about how he always keeps his doors locked in New York. A bald Slav in a garishly bright-blue suit walks in and is surprised to see JP rather than Victor. "Oh, I just heeerd de news from Anya. Where eees Victor? I must give him my sympathy."

JP stands up and folds his arms, signaling distrust. He asks with his deeply commanding voice, "May I help you?"

Oleg advances, offering his hand to shake. JP keeps his hands folded. Oleg continues, "Oh, you must be de son. Yes. You must be JP! How good dat you are hhhere. I am Oleg, Victor's partner. I . . ."

JP whispers in a frighteningly low decibel, "Partner? I don't think so! I am Victor's partner. You have business with Victor? In a week or two, maybe he'll see you. He's in mourning now, and you will not disturb him. Not under any circumstances. The funeral services will be noted in the newspaper, should you wish to attend." Then raising his volume to a stern command, he says, "Goodbye, sir!"

Oleg stands still, puzzled as to what to do next. JP doesn't let more than five seconds pass. He opens his pipes and thrashes Oleg with, "I said goodbye!"

***

Over the next few days, JP helps Victor grieve and find some strength. They sit together in the garden, drinking coffee and telling nostalgic stories of their old life in Paris with Frida. JP texts Iris a bit about Catty's death and tells her that he will stay with Victor for several days and get back to her as soon as he is able. Again, she doesn't respond. This is strangely worrying, but he makes himself disregard any distractions. He emails Vivi similarly.

The funeral service at Chartres Central Synagogue is brief. The priest from Chartres Cathedral, Jennie from the café, Frankle from the lumberyard, and other friends of Victor's attend. Several of Catty's girl gang of Russian Mafia come to pay their respects. Victor will not recognize these people, looking through them as if they aren't in front of him. The rabbi is sensitive and generous in his sermon, addressing the Russian diaspora that seeks safety, security, and fulfillment away from Russia. JP enjoys sitting in the synagogue, adorned similarly to the stately cathedral, with the blue light from the stained-glass windows streaming in on him and Victor, binding them together. After Victor refuses to acknowledge their presence, the Russians keep to themselves, staying across the room.

JP cooks and cleans and helps Victor get out of his bandages and into a physical therapy program. Victor's strength is slow to return, but JP is patient and calm. Anxious productivity of a few weeks ago is far from their daily routine. JP's confident that all else in his life can wait. He hardly explores Luisant or Chartres, beyond the boulangeries and farmers markets. He's contentedly at home with Victor, cooking and tending his garden. Occasionally, he worries that Iris's silence suggests her possible anger at his absence. But he returns to confidence in her steady management. She knows how much he relies on her. He's focused; this is the first time that he can remember Victor really needing him. And it is their first extended time together since Frida died. They read the newspapers and catalogs together, sitting in the sunshine, planning for their steady business growth.

On the afternoon after the funeral, Vivi texts JP that the concert contracts are all signed. He waits to hear from Franny about moving his personal items out of Ocean Manor for Troofi to move in. He texts her and Iris several times, with no response. This radio silence is alarming. He writes to Iris: "What's going on at LBC? Where's Franny, and has she moved my stuff out of Ocean Manor to the store?" She responds quickly, assuring him not to worry. It's busy at the store, and she and Franny have all the details under control.

***

Together, JP and Victor decide that JP should return to New York soon, but JP wants Victor to understand and possibly embrace Vivi and the mission of Whole France. He invites her to come to Chartres to meet Victor's bankers so that Whole France can establish a working relationship with them and, most importantly, to meet Victor and explain the Whole France mission in her words.

As agreed, he picks her up at the small regional airport. She greets him with a handshake, and he feels the freeze between them. His neck and back flush hot and red. Their banter is all business, reviewing the concert details and profit forecasts. They drive directly to the Chartres bank. Victor's friend Antoinette, whom JP met briefly at the funeral, greets them. They have coffee in her office, where Vivi explains the revolving loan fund that Whole France intends to initiate. Vivi tells Antoinette about the sophisticated qualities of her database; it documents specific addresses, including any unique attributes an address may have; the year the building was built, if that is known; the condition and status of the environs around it; and the holder of the title, if it is known. It names nearby real estate agents, banks, and developers that might be supportive or destructive. Antoinette, JP, and Vivi imagine the success of the Prized Troofi concert. "My grandkids played his music for me," Antoinette gushes. She talks about Victor. "Your dad has been a very good client over the years. I'm excited to help support Whole France. Your mission is admirable! I love our old villages."

The bank will file the paperwork with the appropriate authorities. Once Victor signs the appropriate documents, Whole France can parallel an account of Victor's. JP insists on these agreements because the international money-laundering restrictions are complicated and redundant. "I know that Victor will stay up to date with Whole France's work and necessary financial filings. Of course, all this is predicated on the bedrock that the concert will be a huge success." They all smile with pride at their contribution to this worthy cause. Vivi quietly applauds JP.

He and Vivi kiss coolly and briefly in the bank parking lot and drive on to Victor's house, where JP has organized lunch. He's bought baguettes from the three local bakeries—Chartres is a big enough town to merit three—local cheeses, smoked fish, local berries, and wines.

Victor is slow to warm to Vivi's plan. He resists, saying the obvious, that Whole France will put them out of business. But as she begins explaining the nefarious work of big Russian money and their conspiratorial methods to ruin villages and install their own patriots to dominate them, he nods his head in knowing agreement.

"I've also been a victim of their ugly work. I know Oleg, one of many Russian mob bosses here. I know what they do. But your Whole France, you'll put my boy and me out of business. We can't abide by your mission. And the Russians . . . they'll eat your lunch! Errr, I mean, I like you, and so does my son, clearly, but we do salvage. We break apart buildings, rooms, taverns, bakeries, and village squares and sell them to Brits and Yanks. How can we endorse, no, support your plan?"

He leans back into the couch, breathing hard. This threat to his and JP's livelihood seems to exhaust him. JP wants to soften the explanation, but he will let Vivi lay it out.

Victor and JP nod in agreement as she explains their methods and principles, but Victor sees their respective business models as being at cross-purposes. JP explains how Vivi's workers are well trained in collecting and preserving artifacts. Maybe there can be a way for them to work together so that Victor can be the selective aesthete, and Vivi's crews can be the highly skilled muscle that he needs? Vivi smiles, not disagreeing.

"I'm sure that Veronique will agree that not every farmhouse sink here in France needs to be preserved."

Victor and Vivi say in unison, "I'm not sure how that'll work out."

JP is relieved to see Victor warming to Vivi and debating the ideals of Whole France, if not fully buying into the mission.

Later, JP drives her back to the airport. He kisses her passionately. "I want to love you passionately and persistently. I—"

She stops him, putting her hand on his cheek. "JP, I can't do that with you anymore. I'm married. I loved our fling. I think of you often, but we're going to be about business going forward. I warned you that

I'm complicated. I'm sorry, but if I'm going to make this plane, I've got to run. We can talk tomorrow."

With that, she quickly gets out of the truck and runs into the airport. JP feels an icy spear slice through his heart. He sits in the parking lot, feeling pitiful, crying for a spell. Unrequited love, the theme of music, poetry, and heartache whined about for millennia, feels so personal today. He can't just put out the fire that burns so deeply for her. Why can't she feel the same as he does? Why is she so damn practical? He wants her. He misses her. Can't she feel what he feels for her? *Merde!* Alone in his grief or not, his time with Victor is fast ending. He needs to get back to the house in Luisant.

Their last dinner is surprisingly upbeat and happy. They drink heartily. Victor uncorks a second bottle of his favorite burgundy as he talks about Veronique's database. With an arched brow, he says, "It's a powerful weapon against those Russian dogs." They agree that Victor'll contact her to add his valuable details to populate the database. JP hopes that he and Victor will have a future working together with Whole France. He desperately wants to stay connected to her.

After dinner, JP is a bit unsettled as his texts to both Iris and Franny bounce back as undeliverable. He figures it must have something to do with the cellular system in France's hinterlands. He isn't thinking about returning to New York; instead, he focuses on changing Vivi's mind. He loves her. They'll be working together for a long time to come. He'll figure out a way to make her fall in love with him. He'll bring her to New York. There won't be French distractions there, and he can be his American self. He fantasizes that she'll love that. Thoughts and images of Vivi hardly leave his mind's eye.

Victor recognizes JP's distracted attitude. With the second bottle almost finished, he blurts out, "She's not for you! You've been away from your store for a long time. The best thing that you can do for Whole France is to keep Les Beaux Châteaux strong. Change channels; let's think about business!"

JP recognizes Victor's wisdom. "Right. I didn't know how much I needed to spend time here with you and to be here, in France. I'm so deeply sorry about Catty, but I am grateful that we got to be together."

JP can't stop from dreaming up ideas that he can continue to support Whole France. He'll be very enthusiastic and helpful—no doubt! But he is also excited at the prospect of finding and restoring a new home near New York City. He wants to transplant elements of France's true beauty to a new project in New York. Installing this Gallic panache into an American landscape is, he has now concluded, his specialty, his raison d'être. He didn't expect to stay so long or to be so proud of what's happened here, but he's fully marinated now in all things French.

Victor is planning a visit in two months to coincide with the US Open tennis matches. JP will have to ask Iris the name of that ticket broker who buys stained glass. He'll trade for great tickets to the tennis matches. They leave for Charles de Gaulle Airport in the cool of the morning. The dew is thick on the big truck's windshield. Victor is back to driving now, and JP is ready to get home. Their goodbye is heartfelt and joyous; they'll be together again in a few months for Victor's visit.

Chapter Six

The immigration line is slow and crowded but very quiet. Again, no upgrade for his seat. Surprisingly, when he gets to the desk to make his seat request, the agent needs to run his credit card again, as the ticket that Iris purchased apparently hasn't gone through properly. And to add to all that confusion, two of his three credit cards are turned down. He didn't charge very much on this trip. None of that is right, but he did forget to call the banks to alert them of his French travel before he left, and they have now put fraud alerts on his cards. He'll get it straight when he gets back to the office at LBC.

Back at Kennedy, the louder decibels and faster everything jar him. He pulls up Uber on his phone, and the app continually denies his request. Frustrated, he hails a taxi and heads to LBC. Traveling in the afternoon from France to New York is strange, as you arrive at nearly the same time that you left. Anyway, LBC will be open at this time of the afternoon. He sits back and indulges in the skyline and the bridge views. New York is truly a majestic wonder. New York will help him seduce Vivi.

The cab pulls up to LBC. The doors are closed, and there are no lights beckoning him or any other shoppers inside. He pays the driver and slings his bags against the closed and locked front doors. He knocks and rings. No one is inside. Not Iris, not Dolly, not Fargo, no one!

He dials Iris's phone. It's disconnected; Franny's, the same. Damn! Dragging his bags, he goes into the next-door ice cream shop.

He smiles at the owner, realizing that he still doesn't know her name. "Hey! How are you? Have you seen Iris? Where is my crew? Do you know why the store's closed?"

She shrugs. "No. The store's been dark for a few days."

Chills flash up his spine. "Closed? For days? I hope they're not hurt. Closed? Is someone hurt? What's going on?"

She shrugs. JP wrestles his bags out the door again and then drags them back to his locked front door. He searches online for a locksmith as the phone's battery dwindles. Ugh! Why didn't he bring his own keys with him? He doesn't know this neighborhood locksmith; Iris has managed all these details for so long.

After an hour's wait, Rocco's rusty "Emergency 24-Hour Locksmith" truck rumbles up. Rocco saunters up to JP. "What's the problem, Mac?"

"My store is locked, and my manager isn't answering her phone. I've gotta get inside!"

Rocco backs away. "Your manager's what? I mean, who are you? You can't just break the lock. This is a business. I mean . . . I can't . . . Who are you?"

JP exhales loudly. Rocco's gaze hardens. "No, sorry. This is my store, but the manager's closed it up while I was away. Just open it up, and we'll put on a new lock." He pulls a business card out of his wallet.

Rocco shakes his head and says, "Why don't we call the cops, 'cause I just don't like this."

JP nods. "Sure, man, whatever."

JP continually checks his watch until a beat cop JP recognizes pulls up with lights flashing. JP looks away from the blue piercing flashes, protecting his eyes and trying to ward off a migraine. Jacoby, a police veteran, moves gracefully in spite of the bulky police tools that jangle with his gait. "Hey. How can I help you guys?"

Rocco lurches to speak first. "Hey, I'm not responsible for any manager gone AWOL, and this clown acts like he owns the place."

Jacoby nods. "Yeah, he does own this store. I drove by yesterday and wondered where the heck Iris could be."

JP jumps on that. "Right! You and me both. Where are they? I hope she's OK. I haven't been able to get ahold of her and—"

"Can't get ahold of her?"

"Her phone's disconnected. And her sister's, who also works for me. And come to think of it, I keep getting fraud alerts that I haven't paid attention to, thinking that it was because I was out of the country."

He scrolls back to the messages warning of negative balances. He sits down on the curb. A wave of nausea rolls him. *Here comes a blinding migraine.*

"Rocco, please just open this up for me. This is bad."

Jacoby nods to Rocco. The lock breaks open, and the alarm blares. JP stops the screeching, remembering the password, "WOLF," at the last minute.

JP and Jacoby walk inside. It's musty and still, like a month of Sundays have settled here. Rocco stands on the showroom floor with the ruined lock in hand.

An anvil of pain cleaves JP's head. "Please put a new lock on the front door," JP pleads. "I'll need you to come back tomorrow and change every lock here. But tonight, I've gotta sleep."

Rocco nods. "Payment first, to be sure that you can pay for tonight's work. Eh?"

JP won't argue. Rocco returns with an itemized invoice for $1,149.50. JP has to look twice to believe it.

JP tries to stay calm, with black calamity clenching his ribs. He hands Rocco the credit card that didn't work back at Charles de Gaulle Airport. He needs to see if it will work here. Rocco slides it through the portable card reader, and it is immediately rejected. Ugh! Maybe there is cash in the safe? He walks into the back office and sees the safe with the door swinging open, but it is not empty. His birth certificate and copies of his green card and passport sit alone in the dusty felt-lined safe that, only days ago, was full of documents that represented his financial accomplishments. There were titles and bank statements, property tax receipts, car titles, plats of survey of dozens of properties, and cash. How *much* cash is anyone's guess. They always keep lots of cash on hand to pay a special garbage collection or unexpected licensing fee or who knows what; it has always been very useful. A deep pain of insult from Iris surges through his gut. Why is he worried about some small bit of cash? There are bank account numbers with login passwords, as well as stock portfolios and passwords for each and every one of these . . . all gone.

He walks back to speak with Rocco. "Hey. I don't have enough cash right now. I'll need you to come back tomorrow to put all new locks everywhere. Could we just include this payment with the rest?"

Rocco's face darkens. "You mean that you're cleaned out, and you want me to wait to see if you have any money? No way, man! Pay me now! This emergency work isn't easy. I'm on call."

JP exhales too loudly. "Right. I know. I understand. I really don't know what to do." He pulls out his wallet again and hands Rocco the card that worked in the airport the night before. Rocco slides it into the reader as JP's heart races with worry. Success!

JP walks with Jacoby around the store. There is a vacuum—an emptiness as if no one has walked these aisles for days.

Rocco heads to the door and calls out behind him, "Get ahold of me when you're ready for the new locks!"

Jacoby looks at JP with an arched eyebrow. "This is a crime scene." He pulls out his pad of paper and begins writing. "Don't touch anything!"

JP is exhausted from the jet lag. His mind is whirling a million miles per hour. Iris and Franny have cleaned him out. Through the dust air, he moves around the showroom in a tense, sleep-deprived, arrhythmic trot. The showroom floor is full—fountains, benches, consoles, bars, statues, all looking adrift. No, it is he alone who is adrift. The anthropomorphic faces on the artifacts and furniture intended to bring personality to an ambiance—today, they are vapid caricatures that taunt his loneliness. Surrounded by beautiful French artifacts, his mind bounces back to Vivi. He'll have to give that up for a while.

A dozen more police come into Les Beaux Châteaux; swirling blue cop lights illuminate the nearby storefronts with their alarming twists. He walks around, touching the cool marbles and patinaed bronzes. He can sell this stuff. Every marble garden statue and copper farm sink, bronze console table, the weird glove molds, and the stained glass—there isn't one extraneous piece in the entire store. He can feel the beauty and history and craft, but he alone will now hold their weight.

Jacoby looks at him with a sympathetic smirk. "No sleep for a while, my friend. And for sure, don't touch the computers. First thing, get a freakin' forensic accountant here ASAP!"

JP feels a molten rock of self-pity expand in his chest. So much for buying Lark's Lane. He'll be sleeping here at LBC like he did in the old days.

Damn Iris and Franny! He'll catch them. He won't let them get away with his nest egg, with all that he's worked so hard for. He's sick, knowing that he'll press charges against them. He'll need to have them hunted down; he'll have to put them in jail, but he loves them. Is he to blame for this theft? He didn't take the time to create an equitable stake for them. They were paid for their work, no doubt, but they are thieves, cheats, bad bitches. But he was too damn lazy, and they were so damn sharp. They played him. How long had they been planning this heist? Ugh!

He thinks of Victor and the Russians and how he felt that they had played him, ha! That is nothing compared with what he's laid himself open to. Is he broke? He goes to his laptop and opens bank accounts; one after another has fifteen dollars. His fingers freeze on top of the computer keys—he can't bear to open another account. He closes his eyes, trying to calm himself. It'll take some time to figure all this out. He'll have to thrash his way through years of a legal morass without a cent of reparations. The money is gone. He's let himself be distracted. Damn! He wanted to be distracted. If he had given them equity in his business, would they have done this anyway? He'll never know now. A horrible vision of a judge adjudicating over unpaid tax bills, where he loses ownership, flashes in his mind. Terror whirls through his body. Losing his balance, he reaches out to hold the wall. His back is wet with sweat, and he's chilled to freezing. This stark possibility may be on the horizon. *OK, man. Slow down.* He owns the building, but what kind of debts have they run up, and will he be able to protect himself? He'll triage his efforts and focus.

He walks through the store, dodging cops who are writing notes and sword playing with the glove molds. A huge stained glass in the west window spills blue light on his shoulder, much like the blue light in the Chartres Synagogue a few days earlier. He misses Victor. It will be difficult to tell him about this financial wipeout, but he isn't afraid. He imagines how nice it will be for them to put these horrible thoughts out of their minds when they go to the tennis tournament together. His mind is spinning a million miles per hour. Shock and fear and anger pulse like thunder at his temples. Did Iris imagine him in this state? Surely, she played a thousand scenarios in her mind as she picked apart his finances.

He sits for hours while the cops write their initial reports.

Jacoby pats him on the back sometime after 11:00 p.m. "Hey, guy, get some sleep. I'll be back at ten tomorrow and we'll finish up. I'll help you get a plan together."

JP is so tired. He finds an old sleeping bag in the office closet. He knows that there are no pillows—he threw them out himself—so he tucks his small duffel bag under his head and closes his eyes to all the destruction swirling around.

***

JP wakes up on the floor of the office with certainty that last night's nightmare was no sleep-time fantasy but the horror of reality. Soon, life in NYC with limited money will feel bleak, but now, in this limbo, his mind is in the wrong place. Mostly he is worrying about how he will support the Whole France movement with no disposable money. How will he keep Veronique's interest with no money? He can almost feel her wild hair slipping through his fingers—indeed, a sad mirage.

He hates being alone in this hardship—his self-created loneliness. Why doesn't he have a wife, a partner to share everyday nonsense, as well as joy and pain, with? He knows better now than to believe that Iris and Franny were his friends, that they cared for and about him. They were employees, and he should have treated them with due respect but not laid bare his personal everything. What a fool! Obviously, they are not his friends. What an idiot!

He knows that he should be mad, really angry at Iris and Franny. Instead, he is angry at himself for loving someone married, for believing that a partner would drop out of the sky to share his life with him. He is so angry with himself for wanting Vivi to be here with him. What a stupid ass. She never wavered in her commitment to her family. *Fucking idiot, get your own stupid family!* Even Victor made efforts to create his own family. It's sad that Catty died so suddenly, but JP imagines that now that Victor knows the joy of love, companionship, and partnership, he'll seek it out again. Damn Vivi for not being here to share his life! He misses her! He loves her. Stupid fool.

Clearly, Iris sensed that he was distracted and that it was time to make her move while he was blind to goings-on at Les Beaux Châteaux. He has to share the blame for this theft. He practically laid this all at her feet. Well, damn it, yes, she did this ruinous crime against *him*!

Jacoby knocks on the front door. With his hair askew and not properly washed, JP lets him and another cop in.

"Hey, guy, this is Arlett. He's gonna look at your computer. You haven't touched it, have you?"

JP shakes his head. "Well, I checked several of my bank balances on my laptop, I'm sorry to say."

But Jacoby and Arlett don't hear him. Jacoby walks back into the office. Searching for clues and information about Iris's work and theft, he scans the room methodically. Her desk is cleanly swept of everything. There isn't a note, a receipt, a pen, or a dog biscuit, nothing that gives the slightest hint that she once occupied this place. Not even her ubiquitous clipboard—gone. JP stands behind Jacoby, similarly looking at every corner. Seeing few clues and nothing out of place, save the open safe, he wonders what Franny took or left at Ocean Manor.

JP looks at Jacoby, who looks at Arlett. Arlett nods his head and turns on the big desktop computer that was the brain center, the recording vault of all the transactions of LBC. It boots up slowly. JP watches the blue screen populate the standard features: calendar, photos, music, pages, numbers, settings, and so on. Hot fear surges through his lungs as the entire desktop fills with empty blue—there are *no files*. No photos of artifacts, no records of sales, no customer mailing database, no bills of lading records, no personnel files, no sales tax collection documents, no trucking documents, no database of designers, not one shred of their work together for the last ten years remains on the desktop.

He asks Arlett, "What's on the hard drive?"

He knows that he will be able to reconstruct some of the important infrastructure that's supported and made LBC function. However, his slow work will be painful and incomplete. He looks down at his feet, stretching the long tendons on the back of his neck that have constricted to knotted rope in his realization.

Arlett answers, "Lemme see."

Instead, he decides that whichever forensic investigator JP hires will be better suited to look at this computer. JP's stomach starts clenching and seizing. *Oh man, this is going to be a full-time mess to unravel.* Iris is so clever, he knows she will have left few if any clues about her whereabouts and how she stashed his money.

Last night's horizontal time on the floor was not nourishing sleep. He tries to make a mental to-do list that he'll work from, but instead, his mind wanders from Vivi's beautiful hair to how he'll get Prized Troofi to change the locks at Ocean Manor. He can't tame his far-flung fears.

Jacoby and Arlett promise to return the following day. JP dials Victor, who picks up on the first ring. "Hello."

Tears burn at the tip of JP's nose, but he steadies himself. "Dad, I've been irresponsible. I guess I got lost in myself, and I exposed our store— our business, our family—to being robbed. Iris has stolen everything." He recounts the events of the last thirty-six hours. "The best thing to do now, Dad, please call your bank in Chartres and change your passwords and account numbers on *everything*. I doubt that they'll reach across the Atlantic, but those women are very, very smart. I know how incredibly stupid I've been, and we can talk about this in fine detail, but I've got to get moving to try to stop the bleeding and find out all that I can. I'll get back to you as soon as possible. Let's mark in ink the dates for the tennis competition. I'll need something wonderful to look forward to. I'll get us tickets; I'll sell something really expensive today."

Victor signs off, saying, "Don't be too hard on yourself. We'll be fine."

"I know. I'm trying to forgive myself, but of all the stupid—"

"Is this tantrum about what Iris did to you? 'Cause if you're trying to get over Veronique, that's just not going to happen overnight. You lost at love. I saw that the minute she walked into my house. That's the way it is. Iris's insult deserves serious penalties. You've got to be strategic now. Can you think like Iris?"

JP inhales a cleansing breath, exhaling slowly. "No, I'll never be as procedural and intentional as she is, but I am determined. The cops seem quite capable. I'll let you know the details as they develop. Talk to you later."

He texts Rama about the locks at Ocean Manor.

He walks through the aisles of LBC. The rhythm of his footfalls quietly echoes against the brick walls. He glances at himself in the three-way mirror that sits on a green Bakelite vanity. The mirror's silvering is no longer uniform, and its light fractures his image. A dozen unrecognizable JPs repeat themselves into the infinity of the mirrors.

***

Tired and wired, he pushes on to take control. It's been years since he's even touched the dusty file cabinets that cower in the back of the office. He riffles through yellowed, brittle folders to find the name of LBC's accounting firm, which he's forgotten. Today is training day; he's going to execute and know every procedure that makes LBC function. Voilà! Here it is! He dials Geffin, Geffin, and Eisenberg's number.

The receptionist answers, "Geffin, Geffin, and Eisenberg."

He listens, imagining having to say that on the phone, all day, every day. Swallowing his impatience, he slows his honeyed greeting. "Good afternoon, madame. Jeremy Miller, please."

Slowly, he is connected to Jeremy's receptionist, who finally puts JP through. "Hey! Jeremy! I should be polite and ask about your good health and Elaine's, but I've got to get right on this! I've got big, big problems. I've been wiped out. It's crazy but—"

Jeremy interrupts. "Wait, wait, JP. Put Iris on the phone. She knows what's going on."

Exasperated, JP meekly answers, "Right. That's just it. She's stolen everything, and I'm the one who gave her the keys."

"Wait, what?"

***

A loud mix of Sly and the Family Stone with Aretha and Stevie Wonder beats through the many speakers in LBC, announcing that he is open for business. Rocco the locksmith is working with a team, putting new locks on all of the doors, and Officer Jacoby is sitting at Iris's desk, making notes as JP explains what he knows. Every twenty minutes or so, he returns to check on Rocco and his crew, asking, "These are state of the art, right? These'll be secure, right?"

"Look, I already told you, these mortise locks are the best. I can't put smart locks on all of these varied doors. This is the state of the art for this chaotic situation."

"Chaotic situation?"

Rocco doesn't quite give JP the finger, but he turns his back as slowly and insultingly as possible.

JP returns to sit with Jacoby to try to include, in his complaint against Iris, all of her offenses. He's already called the credit card reporting agencies and the banks. His Fidelity brokerage account was cleaned out, all the securities sold a week ago, and cash paid out to his own bank accounts. Years ago, Jeremy suggested that he put some of his assets in less liquid trusts or bonds, but JP always felt that one day he'd just sell everything on a whim and split—travel the world. Iris has just beaten him to it.

Jeremy calls. "A forensic accountant and computer whiz are en route to you. Be polite and cooperate with them, eh?"

Annoyed, JP bites back. "I'm paying them. Of course I'm going to give them every bit of information as concisely as possible."

In all this, customers are coming and going, but JP isn't making any of them feel welcome. Maybe he's lost his touch anyway; he hasn't sold anything in . . . well, since he moved out to Ocean Manor . . . must be at least a year now. He tries to calm himself. He owns a few commercial buildings that pay rent, even though the titles are missing. She can't sell those, can she? The bank and title companies have records of his ownership, and without his signature, those can't sell.

He is about to call Jeremy back when an art student approaches his desk. Her multicolored hair, ripped jeans, construction boots, and necessary fold-up easel give her away.

"Hey, I'm Kelly. First year at Parsons. I love your store. The other lady who works here told me that it was all right to draw here. I love that Nike in the garden ornaments area, and this morning light on her is perfect."

JP is about to explode; he surely doesn't need any cheap-ass art student bothering him today. He stops himself. She doesn't deserve his wrath. He could be in her shoes someday. "Sure! Enjoy!"

He isn't an art student or a new immigrant. He is an American success as much as anyone. Iris helped him get here, true. He hates her theft, but even in her evil deeds, she is teaching him. Anger burns behind his eyes. Love the art students.

The day flies by as he juggles the detailed police reports, the accountant, the forensic computer investigators, and thankfully, a regular flow of motivated customers. He doesn't sell anything, but there are multiple interested types who he believes will return ready to buy. He remembers Iris's proclamation that this is the pattern of LBC's sales. Closing the deals is mostly a two-visit process, where inspiration takes hold, and then the numbers (measurements and bank account evaluations) and logistics are worked out. So many subtleties and etiquettes that Iris mandated ring in his mind as he welcomes customers and tire kickers alike. A friendly interaction might not result in a sale today, but it might lay the ground for one in the future. No more feet up on his desk and no more loud, rude phone conversations where listening customers might be embarrassed. He follows the sales pitch with anecdotal and personal information about a given artisan (even if it is made up that minute) and its historical value, and then he leaves the customer to think and feel the rich beauty on their own.

He stops in his tracks: he needs a dog. A dog is the commitment he's always shied away from. In the past, he wouldn't be able to leave town on a moment's notice as a dog owner. Well, with his finances such as they are, that won't be a consideration. For the time being, he'll gladly consider a dog's needs ahead of his own. Dolly was so smart. Of course, Iris taught her everything. What kind of dog does he want?

JP endures weeks of investigations and sworn affidavits, bank investigations, filings of lost and stolen this and that, and a thousand other things. Jacoby itemizes the numerous complaints against the sisters Stryker (Franny was once married and now uses her married name, Lofton), or whatever their real names are.

JP adjusts his honeyed voice when speaking with clerks calling from the various bureaucracies that have an interest in his theft. He has to sell them on his needs.

The calls become routine: "Hello, may I speak with Mr. Jean Paul Marchand? This is Ms. Albertson from Bank of America calling about a claim that you've made and a theft of your personal information in June 2021."

JP tries to imagine what Ms. Albertson looks like. Is she in a giant call center in India or calling from a stateside office? "Yes, this is JP. Please call me JP. Thanks for calling. You all have been so helpful. I really appreciate your kind efforts . . ."

The clerks can only do what they've been charged with, but moving queries and filings up the chains of decision-makers' steep hills takes momentum from the bottom.

JP finally decides to go to Orphans of the Storm, a dog shelter on the Lower East Side. So many of his customers have loving dogs from that shelter. He closes LBC at 5:00 p.m. on the dot and hurries the seemingly constant investigators out so that he can get to the shelter before six.

Inside Orphans of the Storm, his senses are assaulted. The smell and the racket are so striking, he can't decide whether to close his ears or his nose first. In a few minutes, he grows calmer. The front desk attendants, all young women, are businesslike and friendly. A young art student (didn't he always attract the art students?) escorts him through the cages. There is a beagle mix that cowers in her cage and won't come out to greet him, a dachshund mix with a beautiful coat and loving eyes but a piercing, yappy bark that instantly puts him off. He passes larger lab and mastiff mixes with lovely statures but uncontrolled drooling—no, that won't do for a dog who will have to charm customers. There isn't a good fit in the place.

He leaves feeling a little low, but there are many choices for dogs, and he'll find one eventually. As JP rides back to LBC in an Uber, Jeremy calls. "We've cataloged everything that she stole. I know that you know this, but she was calculating and planning this for a good long time. OK. Losses everywhere: equities, antique cars, CDs, mint sets. Why, man, did you collect mint sets? She liquidated everything— loss or gain, she was on a mission. I know that you know it. One saving grace, she didn't mess with your buildings. Changing signatures on titles would have been beyond tricky. So the four big commercial buildings that pay you rent are in good stead. And of course, your main building, Les Beaux Châteaux, is solid."

"Yup. Maybe she knows that I'd personally strangle the breath out of her if she took my building. I have to make a living. Maybe she believed that those other assets grew at the expense of her sweat equity and . . ."

Jeremy continues. "Well, that's peachy keen. Remember, she and Franny are thieves, and they stole a whole lot of *your* money! Don't go all mushy. You've got other problems right now. Real estate taxes are due in thirty days. You've been reassessed, and the taxes on Les Beaux Châteaux have increased fourfold."

JP scrambles on the floor to pick up the dropped phone. "What?"

"Right. You were so smart and bought that building before the Whitney Museum opened blocks away. Your business is in the single-most escalating census tract in the city in terms of increased assessed value. So the good news is the bad news. You'll get a bank loan."

***

JP sits at his desk with a salad from the bodega down the block. The night is quiet. The doors are locked, and most of the lights are off. JP writes an email to Victor—it is too late to call. He details the depth of their losses and breaks the news that he won't be able to buy tickets to the tennis tournament, not this year. He sends it, and Victor calls right away.

"What are you doing up so late?" JP asks.

Victor chuckles. "I just know what you are thinking. I'm up. Don't worry. We'll go to the tennis next year. I could send you more money now, and we could go, but I think that you've first got to sort out all that shit Iris sent your way. I can't help you much with that. I'm still trying to accept that nothing is permanent—not things, not money, not love, not wives. Hey, better thoughts! Your friend Veronique was here today. I bought a bronze sculpture honoring fallen soldiers. The sculpture is from Bogny-sur-Meuse. Their ironmongeries, errrm, forges, closed in the fifties after this was made. Vivi and her crew—and man, they are so good—crated it all up, and she came with the crew to put the sculpture in my truck. I really didn't believe that she'd help me, even though you two struck an agreement. It's a surprise that Whole France would help me, a picker. And good to her word, her crew came through. She must hate those Russian dogs as much as I do!"

The familiar burn at the tip of his nose distracts JP. He still withers at the mention of Vivi.

Victor senses JP's disengagement. "Can you hear me?"

"Sure, Dad, I'm here."

"It's ready to ship, but I wonder if your customers, Americans, will understand the pride and sentiments that inspired this sculpture of soldiers. So many men from both wars were taken from these tiny villages. These bronzes are valuable to French people, but I don't know about folks over there. You'll have to figure out if they'll even sell. This one's rare. Even the really poorest towns haven't sold them, although there are lots of them across the countryside. I know that Veronique understands their value. I'm surprised that Whole France approved of my purchase, not that I need her to, officially. I intend to stay on her good side. Well, there was nothing left of that village. If there are descendants of those warriors, they don't live there anymore."

JP's heart sinks. He wants to focus on the commemorative statues and how he can get Americans to recognize the sacrifice that France endured in the war. He tries to center on the cultural shifts in France, but all he can imagine is Veronique's wild hair and square jaw. What he wouldn't have done to see her, to touch her face.

"How is she? I emailed with her a few weeks ago, but we haven't spoken in a while. I think that everything is on track for their Troofi concert in February. Whole France stands to make a lot of money. I won't be able to go. I hope that you'll go anyway. And about the statues, thanks for reminding me of how important they are. I'll sell 'em well. Gotta hit the hay, Dad." Exhaustion was slithering through his joints.

"Hit the hay?"

"It's American. Right. Good night."

"Of course! I know, *hit the hay*. I'm just pushing your American buttons."

JP had a cheap Murphy bed installed in the back office. He pulls it down, and he's about to get under the covers, but instead, he opens his laptop once again and cues up a computer search: "Best dogs with children and crowds." Poodles, standard poodles, are the answer. So many images, from the prissiest coiffed specimens to puppy-clipped regular types, all hypoallergenic and known loyal companions . . . He dozes off with images of beautiful dogs in his head.

A few weeks later, JP moves Frenchy into LBC. He is so proud. She's the pick of the litter from a well-known upstate poodle breeder. He adds to his tax bank loan so that he has enough cash to buy her too. He is so happy! At three months old, she has the stature and presence to fit in perfectly at LBC. Even relaxed, she stands perfectly square—legs, shoulders, and paws all in line under a strong, straight back. Her gaze is up and forward, anticipating life's next adventure. Her unusual red color will fade, the breeder explains, but for now, her red curls are akin to an orangutan. She is a star! Almost every customer wants to be introduced to her, and she is energetic and friendly beyond all expectations. She has a soft mouth and sparkling eyes. JP moves her toy box from the back office to right next to his desk, as customers delight in entertaining her.

Together, they go to evening puppy class twice a week, and they practice manners, behavior, and vocabulary every day. Very quickly, she knows the red ball from the blue ball, and her baby (a special doll with a mechanized heartbeat) from the rabbit toy. Out in the park, her athleticism is outstanding. She can jump like a gazelle, over fences and bushes, and then return to his side with his quiet but intentional commands. He loves her company. She is only a puppy, but on occasion, she inspires thoughts of Dolly. Inevitably, thoughts of Iris revive his heartbreak. JP's relative poverty is becoming a grind. Fortunately, he has Frenchy. His memberships to the Metropolitan Museum, MoMA, and most missed, the Neue Galerie have all lapsed. He doesn't really have time to use them anyway. Driving antique cars seems a dream, and his now-limited wardrobe is adequate but not current. Eating frugally is irksome but not paralyzing. It is the lack of the freedom of being rich that sometimes cuts him deeply. On a moment's notice, he used to eat at Michelin-starred restaurants or shop at stores mentioned in the Style section of the newspaper. Those options are not currently on his roster.

Occasionally, he wonders where Iris and Franny have gone . . . He wonders what Vivi is doing and who she's doing it with, but most days, he and Frenchy greet shoppers with pride and the cheer of the moment.

Everything is new and fun for Frenchy, and slowly, JP, as he retools his life, sees fun too. Walking on streets in their neighborhood can be difficult. On the leash or off, Frenchy stays very close, but the ear-splitting sound of the subway trains going around the Meatpacking District unsettles her so deeply that she jumps into his arms when they cross subway grates.

When LBC is closed, they spend time at the city's various parks. He fantasizes about having her with him sometime at Ocean Manor or Lark's Lane. He wants to swim with her; poodles are known water dogs. He heard that the newest rage in the Hamptons is paddleboarding with your dog on the board. He knows that they'll have a blast trying that sometime. He imagines her with Veronique . . . playful, beautiful, strong. Would Vivi recognize him as a good companion if she observes him with Frenchy? Futile fantasies, but he can't shake them.

At the store, Frenchy's charisma entertains. Like the days with Dolly, Frenchy will sit patiently at JP's heel, waiting as he charms customers. One afternoon, Frenchy's youth shining brightly, she greets a familiar designer, Beverly. Bev sits at a classic Bakelite vanity to check her lipstick, hardly noticing the spinach-green bureau, with yellow contrasting handles. Friendly Frenchy headbutts her, and Beverly scratches Frenchy's ears, making friends.

JP zeros in to make his sale. "Isn't this a beautiful piece?" He leans in, running his long fingers over the smooth top. "My dad bought it in France, but a Belgian inventor created Bakelite in the States. It's a completely synthetic plastic, but, man, I love these jewel tones. It was lauded for its flameproof qualities and because it's so lightweight."

Frenchy looks at herself in the vanity's mirror. Beverly pulls Frenchy up into her own lap; she puts their heads together, and they admire themselves in the mirrors. SOLD! Customers love to pet her soft curly hair and coax her happy puppy smile. She brings an innocence and elegance to LBC that JP didn't know was missing but is surely present now. Frenchy's on the team!

***

JP hires Garrett Investigations, at Jacoby's suggestion, to try to track down Iris and Franny. Garrett agrees to waive his usual retainer, at Jacoby's urging, but his monthly travel and phone expenses are frustrating for JP. He's pretty certain that he won't get any money back if Garrett tracks them down, but he just can't leave them unhunted. Victor agrees.

Beryl Garrett is a former NYPD investigator fired from the force years ago for his repeated drinking-on-the-job offenses. His lazy left eye droops at the same angle that his stomach hangs over his belt, inviting speculation about his current drinking habits. Jacoby insists that Garrett has well-honed procedural and detective skills and an even better instinct. After rehashing with Victor all the reasons why Iris and Franny shouldn't have robbed him, JP's anger is hot. He's determined to prosecute them. It might be years before the New York Police Department gets around to investigating his case, let alone apprehending Iris and Franny. JP and Victor agree that Garrett's fees are worthwhile.

Garrett sits in Les Beaux Châteaux with Jeremy, the accountant, for two days and interviews JP for hours about how he and Iris worked together. He is one of the few people who doesn't like or pay attention to Frenchy. "I don't like to be distracted," he tells JP.

JP recounts Iris's supposed history with a family antique store in Savannah, her self-taught approach to accounting, and familiarity with international money-laundering laws. After that, JP never sees Garrett, only his monthly expense bills. Jacoby assures him that he is getting a bargain and that Garrett's fee after the thieves are apprehended will be reasonable.

The cooler weather sets in. Thanksgiving is approaching. JP thinks about Rama and how they met last year on Thanksgiving. He thinks about reaching out to her, but then he remembers her on the floor of the Millerworks between Norman Weaver's legs.

Frenchy has so much energy on these cool days. Keeping her by his side during the workday occasionally seems cruel, but as much as she wants to play outdoors, she wants to be with him above all else. And her character is an asset to the store.

LBC customers are buying in earnest again. This—after years in retail, JP finally identifies—is a seasonal trend. People want to enhance their homes before the holidays. Victor sends container after container of statues, sinks, stained glass, odd one-off items like glass vats for tanner's chemicals, and a dozen plaster death masks of nuns from a remote convent. Surely Veronique has persuaded him not to disassemble bakeries or city halls that she could possibly save. One container included a few early-twentieth-century steel surgical tools, in addition to their bread-and-butter urns and glass. JP has no idea how to price these grisly, steely tools. He displays them like jewels in glass vitrines, ignoring their intrinsic purpose and celebrating their sculptural beauty. He's resisted selling items in plexiglass boxes as untouchable, unusable museum objects, but he places these surgical instruments in a sparkling case. For all JP's skepticism, they sell in a few days. Somehow Victor knows what will sell: the brutal, the rare, and the truly exquisite.

Container arrival days are always complicated for JP. He has three hourly hauling guys on staff full-time, as well as a few of their friends who don't want to work full-time but love to work off the books on occasion. During the days when Iris kept lots of cash on hand, that was easy, but cash payments off the books now, with so many eyes on his business practices, are more complicated. On the container days, he directs the muscle guys and moves some things himself. That is a job enough. The store, nearly sixty thousand square feet, is always being rearranged, like a game of Tetris; the irregular sizes and logistical needs of any given artifact put every other element of the showroom floor in motion. Because he only employs young, part-time additional salespeople, JP greets almost every guest as if they are a prized customer, so he is all over the place. Damn! Why did Iris screw him so badly? He needs her strict time-management skills now! He thinks many times about closing down for container arrival days, but they are inconsistent, rarely ever on the same day of the week.

One particularly cold container arrival day a few weeks before Thanksgiving, Beryl Garrett arrives at the store with no advance notice or fanfare. The showroom is in chaotic turmoil, and JP is seemingly nowhere in sight. Garrett walks in and sits down at JP's desk. From a far corner, JP watches Garrett. JP wants to go immediately to him, but he is busy trying to extricate himself from a testy spat with an ill-tempered, older woman.

Her slight frame and crumpled posture misinform JP as he speaks with her in his honeyed voice. "I'm so sorry, ma'am. Most everything in this store is for sale, everything except my dog here, and that collection of women's and men's bathroom signs."

He remembers when Iris brought the box of this collection to his desk: dozens of bronze, porcelain, glass, ceramic, and steel bathroom signs. She said that they'd be the single un-French decorative element that makes sense here. She installed them at irregular lengths on the outside doors and the walls of the bathrooms herself. Over the years, he's added a few more.

The elderly woman snaps, "What kind of rinky-dink store is this hellhole? I said that I want to buy those signs. This is a retail establishment. I said that I'd pay you!"

JP is juggling so many things—why is this woman so difficult? "I'm sorry, ma'am, they are simply not for sale. Not today or any other day. Please, look around; there must be other things here that can catch your fancy."

The woman's face darkens as she steps back on her heel. "Don't you charm me, you cheating son of a bitch. I'm—"

JP points to the entrance. "Please feel free to use the front door if you cannot find what you're looking for."

He walks past her toward his desk, where Garrett is sitting. He wonders for a moment if he is behind in his payments to the investigator. What could he want now?

Garrett smirks. "Rough day?"

JP rolls his eyes as the old lady and her companion walk by. JP thinks she has left, and he turns to engage Garrett. Looking at Garrett but listening to the ruckus at the front door, he hears the old woman spit on the floor. JP closes his eyes in resignation, knowing that some customers are simply difficult. "Yes, Beryl," JP says, "a strangely bad day."

Usually a man of few words, Garrett says, "I'm here to change all that. Good news! I found them. I found Iris and Fran. They go by Ellen and Danielle now. They don't know that I've tracked them, but they're in Charleston. They paid cash for one of the bluest-blooded, fancy-pantsy antiques shops in all of the low country, called Silverthorn. They're very careful. The store only opens by appointment, but I watched for days, and I finally saw them."

Frenchy nuzzles JP as he hesitates to respond.

Garrett says, "What? You thought I wouldn't find them?"

JP steps away from the desk and pats Frenchy in his *calm down* manner. He doesn't even know if restitution back to him is a possibility if they are charged and convicted. Will they be forced to sell their store? He doesn't want to present himself as naive to Garrett. "So what's next? What do I do, or what do you do?"

"I'm gonna go get them. I just wanted you to know before I pounced."

JP feels weak as Garrett pounds the desk.

"I found those bitches! I'm going to go and haul their red heinies up here, and they will be tried. I'll bet you didn't know that they were check kiters in Oklahoma in the nineties and early aughts, did ya?"

Silently, JP shakes his head no.

Garrett bellows, "How much did you know about them before you opened your life for them to gorge?"

Embarrassed, JP hopes that Garrett will lower his voice. The nasty tone of the old lady minutes before gave him doubt, and now Garrett's big volume adds to his uneasiness. He hates being public with the ugly theft truths. He doesn't want anyone's sympathy, and he doesn't want to be known as vulnerable. He doesn't want to explain that he did no due diligence on the sisters at all. But Garrett is correct; he's been played.

Quietly, he says, "So what do I do now?"

Garrett rolls his eyes in annoyance. "Well, you get ready to press charges against them, and we'll go to court and get your money back. Or some of it! And those girls, those bitches, are going to jail!"

JP steps back even farther from the desk.

Leaning over the desk, Garrett says in a voice way too loud, "Now don't tell me you don't want their scalps. Don't you lose your fightin' form. This'll be long, and they'll be slippery. We are going to grab them and hold them and shake every nickel out of them."

JP is defeated. "It's complicated. I loved them."

Garrett is quick to retort. "Nahhh, no! They are thieves, and they marked you. They didn't love you, that's for sure."

Resigned to full-on retribution, JP turns away from Garrett, saying over his shoulder, "Right. I'm ready to follow through. Please go and get them. You certainly do good work. Thank you."

The rest of the afternoon is a calamity. Nothing moves easily, and the design and vignettes of arranged artifacts that usually come together aren't working. Nothing looks good together, and dozens of time-consuming tire kickers come and go. They close at five, and the haulers work with JP till nine, yet still nothing comes together for pizazz. His neck hurts, his shoulders are sore, he foolishly misses Veronique, the store is a mess, and he has only himself to put it right.

When everyone finally leaves and he and Frenchy are alone in the store, everything is still in disarray. He puts on pity-party music, Sam Cooke, "Bring It on Home." He and Frenchy walk around, with JP singing at the top of his lungs, missing Vivi, and cleaning up. He wants to possess Veronique's soul. He wants to shelter and thrill her. Damn, she is gone from his life. Sam Cooke's music is so sincere and sad. He feeds Frenchy and takes her out for a walk. He's taken to eating Trader Joe's frozen food. It has little taste but adequate nutrition, and he can stay with Frenchy and save money, too, with frozen chicken cutlets and Trader Joe's famous Two-Buck Chuck—certainly drinkable and effective to boot!

On their walk, JP imagines a sincere partnership; simple exercises like arranging furniture could be great with a partner who agrees with your plans or edits your ideas with constructive success. Of course, the downside of partnership is if you don't agree on a plan or design. He's always been decisive. Victor calls him headstrong, but his mother nurtured him: "Your instincts are great! Trust yourself." He and Iris had a partnership of sorts. She attended to most everything small and routine while he kept a grand vision, and it worked for a long time. Well, maybe she was stealing for years and he still hasn't identified all the losses. Nahhh. The accountants combed through every transaction from the last ten years. Tonight, he really wants a trusted partner.

He thinks sadly again of Veronique. Would she have been a respect-ful partner? *Stop tormenting yourself,* he admonishes. He thinks of her words, "committed to her family," and yet she fucked him. *How many others were there . . . committed to family?* he wonders.

As he and Frenchy arrive back at LBC, he receives a text from Rama: the Valentine's Day concert to benefit Whole France has sold out in one day. She wants to know if he'll send her to France to help make it a success. He thinks to himself, *I'm not even going. I don't think that I'll be sending you.* He decides not to respond to her. He is confi-dent that Veronique is aware of the great financial success, too, but she hasn't sent him any message. *C'est la vie.*

He and Victor have helped Whole France in generous ways. He knows that Vivi appreciates what he has done. One thing's for sure: they have *not* given up their livelihood. He hasn't asked Victor if the nefarious Russians are still ravaging small towns. Better not to bring up a sore subject. Things are good for Victor with the Whole France team of well-trained haulers. Victor is better at and happier with his hunting than before. JP wonders about Catty and how much Victor misses her. He never speaks of her. Victor is focused on their work together. He is a patient partner, and though Victor reminds JP that nothing is permanent, their bond is strong, beyond JP's earlier expec-tations . . . permanent for their lives together.

JP longs for romance like what he believed possible with Vivi, but he is grateful for Victor's trust; he reminds himself that they're not mutually exclusive. Since the theft, he values Victor far more than in the past. For so many years, he was glad they were on different sides of the Atlantic, that he didn't have to interact with or support Victor, but now, things are different. Next summer, Victor will come to New York to watch the tennis matches, and they'll finally get to spend time together in the States. Will he close the store for a week or two and take Victor to the Grand Canyon or somewhere else?

The next holiday months whiz by in a blur. The economy—the Wall Street economy—is growing, and those patrons are buying LBC goods. JP tries to imagine being angry at Iris if and when he sees her in court. He is also aware that these regular, top-spending customers were cultivated in part by her clever strategies. Can he embrace forgiveness and have the strength to press charges against her and Franny? LBC was always his and Victor's creation. Iris and Franny are due no credit for that. And if their ideas for logistical management added to his success, he paid them. Maybe any manager type could have done the same? He definitely made mistakes trusting them, but it was he and Victor who saw the edge in the marketplace for their expertise. Damn right! He is living safely and well enough, but he was rich before her theft. Would he pursue Vivi with more confidence if he still had money? He tries not to mix these two streams of thought.

To JP's surprise, two large and complete bakeries come in at the end of November, no doubt a Veronique-approved haul. The elements arrive in protected crates made precisely by Vivi's team. He knows that there will be few, if any, more whole rooms like this, so he reassembles them slowly and exactly and then prices them exorbitantly.

One sells within a week. He has paid back his bank loan and put money away for the next tax season. Still, he is living frugally. He has bought no clothes and now has a secondhand truck. He isn't traveling. Fortunately, he has no mortgage, but he is very strict with himself. He eats most nights with Frenchy. He indulged himself in years past with new buildings, vintage cars, fine wines . . . That was when business was good and Iris managed the day-to-day paperwork drudgery. And he spent so much money on Ocean Manor. Well, that certainly will pay dividends; he's proud of that beautiful project, and it's paid back in valuable connections and real money.

He has heard nothing from or about Prized Troofi beyond the automatic rent deposit, thank you very much! Will Troofi stay on? He hasn't heard from Rama after the text asking that he send her to

France. Maybe Troofi will take her to France with him? JP is confident that Whole France is on the path to sustainability. Maybe his heart is cauterized, and he is no longer bleeding in pain. Vivi has scarred him.

One dark and snowy afternoon, a young couple comes in. JP greets them with ample hospitality. It has been quiet most of the day. He's been looking online at hotels that allow dogs along the multiple routes to the Grand Canyon—kind of interesting, but maybe not his most productive afternoon. They are dressed like students, and JP assesses that they are not even thirty years old. He has just finished reinstalling the worn marble slabs on the bakery shelves. He added a dazzling center-hung chandelier and a knockout clock for perfect symmetry. He sent pictures to Victor, a rare practice, but this installation was fully satisfying. He watches the young couple admire all the best details, from the matched wood grains of the Spanish mahogany to the smoothed marble slabs. They run their hands over the moldings' curlicues and admire the added clock. He lets them enjoy the details without interfering in their fun. He purposely doesn't have a price tag anywhere in the setup.

The young man approaches the desk. "Hey! Can you tell us a little about the bakery?"

JP doesn't need to be asked twice. He explains that he and Victor are partners in this salvage but that they are now supporting the Whole France movement, and this bakery might be one of the last entire rooms they will sell. He adds that because they are partners with the most respected preservation organization in France, Whole France, this particular bakery has been approved for export, and there must have been a total stripping of that town or building for Whole France to have allowed it to be sent to them. But here it is. Lauren, the female half of the couple, is dazzled.

"So will you sell it?" Bryan asks JP.

"Everything in this store is for sale, except for me and my dog. Oh yes, and the bathroom plaques are definitely not for sale."

Bryan asks again. "So how much for the entire bakery? I mean the whole thing. You sell it as a complete thing, right?"

JP nods his head in the affirmative. "Yes. I wouldn't sell it piecemeal. That would be a crime. This is not only the last of its kind but also one of the best too. I've sold several bakeries, but none as complete or in such great condition as this one. This is a hundred and twenty thousand," he says, expecting them to roll their eyes and guffaw at the fun of imagining such a price.

"How about installation? Can you help with that also?"

"Not likely. I'm full-time here. I can advise on a few techniques, but you'll have to have an experienced carpenter install it."

Bryan looks at Lauren and says, "That's tough, but OK! We'll take it!"

They laugh and smile, and for a minute, JP isn't sure if they're joking or not. He rarely sells an expensive piece without some negotiation or a second visit. But here it is—Bryan has just swallowed hook, line, and sinker. Wow! This will help put him on the path to profitability sooner than anticipated.

JP helps measure the walls and photograph the details. Frenchy is a great model for their photos. Her charm is not lost on Bryan and Lauren.

After they leave, JP realizes that he should be promoting Whole France, like a *Good Housekeeping* seal of preservationist approval. He is their American partner now, and he should use that for promotions. He writes a long businesslike email to Veronique, asking for their promotional materials and a large poster or two. The body of the message is all business, but he signs it *"tu me manquez,"* missing you.

JP realizes that his promotional acumen has been on hold since the theft. Now that he has an idea to leverage Whole France, maybe he should reach out to Goldie to see if the Millerworks would do a joint promotion or event with LBC. He emails her and suggests a small winter solstice auction at LBC for Millerworks' bigger donors. He'll host, with all the bells and whistles, and he'll donate a small stained-glass piece. He pushes "Send," and a satisfied warmth spreads across his chest and arms. He helped Goldie; it's time that she reciprocates.

Later, he and Frenchy are out walking past their usual boundaries into Chelsea. At St. Peter's Episcopal Church, there is a hand-painted notice on the mostly staid marquee that reads, "Pet blessing, Sunday at 10:00 a.m." Then, written across it in bold red marker, "SOLD OUT."

Drat! he thinks. He has never been spiritual or religious, but it might be a fun way to meet New York pet owners. He jots down the pastor's name from the marquee and the address of the church. Back at his desk, he googles the church and the pastor and reads a few of their weekly newsletters. Why hasn't he done this sooner? No, he isn't spiritual, but the newsletter has so much neighborhood information: from a garbage truck driver's broken leg to a kindergarten parade and new moms' group. Ideal marketing foci.

He writes an informal note to the pastor saying that he isn't new to the neighborhood but that he's a new dog owner and is sorry to miss the pet blessing. Could he possibly host a second event at LBC with the pastor officiating? Within a few minutes, Pastor Mike, as he calls himself, writes back. He knows LBC; he's cruised inside many times. JP wonders if he would recognize the man, but nothing comes to mind. Mike continues: he has a waiting list of pet owners who wanted to be included in the pet blessing, and maybe they could arrange it for the same day as the earlier scheduled event, but later in the afternoon? Mike warns that no matter what number they agree to host, it will sell out. There will be more pet lovers who want to be included. JP has never even heard of a pet blessing before, but this is surely a new demographic group that he has not yet reached out to. Maybe there is particular French pet paraphernalia that he should be selling? He makes a note to ask Victor about that.

Two weeks later, on a crisp and cold November afternoon, 125 dogs and even a few leashed cats and their owners come into LBC's large main showroom floor, now mostly cleared for the event. There are some familiar neighborhood faces, but on the whole, JP knows very few people or pets. Pastor Mike is friendly and casual, and JP does recognize his face. JP is amazed that most of the pets seem to be on their best behavior; there are only a few snarls or hisses, and the people attached to the pets are every color, age, and orientation. JP doesn't call the event to order right on time; it is so fun to watch all the pets. Finally, Pastor Mike nods to him to get the show started.

JP and Frenchy stand on a small stage that he has pulled out from previous benefit events. "Hello, New York! Les Beaux Châteaux has been here for a while, but I intend to be much closer to the pet community going forward—"

Interrupting him, there is a kerfuffle at the front door, and the crowd parts like the Red Sea. In walks Rama, Prized Troofi, and a woman who could only be his mother, with two black standard poodles. A hush rolls over the entire audience. JP looks at Pastor Mike and hands him the mic.

Pastor Mike's prayer is fresh and poignant, reminding everyone to learn tolerance and patience from their pets. He wishes everyone a happy holiday season, and then it's over. The pets and their people fan out into the store. Rama and her entourage approach JP. Frenchy and the other poodles quickly start playing happy dog games.

A crowd of gawkers surrounds Troofi, and though JP doesn't know exactly what to do, Troofi pays no attention to the onlookers as Rama makes the introductions. Dressed as a big star with thick gold chains on his bare chest, a close-fitting leather blazer, and dark glasses, he draws everyone's eyes. JP can feel dozens of cameras trained first on Troofi and then on him and Frenchy. He glances at his desk in the distant background with the big, well-framed Whole France poster waiting to be his promotional tool.

JP is eager to express his gratitude to Troofi. "Thank you for agreeing to do the Whole France promotional concert. The leadership at

Whole France is very grateful, as am I. It's giving them the foundation to do systematic and careful preservation of antique towns that might have vanished or been disastrously changed if not for their and your efforts."

Troofi smiles. "Yeah, man. I researched their mission and work before we agreed to help them. I like them. And I've never been to France. It's great to be able to go on a working trip." Troofi winks at his mother. JP watches the dogs circling each other. He's not paying attention to Troofi or Rama, but he hears a loud, unified laugh from the group surrounding them. Troofi's mother has all three dogs sitting at attention, waiting for treats.

Rama looks at JP coolly, giving nothing away. The store is sizzling! He is glad to have brought on the part-timers. He would never be able to handle the crowd. Politely, he extricates himself from Troofi's circle to explain the wrought-iron processes to a family with a collie.

Pastor Mike interrupts him with a squeeze to his elbow and a warm "Thank you!" and leaves.

Frenchy is by his heel most of the afternoon. She identifies or introduces herself to many of the other pets but always returns to his side. She is both nervous and excited. It has been an exhausting afternoon for both of them but lots of fun. Never has he been introduced to pets along with people in quite the same way. And yes, he concludes, it is true: American dog owners look so much like their dogs.

After hours of rearranging the store and cleaning up, he and Frenchy finally settle down to a contented, quiet night. Then his phone starts buzzing with people texting pictures of the pet blessing from social media. Pictures of Troofi with his mother's dogs and Frenchy are being sent to him from people he knows and lots of people he doesn't know. How have they gotten his number?

Veronique sends a text: "Master of ceremonies, it seems. What a lovely event you hosted. I would have liked to have been a fly on the wall. I didn't know that you had a dog. Prized Troofi's concert is sold out, and Whole France is so proud and happy for our partnership with Les Beaux Châteaux! I have lots of plans. Let's talk soon."

Right, he thinks, *Whole France partnered with LBC, but not by my design. I'd have made the partnership you and me.*

The following morning, Goldie calls to accept his offer of a small, exclusive benefit auction event at LBC for the Millerworks. She is excited but hopes that it can be scheduled some months out, perhaps next September? She has obviously seen, on social media, all the attention that he and LBC have gotten from the pet blessing. With a high-pitched thrill creeping into her voice, she asks, "And can you invite Carter?"

JP thinks her cavalier reference to Prized Troofi by first name rather than his stage name is ridiculous. He answers without a hint of irony. "Actually, Goldie, he came here with Rama. You could call her and ask her to bring him along."

There is a long pause, and she finally says, "Well, let's not fuss about that. I'll have the office send you an agreement for the auction. How many people would be ideal?"

"That's up to you. Seventy-five people, a hundred looks full enough in here, but of course, we can accommodate many more. I'm hoping that you keep it exclusive. If you want to wait for so long, why don't we wait to confirm a count for a few months." As he hangs up, he thinks it ridiculous to be planning so far in advance.

JP keeps his focus on restoring his credit and his confidence through the coming winter months. It is an especially cold season, but Victor's supply of extraordinary artifacts keeps a steady flow of top-shelf customers shopping.

JP and Frenchy have been frugal enough for JP to plan for a bit of luxury during the summer. Sight unseen, he's rented a small Hamptons house blocks away from the beach. Over the winter months, he hires several assistant-manager types and separates their responsibilities so that not one of them is indispensable—and not one of them can get into the safe!

Christmas comes and goes. He sends Victor a handsome set of leather gloves and a cashmere scarf and hat. He and Victor speak almost every day. Their mutual trust and admiration are a revelation. They have never before been so close or relied on each other for advice and recognition like partners, and like father and son. To JP, the Atlantic Ocean has never felt so small. He knows what Victor is doing, where he is scouting, what he is buying, who his competitors are (all Russian), and how confident he is in working with the Whole France demo teams. Victor is less interested in New York life, but he truly loves Frenchy, even though he hasn't yet met her. JP has learned to photograph her at her silliest, her most athletic, and her cuddliest. Victor is smitten. JP spends the festive New York season in the Meatpacking District holed up with Frenchy. No prix fixe dinners or holiday champagne brunches draw him away from his disciplined savings and austerity. Adequate money for a relaxed summer with Victor stays in his sights—time in the Hamptons and, likely, a road trip for the record books.

***

In France, St. Valentine's Day isn't the huge holiday that it is in the States. People do send cards and buy candy or roses, but not quite in the volume or with the overenthusiasm in which it's done in the States. It's more of an in-person dinner event. But this year, with Prized Troofi coming to town, shopkeepers and T-shirt hawkers on the Quais de la Seine are conflating Troofi with the lovers' holiday. The weather is bright and crisp, and even those without tickets to the concert have Troofi fever.

Posters of Prized Troofi are plastered on alleyways and subway entrances and billboards, with Whole France named in the requisite bright-yellow lettering under his image. With Troofi fever comes Whole France excitement too! Veronique is interviewed on radio and TV, and suddenly, Whole France and its virtuous mission are on the lips of hip French patriots. Preserving France for French people is the mantra of the hour. Victor is pleased that Marine Le Pen has nothing to do with this latest vogue. Donations to Whole France balloon in the weeks up to the concert, and once Prized Troofi arrives, the Whole France website crashes because there are so many online donors. Russian developers (*dogs*, as Victor has named them) are in hiding.

Veronique sends JP two huge envelopes: one with a collection of Prized Troofi posters, and the second stuffed with newspaper headlines explaining Whole France's mission and partnership with LBC and the work that they've done and will do together. He's carefully followed the media frenzy online, but he's touched by her gesture. Rama (obviously in attendance) sends JP a video of the concert from backstage, and Victor sends a picture that Vivi has taken of him and Troofi in the greenroom. The concert and the aura surrounding Troofi's blessing are a huge success for Whole France. Troofi, Paris, and hopefully the future of France's ancient villages will have Whole France as an important resource for years to come. JP is surprisingly ambivalent as he reads the various media reports documenting the event that he conceived of. The success will be Vivi's and Whole France's. They have enough money to identify troubled homeowners or villages, find verified buyers, and help bridge the financial gaps to maintain even a small bit of integrity in the blighted areas. For now, he doesn't feel like he needs to be there. His place is at LBC. It doesn't feel like his fight or his victory. LBC's partnership with Whole France is welcome but not currently valuable. American buyers read his brochure about his partnership with Whole France, but that doesn't close the deals for him.

***

Easter plans are in the air for Les Beaux Châteaux customers. JP realizes that he hasn't heard from Garrett in months. Where is the big showdown? When will he have to go to court to testify against Iris and Franny? When will he recoup some of those lost assets? Forget about Garrett—what is the status of the NYPD investigation? Is Jacoby still on the case?

JP's seen the car he restored so beautifully on an internet bulletin board for MG collectors—for sale for almost double what he put into it. Perhaps few collectors are meticulous enough to have had the metallic elements re-chromed as he did. He knows in his bones that it is his car. Is this Iris selling under a false name? Who has signed the title for the sale to be executed? Older cars can have duplicate titles issued with ease. Maybe they sold it to this seller? He should call Jacoby and tell him about this car on the market . . . Following up on all these details makes putting the theft behind him difficult. Maybe someday he'll buy another one . . .

Good Friday is a beautiful day. The Highline is buzzing with activity, but there aren't many shoppers at LBC. Everyone is in food halls and liquor stores, stocking their larders for the weekend. These quiet holidays used to magnify his loneliness, but now, with Frenchy, he isn't searching to escape the quiet. He and Frenchy stand outside the store. This is the one place where she is nervous, anticipating the horrid train noise. He is ready to go back inside . . . Or should he get an ice cream for each of them? He pulls his keys out of his pocket; he'll lock the door for just a few minutes while they get ice cream. But as he looks up, there are Garrett and Jacoby together, walking toward him. Their flushed faces say it all. They smirk and grin as if they've won the Mega Millions lottery.

Jacoby yells ahead, "He did it! I told you that he'd get 'em. They're locked up downtown right now."

JP feels dizzy for a second and then pushes the men inside. He doesn't want to make Frenchy suffer the noise that will screech by in a matter of seconds.

Inside, JP watches Garrett strut with a posture that he's not seen from the man in the past. Garrett begins to tell the story. "Oh yeah! I made an appointment to see a particular eighteenth-century desk that they'd advertised in a southern design magazine. Oh, they wanted to unload that piece of garbage, and I was gonna be their live one. Iris, errr, Ellen came to the door to let me in. We chatted about my made-up story of a granny in St. Louis who once had . . . blah, blah, blah. They said that they had been managing a store in the Northeast but that the South suited them, and when Silverthorn became available, they made their move. That's when I made my move! I'm not sure about the slow churn of New York justice and you possibly getting anything back, but they'll be arraigned on Monday! Even when they post bail, they won't be able to go to Charleston to oversee the liquidation of Silverthorn. Maybe there'll be an agent appointed to do it. Maybe the court will compel them to have an agent do it, or maybe it'll sit for a good long while. I'm still looking into what other assets they may have. I think there'll be fungible assets that will likely come to you sometime down the line. I emphasize *some*. Clever as that Iris is, I wouldn't be surprised if they stashed the assets in Bitcoin, untraceable unless you've got the FBI unlockin' their secrets. If there are other people who have been defrauded by them, you may have to share in the assets' liquidation, but as far as I can tell, there weren't any others, recently, that is."

JP swallows the lump in his throat. A strange relief warms him— love 'em or hate 'em, his ordeal with Franny and Iris is almost over. He hadn't perceived that this unresolved trauma was causing his stress, but now he feels lighter.

He turns to Jacoby and asks, "So what do I do next?"

Jacoby's calm smile often masks the urgency of events to come. "You can come to the arraignment, but that'll be all of five minutes.

Garrett here has assembled the evidence for me and my department to go to the DA. They'll take it from there, but these women are repeat criminals. No one's gonna go lightly on them. You can read about the arraignment in the paper, and after that, I'll keep you up to speed as to when we'll need your testimony."

Garrett stands tall and pulls in his gut. His eyes brighten. "I know what you can do; you can pay me. I'll send the billing and invoices to you on Monday."

JP answers, smiling and half-heartedly joking, "Oh great! I just finished paying the forensic accountant. If I get anything back, it'll help pay for these professional services."

JP's nervous laugh is not lost on Jacoby or Garrett.

***

Filing insurance claims precisely, like finding the prime spot for a giant bar in the showroom, requires concentration. JP does the fine-detail work more easily after he buys stronger eyeglasses. Insurance claims, with their exactitude, are time-eaters, yet he's filled with satisfaction after completing them. Bigger, more impressive pieces from Victor brilliantly placed on the showroom floor make him proud.

He and Victor speak during Victor's long drives in the country. He detests the commercialization of French life. "Even in these remote areas, people seem hungry for a commercialized, Chinese plastic window-box life! Fast tourism, I hate it. The more stable villages and towns' flowers are displayed in artisanal ceramic or very French lead pots."

"So you can assess the health of a village by the quality of its flowerpots?"

Victor laughs. "You've summed up my philosophy for the day exactly!"

JP assures him that the cheap, throwaway mentality isn't just in France; New York is full of saccharine hollowness.

Les Beaux Châteaux stays open long retail hours. JP occasionally resents this grueling schedule, but he's calmer now with the ebb and flow of business. He can categorize his customers: informed, rich, slim, mostly fashionable women. Yet there are wonderful surprises. An older couple who taught theater and drama in a public high school "had always wanted to check out Les Beaux Châteaux," and now that they're retired, they finally stop in. Four older Black guys come in looking for vintage wooden shoeshine kits. A bagel baker comes in looking for antique display cases; he buys a big chrome-and-glass piece. JP keeps notes to share with Victor. And they speak often about various customers at LBC and the different sellers that Victor is negotiating with.

Victor's disdain for Russians in France has fully crystallized. "They're always trying to impress the world with their gross thefts and ugly gold-plated copies. Ugh, they're a menace!" He avoids the Russian pickers at auctions and the Russian real estate agents smothering ancient villages. Victor is keenly interested in the case against Iris and Franny, and JP keeps him apprised, especially as Garrett caught them.

"I would have liked to have seen that fat slob Garrett's work at Silverthorn when he nailed 'em, eh? They had covered their tracks so carefully, but you got them anyway. Les Beaux Châteaux is our creation!"

"Dad! Iris worked so hard here. She's really smart and so knowledgeable. It's a tragedy that she'll rot behind bars."

"JP, you're looking at this the wrong way! Go to the court appearances. You've got to see them for what they truly are, cheaters and thieves!"

Though Jacoby advises JP to read about the arraignment in the newspaper or online, JP staffs LBC with a young crew so that he can go to court to see American justice in action.

Jacoby meets JP in the parking lot of the Bronx Hall of Justice. The modern glass structure isn't the ominous dungeon that JP has read about in *The Bonfire of the Vanities*. New York does make progress. They walk to the DA's office. Jacoby gives JP a little background. "Sharon Tracker's our prosecutor. She's the smartest person in the building, one of New York's best legal minds. When I first met her, I wrote her off as some affirmative-action darling. She's Native American. Forget that! This woman knows the law."

JP's stride slows. Jacoby reads his tell. "Affirmative action. Oh, you stupid Frenchy. Like when minorities get jobs or entrance into fancy universities over white guys because they're minorities. This is very controversial and political, and you and I are not gonna get into that. Not now. Anyway, I've had a few beers with Tracker. She's not any old prosecutor. You should google her when you get to your desk. She does solid work. She's definitely the one we want on our team!"

In the purple-blue fluorescent light of the Hall of Justice corridor, Jacoby introduces JP to Sharon. Her hair is so black it shines, mirror-like, back at him. She is looking down, assessing the thick file with all the charges and evidence against Iris and Franny as she speaks. "Right. Nice to meet you. These bitches are real movers—Oklahoma, New York, Charleston. They worked for you for a long time, eh?"

Sheepishly nodding, JP is glad that she isn't looking up at him to see his embarrassment.

"Don't be shy; these cu—these cats were professionals. They were patient, pugnacious cunts, errr, cats. They weren't gonna leave New York until they had their prey. We'll see what we can do."

Finally turning her head up, she winks at Jacoby. Then she turns her wide black eyes on JP with laser focus. The slow cadence of her language and low decibel of her voice draw him in to listen carefully. Though the hallway is full of loud conversations, everything disappears from his periphery as she articulates her plan: "I'm concerned that we'll never find their stash of cash. Obviously, Iris is well versed in money-laundering controls. I'll bet their money is carefully hidden. If that's the case, we'll have to push her hard. We'll have a solid case."

She holds his gaze. She has russet skin and large features that punctuate her powerful stature. Her geometric shoulders and long arms that stick too far out of her jacket are graced with large, widespread fingers. Her gesticulating hands animate her thesis: "They're crooks!"

Jacoby was right; she's impressive! JP tries to remember if he's ever met a Native American before. He can't take his eyes off her; she is so striking, both in size and command.

JP looks at Jacoby, remembering that Garrett suggested the same thing about hiding the money in Bitcoin. Her concurring theory is disappointing. He's told himself that he'll never see any money from chasing and catching them, but now that this reality seems more real, he feels sick. He thinks back on the lean year he has spent rebuilding his credit and self-confidence. He was once tenderly sympathetic to Iris and Franny; now his black anger is front and center.

"You mean, errr, I won't get my money back?"

She shakes her head. "We'll have to see how this plays out—where they've buried these assets is anyone's guess. Don't hold your breath, my friend. You hired them because they're smart. We'll see who has the last word on this. They're scheming, thieving criminals; they'll serve time!" Sharon Tracker starkly frames their crime, and their violation finally pierces his ambivalent armor. Maybe Garrett and Jacoby also tried to rile his anger, but it is her focused passion that finally shakes him.

She continues. "They'll plead for short jail time so that when they get out, they'll still have years with their—or I should say, with *your*—money. I'm gonna, well, the people are gonna fight hard for real restitution. And there's no reason that they should have a short vacation in jail. They're regulars at this." She tucks the file under her arm and turns to Jacoby. "I'll see you over there."

Once she's out of earshot, Jacoby turns to JP. "Yeah, hasn't she got it all? Great legal strategy and stunning!"

The arraignment is over seemingly before it starts. JP only sees Iris in profile and the back of Franny's head as they walk, hands bound, into the courtroom, and then, a few minutes later, they leave.

On the walk back to the parking lot, JP asks Jacoby, "I thought Native Americans lived out West. She's as New York as the Statue of Liberty."

"Sometimes you seem so savvy and cool, but . . . yeah, there are dozens of Native American tribes. Some in the West, but, man, they were here long before white folks, so they're across the continent. I think that she's Oneida, rich. But I don't know, man. Ask her yourself."

"Nahhh. I'm sure she thinks I'm stupid enough. Better not to get personal."

***

The following week, Sharon calls JP. "I'd like to see Les Beaux Châteaux and read the original report from Garrett. I'll swing by on my way home."

JP is slightly hopeful, as this is an errand that any clerk in her office could handle. She is coming in person. Will a firsthand look at his store amp up her efforts? Will that make a difference in getting his money back? When they met, he was confident that she was invested in Iris and Franny's conviction. Clearly, she understands that seeing Les Beaux Châteaux in person is really the only way to understand the store.

At six o'clock, an hour after closing, he doesn't want to lock up. He turns his back to the front door, thumbing an auction catalog, but he can't concentrate on the offerings. Frenchy knows it's past time to close. She throws her toys up onto the desk, eager for playtime. Six turns into seven o'clock. He and Frenchy stand outside, watching both directions of the street. His mood sinks—the evening is dark. They lock up and begin turning off the lights when she knocks.

"Didn't think that I was coming?"

Wooden, he stands still, trying not to reveal his earlier disappointment. He watches her large-boned, gliding movement. She doesn't carry a big backpack or briefcase, only a small cross-body pouch. Is she really here to collect documents? Frenchy brings Sharon her red ball, breaking the ice. They laugh, and JP throws the ball far into the narrow aisles to keep Frenchy distracted.

Seemingly trying to brush off her embarrassment at being so late, Sharon squares her shoulders and stands tall. "Wow! I'm so glad that I came down here. I had no idea exactly what kind of store you ran. Even photographs couldn't have explained this to me. This is kinda like a museum. I'll have a hell of a time explaining this to the jury. Oh, and *Les Beaux Châteaux*—I speak several languages, but I had to look this up: the beautiful homes."

"Oh, I studied a little Spanish and German. What languages do you speak?"

"I speak Oneida and Iroquoian."

JP is silent.

Sharon turns 360 degrees around to take in the entirety of Les Beaux Châteaux. "I can see that this place needs a front man, a logistics expert, and lots of support staff to function well. No wonder you leaned on her. How did you meet her?" Not waiting for his answer, she beings walking toward the dark periphery of the showroom. JP turns the lights back on. "In or about 2010, they fled Tulsa," she adds.

He nods his head in agreement. "She first came in October, and I hired her after Thanksgiving that year."

Sharon stops at a French garden vignette, complete with a stone bench, a wooden trellis, and a carved well cover. She looks out across the aisles to the artifacts displayed throughout. "I don't know much about antiques, or art, or European stuff."

"These pieces are almost all from France."

She walks silently, stopping at the glove molds and wine-bottle dryers and an art nouveau pharmacy sign. Frenchy prances along, looking up at Sharon every third stride. JP stands silently at his desk.

She cuts back across the showroom to him. "Do you think that people are born with good taste, or is it learned?" His surprise keeps him quiet. She continues, "I suppose that good taste, whatever that is, is cultural, right? It's not simply that these pieces' proportions and prized materials make them valuable; it's their context, too, right? And does the age of a thing add commercial value?"

The bronze statue of military heroes that Victor is so proud of arrived that afternoon. All three life-size warriors are ready to protect their turf, each weapon cocked and aiming in a different direction.

"Yep. That's the question I get asked the most: 'How old is it?' And the age of a thing, and its relative value, is specific to the thing. Technological breakthroughs often determine exactly what a thing is. Relative age is a discussion on its own." This philosophical groove gets her attention. JP turns to the warrior sculpture. "In both world wars, the men of France fought in battalions with their neighbors from their own hometowns. Whole families of fathers, sons, brothers, and uncles died together on the battlefields. In the forties, or, I guess, the fifties, most villages in France raised blood money to memorialize their fallen soldiers. This particular village was so desperately poor this year that they sold their memorial, sold it to my dad. The bronze craft is notable, but maybe its real attraction is in its tragic existence?"

Sharon touches the cheek of one of the bronze soldiers. "Do you recognize particular artistry in this beyond the backstory?"

"Of course! It wouldn't be here in Les Beaux Châteaux if it didn't have an intrinsic beauty. Can you feel the essence of these men? Their worry, their instincts? I can. That's certainly part of the art."

JP gives his canned speech about the artisan's control of his materials and the variation in the texture and color of the bronze, and then he goes off script. "You know that I'm here in the States like any other businessman, but I'm not, you know. I'm French."

They stand in the silence of LBC, with only the sound of Frenchy squeaking her red ball. A thoughtful moment stretches between them before Sharon breaks the spell. "What else is truly exquisite here?"

They both smile, and JP feels an imaginary barrier begin to melt. He waves her to follow him. "Likely, we won't be seeing more like this bakery. This one is sold and will be delivered next week. But look here, book-matched mahogany walls with classically carved columns. Pleasing to look at and impossibly satisfying to know the various techniques." She takes in the woodwork and shelving. "I'm so busy trying to impress you. Please, tell me about you."

"Yes, impress me! I'm learning. Promise that you'll explain more . . ." He smiles and nods. "I'm a proud Oneida and something of a spokesperson for all Native peoples. There are officially five hundred and seventy-four recognized Native tribes. Maybe you've read about the Lakota Sioux of Wounded Knee, as they're in the news of late. I'm Oneida first, but like you, I've adapted to mainstream life here in the city—"

"Wait! What about Wounded Knee?"

"You know Native American history?"

"No, not really, but in high school, we read excerpts of *Bury My Heart at Wounded Knee,* so I am kind of familiar with that."

"Only a few weeks ago, Lakota leaders requested that the medals of US Army murderers from those battles be rescinded and the remains of the Native people held by institutions be returned to their families and tribes. Just the opposite of the memorialization of these French soldiers. The Lakota Sioux nation has suffered. We Oneida, not so much. My story kind of sounds sad, but it's not, not at all. I never knew my dad, and I don't remember knowing my mom. She died when I was three. We Oneidas, we are not the destitute Natives that you read so much about. Four elders—well, four aunties—raised me, so I sort of had four moms. They were very strict, and because there were four of them, I was never without love, support, and very high expectations for accomplishment.

"They sent me to the whitest white prep school, where I was the Indian weirdo, but amazingly, that wasn't horrible because I had my aunties. And home was at the Dream Catcher Community Center, where Auntie Elma was the boss. We were always workin'. That sounds bad, but it wasn't. We were busy, and we knew everyone's business. It was home. That's what we did—we organized health-care plans, voter-registration drives, elder care, heritage education, language-preservation classes, and other culturally centered programs. Against all of our oral traditions, Elma and the other aunties computerized and digitized these Native programs for the entire community, and I learned at a very young age to keep track of records. And I am a whiz with numbers, at Elma's insistence."

JP laughs. "I'm allergic to numbers."

"BS! That's a jerky cop-out. I was very lucky. Affirmative action was the fashion when I was growing up, and Elma enrolled me in every program that I was even remotely qualified for—and several that I wasn't at all appropriate for. She wanted me to find success."

JP looks at her quizzically, remembering that he didn't understand Jacoby's earlier reference to the same.

"You know, giving scholarships and opportunities to previously discriminated-against groups, like First Nations people. I'm very good at standardized tests—my scores are great. That sounds easy, but I assure you that I've worked hard and prepared twice as vigorously as others. I was given opportunities to compete with others, but I got top scores fair and square! I've gotten almost every scholarship that I applied for."

"I don't think that we have that affirmative action in France," JP interrupts. "I'm not certain because I'm white. I never had to worry about that."

"Lucky for me, I never had to worry either. I was a shoo-in. I'm making fun of it. I could never have afforded to attend Cornell or Yale. I'm Ms. Gratitude USA 'cause lookee here!" She gestures to herself. JP looks at her in admiration. "After Cornell, the aunties made sure of two important things: Firstly, that I was awarded my full birthright ownership as an Oneida Native, which means that I have lots of shares in the community corporation, which is essentially the profitable casino. And secondly, that I got a great job at the Oneida Touch Stone Casino in the back offices, with plenty of time off to study for the CPA exam . . ."

"You're a CPA, and you're rich too? Oh my God! I'm such a slacker. But here's the loaded question: Jacoby told me that you cuss like a sailor. Where's your cool language?"

She waves her hand, dismissing that gossip.

JP continues. "So you worked really hard to get to this exalted position. What else are you interested in?"

"Well, I'm committed to my job. I'm not wealthy rich, like Wall Street rich, but I don't need my job to pay my mortgage. Honestly, I've never considered other interests beyond being the best spokesperson for Native people. I have so many titles, though. I'm it: a single Native woman, lawyer, CPA, assistant district attorney, Queen Bee. And I'm the prosecutor tryin' your lock-'em-up case."

"I'm so glad that you believe that this is a 'lock-'em-up' case. Until I listened to you describe their offense, I've felt guilty, like it was my fault that they did this."

"Do you think that if you'd paid them more, they wouldn't have defrauded you? Think again, bud! I think that they were scheming for a long time. No matter how much you respected their good work, they were gonna get theirs. They focused entirely on gaining your trust and finding the perfect opportunity to run with your money."

"I wasn't focused on Les Beaux Châteaux. I was busy finding myself, err, looking for myself."

"Did you find what you were looking for?"

He holds up a folder from a pile near the copy machine. "Not really, but now I'm too busy fixing everything to be looking for bullshit. So maybe I have. Here's the report that you'd asked for. I thought that Jacoby already had this?"

"Maybe he already gave it to me. I can't remember. I wanted to see this place to imagine Iris here, to—"

"She was a huge presence here. I would have gone out of business long ago were it not for her managing the logistics, her systemization of our practices. She knew what she was doing in the theft, but she really knows accounting and trade guidelines. She knows people's vulnerabilities . . . She knows me."

Sharon turns her black eyes unflinchingly to look directly at him. She's steady, calm, self-assured. He breathes in a cleansing breath and feels her strength.

As she is leaving, Sharon warns him that the case against Iris and Franny will proceed slowly, noting the high-priced lawyers Iris and Franny hired. "There'll be procedural trickstering and legal mumbo jumbo to grind your justice to a glacial speed. Don't worry. Be patient. I won't let them out of my sight."

***

JP tries to go to all the court dates to own some satisfaction after Iris and Franny's assault on him, but mostly he goes to watch Sharon in action. He develops a crush on her, but after enduring Vivi's rejection the year before, he's circumspect and careful to keep the scope of their conversations about his case. He reads everything about her online: Her scholarly awards in middle and high school. Multiple profiles of her in the *Cornell Chronicle*, the first a story about her arriving at Ithaca as the lone Native American student, and the second after she was named captain of the championship debating team. She is well known by the *New York Times*, the *New York Post*, and local TV channels. During her first year as an assistant DA, she helped build the case against Bernie Madoff. JP searches into the bowels of the internet to find more on Sharon Tracker; are there gossip pieces about her personal affairs, her lack of fashion style, her friendships with cops? He searches and searches but can't find much of anything beyond her professional record.

One hot summer afternoon, he calls Jacoby. "How do I get to the Hall of Justice on the subway?"

"Are you nuts? It'll take two hours, and I have no idea. I drive the car all day. What do you need down there? Just take an Uber."

"I'll figure it out."

"No, wait; there's guys here who really know the subway. I'll text you in a few minutes."

JP closes Les Beaux Châteaux promptly at five and walks to the Fourteenth Street station. He's ridden once before, trying to get to the Neue Galerie, and wound up on the West Side and had to take a taxi to the gallery from there. He follows Jacoby's instructions exactly, and it takes almost two hours to get there. Will she still be in the office so late? It doesn't matter; the adventure is exhilarating. Passing through security is a breeze at this hour. Alone in the creaky elevator, he realizes the foolishness in this foray and turns around and retraces his steps. The whole subway experience is easier, slower, and hotter than he expected. As a kid in Paris, he always used the Métro. He is glad to finally get past his New York subway jitters. Back to LBC and Frenchy. He's safe.

A radio silence from Jacoby and Garrett lingers.

***

Business is steady, Victor and JP are stronger together, and JP's life feels normal. Days are long at the store, but his personal discipline has become second nature. Sales, hospitality, and the constant rearranging of giant artifacts fill his time. While his body is hauling stone fountains, wooden bars, and crystal chandeliers around his giant showroom, he's wondering what Sharon is doing. Will he tell her about his curiosity and feelings for her?

One quiet evening, he takes the subway to the Hall of Justice again, without advance notice or even a query to her. Nervous excitement flutters in his stomach. Why does he keep tormenting himself with this adolescent thinking and behavior? He gets off the elevator on her floor. It's only seven thirty, but no one's about. The halls are empty, and he knocks on the antechamber of her office. He should have called first. He should have thought up some important reason to be here . . . He just wants to talk to her. No answer, but it isn't locked. He goes through the next door, and there she is, shoes and blazer off. She isn't looking at the computer, however. Her angry face is looking right at him, and he sees that she has an iron grip on a black police truncheon raised over her head.

"Oh! Sorry! I know that this is crazy, but I just wandered here to see you."

Sharon touches her brow and breathes deeply. "Did we have an appointment? Wandered here? What kind of nonsense are you talkin'? How did you get past the security? You can't just fucking . . ."

"I guess you're prepared for danger here when you work late, eh? I'm sorry to scare you."

She waves the truncheon above her head again in mock aggression and then slips it into her top drawer.

He moves forward half a step. "Have you eaten dinner yet? I've read about a Haitian restaurant nearby. Would you join me for dinner?"

"No! No, I'm busy. I've got a . . . You can't just walk in unscheduled . . ." She stops herself. Red anger melts from her knotted brow, followed by a widening smile. "Nope, I haven't eaten. Haitian? I've never tasted it. Frenchy food. I'd love to hear you speak French. It's down the block? Really, I've never noticed. Let's go!"

Le Soleil Brillant is casual and colorful, and the fried snapper with rice and beans is new for both of them. The hard chairs and stark light from the naked light bulbs don't hinder their laughs and smiles. Iris and Franny aren't mentioned once during the entire meal.

At 11:15 p.m., the owner, Monsieur Rick, asks, "Excusez-moi. Please return during our open hours!"

They walk several blocks together. The nearby environs are chock-full of ethnic delis and quick-serve restaurants . . . New York's unique tapestry. JP holds Sharon's hand. Their strides match easily. They are briefly quiet. "My accommodations aren't cushy, not really even comfortable," JP says, "but would you please come to my place? I think of you so much, and I want you."

Sharon turns to face him, taking hold of his other hand. "Monsieur JP, you are very pretty. I like you." He smiles. "I do want to come with you, but I'm not exactly experienced in the ways of romance. I'm no virgin, but I might as well be for all that I know about being turned on or even turning you on. I spend my time working or preparing for work. I haven't spent much time or effort on being romantic. None at all."

He takes her face in his hands tenderly and kisses her passionately. Her kiss answers affirmatively.

"Let's see if we can get your romantic record to match your amazing professional accomplishments, shall we?"

✴

During the next months of the trial, Sharon and JP are very discreet, though JP doesn't think there is anything illegal about their romance. No need to draw undue attention when their personal relationship has nothing to do with the alleged fraud and thefts that Sharon is prosecuting. Their time together in her office is official as she prepares JP for his testimony and her case to convince the jury beyond a reasonable doubt of Iris and Franny's crimes. They spend time together but rarely stay over at her place, as Frenchy isn't allowed in Sharon's building (though they slip her in a few times).

One night, hours after LBC has closed, Sharon calls him. "I've just picked up fried snapper with rice and beans. It'll be cold by the time I get to Les Beaux Châteaux, but that Trader Joe's wine you have'll make it just fine. Shall I bring this dinner to you?"

She parks in the back, and JP and Frenchy let her in through the loading area. Careful not to spill the packages of food that she's balancing, she doesn't pay much attention as she walks in. She looks up; most of the lights are off, giving the cavernous place a creepy look.

JP immediately notices that her antennae are up. "I'm not being stingy on the lights. If I turn them on, people think that the store's open, and the bell will be ringing all night. People love my store, and they'll come here at all hours. It's really a blessing, but sometimes it's a curse."

He takes the packages and sets them on the café table that he set up near the nonfunctioning fountain. Frenchy's dinner bowl is close by. JP's mother's favorite French café music elevates the mood, and he lights an art nouveau candelabrum with six candles to brighten the table.

"You might imagine that we're in Paris?"

She laughs and kisses him deeply.

They eat quietly, with Frenchy's collar hitting the bowl being the only sound beyond the music. Being together without any particular agenda is comforting to them both. They walk arm in arm around the block with Frenchy. The same looping songs play throughout the showroom upon their return.

"I love this music almost as much as my mom did."

They dance to a few songs and bump into an old billiards table. He kisses her and lifts her up onto the table, slowly undressing her.

Unbuttoning her business blouse, he rolls the black eight ball over her breasts.

"Stop! You French weirdo, what are you doing?"

"This is how we French play snooker."

"Snooker, as in you cheated me out of something?"

"No, dear one, snooker, as in you're gonna love being snookered on this games table."

By the time they clean up the dishes, Frenchy is asleep on her bed. JP pulls down the Murphy bed. The pillows and linens are adequate, and though its queen size is wide enough for them, the bed is not hospitable for two. Regardless of the limitations, they are very romantic together.

***

Finally, their day in court is on. Opening arguments set the stage. JP sits far back in the full gallery. Iris and Franny have gotten lots of local coverage in the newspapers and on TV, none of it complimentary. Sharon is a master of the media, though the jury is sworn not to read or learn more about the case outside of the courtroom. The jurors sit on the edge of their seats as she explains Iris and Franny's fraud: the planning and the coldhearted theft perpetrated when JP had to go to France to help his injured father. JP feels protected in the back row. The judge, Irene Norworth, is small, and to JP, she looks like Dr. Ruth, but her rumbling voice gives away her cigarette-smoking past. Sharon says that she is known around the judicial circuit as a fair and no-nonsense judge. The courtroom isn't anything like a Hollywood portrayal. It is a dreary gray, and all the players (except Sharon) seem tired; the judge's robe is worn and frayed, as is the uniform of the managing sergeant at arms. The flat-blue environmentally aware lights expose everyone's plain humanity—not a flattering shadow to be found. Gone is Iris's shining silver hair; in this light, its flat gray tone matches the deep-purplish creases on her face. Most shocking is the slump of her shoulders. JP used to admire her disciplined posture. They lock eyes. If mean stares could wield daggers, Iris's are murderous.

Garrett is on the stand for two days. Iris and Franny's lawyer can't get him off track or weaken his resolve. Garrett, led by Sharon, explains to the jury how the greedy sisters calculated their fraud; JP, the hardworking immigrant, was wronged. After Garrett, Jacoby, and the accountant testify, JP is expected to take the stand the following day.

That evening, Sharon calls him as he is about to leave LBC to prepare with her in her office. "They want to plead out."

"What? Remember, I'm not a lawyer."

"They don't want to finish the trial. They don't want you to testify. They've asked for a plea."

"I really don't understand. We're in the middle of this trial. They can't just stop, can they?"

"Well, as an officer of the court, expediency is my obligation, as well as upholding the law. If they do real jail time and make restitution, let's just be done. They should serve five years in jail and pay penalties. If they want to do this deal, they'll have to cough up real money. This is a fluid situation. Plan to come to court tomorrow to testify, and I'll call you if anything changes. I'll see you here, early. I'll be busy with them tonight, so no rehearsal for you."

After a long, relaxing walk with Frenchy, JP feels relieved and sleeps easily. He and Frenchy are up early. Sharon hasn't left a message. Did they or didn't they plea?

As soon as he arrives in her office, he knows that she is tense. "Nope, the negotiations didn't work out. Your testimony is the clincher." She winks at him. "You're the man of the hour!"

Sitting in the witness box, he begins to feel embarrassed that these sharks took him so completely. Then he feels bad for them. Maybe he was a terrible boss? But as soon as Sharon begins leading the questions, his worries disappear. She explains the complexities of Les Beaux Châteaux's many functions and the showroom's gigantic size. JP brings a strong foundation to the changing neighborhood. Most importantly, he needed a logistical-support employee so that *he* could grow the business. "Is that correct, Mr. Marchand?"

"Well, we worked well together. Iris is very experienced in this unique trade. I relied on her knowledge. And then I relied on her more and more to—"

Sharon halts his sympathies for them immediately. "And so her responsibilities included complex currency transfers?"

JP tries to answer with yes-or-no responses but inevitably comes back to sympathies for Iris and Franny. Sharon stops him again and again. Regardless of his repeated mistakes, he can see absolute confidence in Sharon's posture. He watches Sharon watch the jurors, who understand his trust in and reliance on Iris. Finally, the judge excuses him. He walks by Iris's seat with slow determination. Her sour smell projects fear. He knows that his testimony is the icing on the cake. Sharon has built a strong case, and Iris is going down.

Within four hours, the jury has returned its verdict.

Sharon and the justice system finally prevail. Iris and Franny are convicted of conspiracy, larceny, money laundering, fraud, theft, and a host of additional charges. The judge issues stiff prison time of five years each and penalty costs of $500,000, as well as full restitution. These courtroom procedures feel disconnected from any functions of JP and Victor's business. Though he can remember, in vivid detail, Iris's work ethic, it's now unrelated to him, floating untethered in the atmosphere. Iris and Franny are like TV characters he has no intimate knowledge of—people he can turn off at any moment. They are no longer the women he trusted and admired. No, these are the thieves who stole so much from him. Their final exit from the courtroom is anticlimactic. He catches Iris's eye. Her gray, toneless face has aged dramatically since the last time he saw her. Her rigid shoulders are hardened in anger. Franny keeps her gaze down as they leave, handcuffed and escorted by uniformed officials. JP sits alone in the back of the gallery, even after everyone has filed out. The quiet is restorative.

Out in the featureless halls, JP calls Victor. "It's over, absolutment finis," he says.

Victor laughs. "Oh, thank goodness. I didn't want you to be wasting my time with that bullshit when I get there!"

They both laugh heartily in relief.

***

After the trial, JP and Sharon's life together changes. They buy a small apartment where Frenchy is welcome and that has easy access to many subway lines, as JP becomes a subway navigator. They both work long hours, yet they are happy together. They find occasional afternoons to go to museums and concerts.

Though the Whitney Museum's opening in the Meatpacking District a few years prior was a big splash in the neighborhood, JP has never gone. Soon, the huge, open galleries become a regular meeting place where he and Sharon learn together about various artists. Their favorite is Lee Krasner's inspired art, among others. Though Krasner was Jackson Pollock's most significant support, her own monumentally sized canvases are no less masterpieces. Sharon loves Krasner's abstract expressionism, which she describes as "almost the opposite of Native art." The museum's outdoor restaurant and bar is their romantic touchstone for an evening break before Sharon returns to her office.

One late night, returning home after a members' concert at the Met, they stroll on Fifth Avenue and pass the Neue Galerie.

"Sometime I'd like to take you to my favorite tiny museum," JP tells her, pointing to a beautiful large town house. "Do you know the Neue Galerie?"

"I've heard of it, and I've read lots about Ronald Lauder, famed New Yorker. A few years ago, he gave a huge gift to the Met. A whole bunch of ancient arms and armaments. I saw pictures of really old gauntlets and body armor from the fourteen hundreds that he donated. You gotta wonder what was he doing with those articles before he gave them to the museum?

"When Chief White Cloud visited me from upstate, I took him to see that installation at the museum. He laughed so hard at the armor. 'No wonder white men are so stiff on horses,' he said." She and JP laugh. Then she asks, "If Neue's your favorite museum, why haven't we gone there yet?"

JP bites his thumbnail in anxious anticipation. "It is really the gem of New York's smaller museums, but I once took a woman there who didn't like it or the art, and I judged her so egregiously for it. I don't necessarily want to influence what you like or not, but I'm hes—"

"If you don't want to judge me for my taste, then don't. You're in charge of yourself. Don't be a goof. That's absurd!"

It is weeks before they are both able to take off an afternoon to go to the Neue. JP's favorite guard gives him a knuckle bump. They climb the familiar staircase and slowly tour the art deco rooms until they finally arrive at the Adele painting. There, Sharon's face lights up.

"I know this! This was on my Aunt Elma's coffee cup. I always thought that it was a Native image. I was responsible for making her coffee. She was a stickler for fresh coffee. Not quite as finicky as you are, but I was in charge of her morning brew, and someone had given her a mug with this image. She drank her joe outta this mug every morning. Wow! Of course, I love this. And now I understand it, somewhat."

JP cracks up laughing. "Adele, Native, really?"

"I was a kid. Why would she have anything that wasn't Native? Well, I don't know where she got it, but now I know that it didn't come from an Oneida artist."

They laugh. They always laugh together.

***

The US Open tennis tournament is still a month away, but JP and Victor have already planned Victor's American tour. For the first and only time (save when Iris left the store), JP plans to close LBC. He's rented a small camper van to tour the East Coast with Victor and Frenchy, and then they'll drive out to South Dakota to the battlefield of Wounded Knee to meet Sharon, then on to the Grand Canyon.

On a warm summer Saturday, a day that holds great promise for business at LBC, JP and Frenchy are far away from the store. He, Sharon, and Frenchy are in his truck at the Kiss and Fly lot at Kennedy Airport, awaiting Victor's arrival.

Acknowledgments

Special thanks to Iram McGill for reading and critiquing innumerable drafts of my stories. Thank you to David Schaffer of L&G Law Group for advising me on criminal law. Thanks to Stuart Grannen of Architectural Artifacts for explaining many of the dos and don'ts of deconstruction. And, lastly, thank you to Katherine Richards and her team at Girl Friday for their patient wisdom on all things publishing.

About the Author

Dorothy Mackevich Marks is a screenwriter who preserves things. A Chicago-based writer, screenwriter, and producer with a passion for unique and exquisite things and their history, she earned her MFA in screenwriting after studying journalism. Early in her career, Dorothy worked with preservationists in Chicago to conserve and repurpose historic movie palaces—beautiful architectural confections that intrigue. Her passion for the stories entombed in artifacts erupted when she joined the community of Chicago's Field Museum of Natural History. Arm-in-arm with museum scientists and policy makers, she examines cultural change and the future of encyclopedic museums, teaching and preserving authentic history.

With a learned eye for function and beauty, Dorothy passionately delivers fresh news from the past to curious and discerning audiences. Always a Midwesterner but with a wanderlust rooted in childhood, when opportunity knocks, she travels to listen, learn, and share. Dorothy lives on the shores of Lake Michigan with her family and two polite cats.

CPSIA information can be obtained
at www.ICGtesting.com
Printed in the USA
LVHW040115170422
715941LV00001B/2